BIRD HITS GLASS

BIRD HITS GLASS

A novel

Beate Triantafilidis

Matador
Unit E2 Airfield Business Park,
Harrison Road, Market Harborough,
Leicestershire. LE16 7UL
Tel: 0116 2792299
Email: books@troubador.co.uk
Web: www.troubador.co.uk/matador
Twitter: @matadorbooks

ISBN 978 1803131 627

British Library Cataloguing in Publication Data.
A catalogue record for this book is available from the British Library.

Printed and bound in Great Britain by 4edge Limited
Typeset in 11pt Adobe Garamond Pro by Troubador Publishing Ltd, Leicester, UK

Matador is an imprint of Troubador Publishing Ltd

For Nic

Part 1

1

My leaden legs move in slow motion down the corridor. I glue my gaze to the silver doors of the lift, wanting to pull them closer with my mind. With each step, my head pounds like a speaker with the bass turned too high, but the photo Jas posted burns in my mind; I can't stay home, not tonight.

The corridor spins. I place one foot in front of the other with the concentration of someone drunk trying to appear sober. When I reach the lift and push the button, the doors glide open, and I step into the mirrored box. In the bright light, I analyse my made-up face: sweat shines through the foundation and my eyes are dead, but otherwise, I look fine. The outside and the inside of my body are two different people. A wave of nausea rises, and I lean my forehead against the cool mirror, bargaining with my exhausted insides. *If you give me tonight, I will let you lie in bed for a week.*

The metal doors glide towards each other. They are almost kissing, when my aching arm flings itself into the narrowing gap and forces them open again. Stepping out, my body sinks to the carpeted floor and leans against the wall.

As soon as my body touches the floor, it's like the weight of the building and the earth itself latches onto me. My aching limbs feel unfamiliar. Invisible bruises pulse under my skin. Fog fills my throbbing head. With deep breaths, I swallow the surging terror. *You have only gotten worse, not better.* I shout over the frail voice: *I am fine; I am fine; I am fine.*

I roar at my body to get back into the lift, but it ignores me. Clinging to my phone, I sink further down the wall. I am underwater, plummeting. With shaking fingers, I type 999 into my phone. I watch the digits hover, and my heart pounds faster for a moment before I black out the screen. It's *my* body; I own it; I should be giving directions, not taking them. My face burns at the thought of yet another doctor telling me they can't see anything wrong on any of the tests. Their reassuring words do not comfort me. If the tests say I am fine, but I feel like my body is dying, either the doctors have missed something or I can't trust my own mind anymore.

Somewhere down the corridor, a door opens. Muscles bursting with effort, I push myself up, my legs trembling like the elongated limbs of a baby giraffe. I can't let my neighbours see me collapsed on the floor; in my black dress and spiky heels, they will think I am either drunk or high. Dragging my exhausted body back to my flat, I pass the young woman and tiny hairless dog who live across from me. The dog yaps; maybe he can smell that under my shiny surface, I am rotting.

Stripping out of my dress, I crawl naked into bed and curl up in the foetal position. My tense mind unspools. The heaviness pushes me into the mattress. Cradled in my hands, my phone screen shoots light into the dark room like a tiny sun.

'Won't make it' I text Matt. Copying the words, I send them to Jas too. After pressing send, I pull the duvet over my fevered face; I don't want to see my defeat solidified in their replies. From inside the warm cocoon of the duvet, I hear the phone dance across the glass surface of the bedside table, the sound aggressive. I envision reaching out for it, but it's so far away. I'm vibrating too, my teeth chattering.

When the phone buzzes again, I pull the blanket off. On the glowing screen, Matt's face is grinning at me. He will be standing in a corner of the heaving bar covering his ear with his hand, wanting to know if I am really missing the party I've been planning for months. Picturing him there without me, disappointment wraps my comatose body like a corset pulled too tight. *Decline.*

'Celebrate extra for me!'

I add a smiley face to the text, then delete it; I never send emojis – Matt will know I am faking the lightness. We have been together long enough to know each other's habits, but not long enough for our relationship to bear too much heaviness. His reply is instant.

'If you knew you were sick again, why didn't you cancel?'

Ignoring his text, I find the doctor's number in my list of recent calls. The surgery is still open for another half hour; their opening hours have cemented themselves in my brain. Putting my phone on speaker mode, I place it on top of my chest and close my eyes. The phone rises and falls as I breathe. An automated female voice fills the cool darkness.

"Your call is very important to us. Please continue to hold, and we will be with you as soon as we can."

The woman pauses briefly before again shouting her apologies for making me wait. I turn the volume down, but she is still screaming. The beep of another incoming call interrupts her, and now it's Jas's face that fills the screen. I push away her intense gaze. Halfway through the automated woman's speech, a male voice speaks. His tone is flat, as if he has been infected by his disembodied colleague.

"Thanks for holding, how can I help?"

"I need to see a doctor."

"Okay, let's see what we've got."

I hear him type on a keyboard.

"I can do the 24th of January," he says.

"But that's more than two weeks away. Do you not have anything sooner? I could come in literally any time."

"If you need urgent care you have to go to A&E, I'm afraid."

Hanging up, I fall back into the swirling ocean of painful exhaustion. Swiping at my phone screen, I find the photo Jas posted half an hour ago. On the bar's roof terrace, she is posing front and centre in an orange dress, clutching a bottle of prosecco in one hand and a small bouquet of silver helium balloons in the other. Behind her petite body, everyone congregates like a fan club, holding up slim glasses in a toast. Yelling cheers into the freezing air, their bodies are as polished as the champagne flutes. The London skyline glows behind them. I stare at the photo, as if gazing at my stationary birthday party with enough desperation can lift me out of my broken body and transport me across the city.

'Happy birthday Grace!!!'

Jas's overuse of exclamation marks in the photo's caption sparks a flash of happiness, but I want to be on fire all over with pleasure instead of pain; her electronic words should be only the frosting on top of the real celebrations. Thinking of Jas enveloped in the bubble of undivided attention that was meant to be mine, I fill with aching longing. *When I asked you to play host for me until I arrived, I didn't mean you should act like the party is yours.* I should have told the doctor's receptionist that it's my birthday, maybe he would have conjured up an appointment, like a restaurant offering dessert on the house. I consider calling Jas back, but instead I repost her photo on my own social media profile. Head pounding, I type out a caption with shaking fingers:

'Best night out with the best people. Happy birthday to me!'

Staring at the screen waiting for likes, I google 'happy birthday', and a choir of strangers sings me a tinny rendition. Their voices drill into my aching head. Closing my eyes, I imagine myself sitting on a stool in the buzzing bar, sipping on a cocktail, surrounded by my colleagues and friends, my body glowing with vitality.

I revel in the fantasy until the song cuts off. Glancing down at the phone, I see that the screen has gone black, the battery dead, as if my phone and I are one integrated being, powered by a defunct battery.

2

Stepping into the doctor's office from the cold drizzle, I close the transparent dome of my umbrella. The young receptionist smiles at me, her eyes warm.

"Hello! Name? Date of birth?"

I extract the details from my dizzy brain and relay them. She beams, as if I've provided the correct answers to a quiz.

"Okay, honey, take a seat."

I shuffle over to a plastic chair and sink into it. My umbrella drips water onto the floor, forming a small puddle. Watching it expand, I feel liquified too. I melt into the chair, as all my remaining energy leaks out of me and spills onto the floor. I close my eyes. Like an adult version of a jar of lollipops, the receptionist has handed me a different affectionate word each time I've come here: *darling, sweetheart, honey*. I wish she would step out from behind her desk, walk over to me and gently stroke my hair, then baulk at the impulse; craving comfort from a stranger is only yet another symptom of disintegration.

A baby starts blaring like a car alarm. I open my eyes. The mother's pale face looks drained and distracted as she bounces the baby on her lap. Digging in my bag for noise cancelling headphones, I see my phone light up with a new email. Escaping into the white noise bubble, I read work emails, force-feeding words to my burning brain. I manage to leave my aching body for several minutes until a strict female voice calls my name, yanking me back into pain. Heaving my body up to stand, I walk towards the tall woman standing at the edge of the waiting room. Her jeans, T-shirt and trainers are all white; even her thin hair is so light blonde that it blends in with her self-imposed uniform. I follow her down the corridor. Her shoes squeak against the linoleum, as she strides forward without noticing that I am not keeping up.

In the consulting room, I sink onto the chair she indicates, sweat beading on my forehead. The bright artificial light stings my eyes. The doctor plops down in her chair and looks at the computer screen instead of at me. Seeing her up close, I realise she must be only a few years older than I am.

"Okay," she says, her eyes still at the screen. "I see you took some tests a few weeks ago? Everything looks absolutely normal."

"Yes, I know, but I don't feel normal."

She shoots my symptoms into the air, many words sewn together into a long string. In her voice, they sound unproblematic, like they are theoretical medical concepts instead of visceral experiences. Her breath smells faintly of mint.

"How long has this been going on then?"

I scan through the last year looking for pain, but I can't find my body in my memories.

"Just over six months, maybe," I say, picking a number at random. "I have been exhausted before that, but that's normal, isn't it? You know, a London thing."

A laugh escapes me, and immediately, I want to collect the soundwaves from the room the way you pick up dropped coins. Laughing will not make this woman prescribe tests, scans or pills. She only nods, before returning to her typing.

"It's not normal anymore though," I say, concentrating on keeping my teeth from chattering. "I can't push through."

The doctor looks at me with unreadable eyes. Her bright blue irises look fake and remind me of wolves. Fear rises. I swallow. *Fix me. Please.*

"I can give you sick leave," she says. "Three weeks."

I stare at her. "I can't be off work for that long."

She raises her eyebrows. "Twenty-one days is not very long. You need rest."

She says this as if rest is not a remedy that belongs to a different century, like fresh air and leeches. Twenty-one days is how long it takes to build a new habit, but I don't want to learn how to rest, I want to snap my fingers and return to normal. No one I know listens fully to their body; we would get nothing done. Giving up holding my body together, I let it tremble freely, but she doesn't see. I want to lie down on the floor and refuse to leave until she disassembles me, locates the broken part and replaces it.

At her desk, a printer whirs and spews out a piece of paper. She signs it with the speed of a celebrity used to giving endless autographs. Stepping out of the room, I crumple the paper in my hand. With the other, I order a car to take me back to my flat; the ten-minute walk has become insurmountable for my deadened legs.

Collapsing into the back seat of the stuffy car, I text Jas with shaking hands.

'Still no answers or pills.'

A short voice note arrives instantly. Plugging in my headphones, I press play.

"*Eee ooo, eee ooo.*"

'Detection successful, venting aborted' I type in reply, resenting for the first time our ritual of emitting fake alarm sounds at any sign of complaining.

Jas sends another text, a photo of a poster depicting a woman hunching forward and holding her forehead in her palm. Below closed eyes, she purses her plump red lips in pain. Large red letters run across her torso, the shade matching her lipstick:

Cynical and demotivated? Reluctant to go to work?
Irritable with colleagues?
Is this you? The talent management team will help
extinguish your burnout.

I have seen this poster countless times; it plasters the inside of every bathroom stall in the women's toilets at work.

'You know I would sell my hair to be back in the office' I reply. 'And I wasn't complaining, just updating you.'

'Not a pity party invitation?'

I hesitate. 'No.'

'Come back! Lean in with me! We need you!'

'I would if I could.'

Jas types for a long time, but when the next text finally comes, it's short:

'Did you see my email?'

Sinking into the car seat, I close my eyes for a moment before swiping on the screen again to open my emails, just as a text from Matt arrives asking if we are still on for tonight.

'Of course' I reply, overriding my jellied body that begs to lie down in cool darkness.

3

Matt and I sit on the couch, boxes of sushi spread out on the glass surface of the coffee table. Candles fill the living room with flickering light and the smell of citrus. I wanted our confinement to my flat to feel like a choice, but the bare white walls are suddenly too reminiscent of hospitals.

"So, what did the doctor say?" Matt reaches for a piece of salmon sashimi and dips it in the soy sauce.

I shrug. "Nothing really."

"He must have said something."

"She," I mumble, my mouth full. "What kind of solution is sick leave?"

My chopsticks tremble as I talk, and the salmon slips out and falls to the floor. I dive down and grip the slippery slice of pink with my unsteady fingers. Sitting back up, I pop the salmon in my mouth as my head spins.

"No more tests," I say. "No medication either, she just

told me to rest. Haven't we progressed past rest? It's so primitive. And four minutes of her time was all I got."

"Even during speed dating you get more than four minutes to identify all the things that are wrong with the person sitting across from you." Matt sips his beer, a bottle from a microbrewery set up by a friend of a friend. My friends are amassing deposits on shiny flats, while his only want to accumulate experiences.

"And how do you know that?"

Matt only winks at me. "Anyway. This new glow-in-the-dark ping-pong bar is opening this weekend, want to go?"

I shake my throbbing head. "Don't you get enough ping-pong at work?"

"We barely play anymore; everyone's too focused on the investor pitch. They want me to lead it now; the founders say they'll be too nervous and just fuck it up."

"No ping-pong?" I mock gasp. "What's the point of working for a start-up if you don't get to play games? Having to actually work when you're at work... shocking." I roll my eyes.

Laughing, Matt rolls up the sleeves of his sweater, as if our conversation is a form of arm wrestling. Usually, I like that we debate more than we talk, but now my head thumps. I should ask him more about the upcoming pitch, but I want him to leave so I can collapse into bed. I slide down into a horizontal position.

"I hate table tennis," I say. "I'm not any good."

After I got home from the doctor, I tried to have a shower, and I had to sit down in the bathtub because when I stood, I felt so dizzy I thought I would faint and crack my head on the rim of the tub. My sit bones pushed uncomfortably against the hard, white surface, as the water pummelled down on my head and back. My chest and throat burned, but I bit down on my lip until the embryonic tears died. I sat there until my reddened skin felt raw, waiting for my depleted body to behave itself. Steam filled the room before I forced myself to step out of the shower. I wiped the moisture off the mirror and stood there evaluating my naked body, as if it would suddenly reveal through the fog where and when everything had gone wrong.

"You could just play for fun." Matt nudges me with his elbow. "Fun? Heard of that?"

"I told you, I can't, okay?" I snap.

"Come on."

"I have to work."

Matt stares at me, then lunges for my work phone and laptop on the table. He jumps up from the couch and holds them above his head. As I stretch up, my head spins again. I am tall, but he is taller; my fingertips touch only air. White spots litter my vision, and I sink back down into the cushions.

Matt looks down at me. "In Japan, workaholism kills people so often they have an actual word for death by overwork."

"I'm sick, not overworked," I say.

"And sick leave is not a synonym for working from home."

"Endless pleasure is mind-numbingly boring," I mumble.

Matt shoots laughter at me. "Is that your problem right now? Too much pleasure?"

I lean into him. His soft lips press against mine, his mouth slightly open. He tastes of beer. Our tongues dance, but I don't want to put too much force into it; I want to go to sleep, not initiate anything.

Matt reaches over to stroke a finger down my chest; he traces down my stomach. I look at the bronzed Cleopatra figurine on the end table behind his shoulder. She mocks me with her surplus of sexuality and power; her head adorned with a golden helmet shaped like a bird, she lounges on a sofa, her bare legs sensually crossed. I want a body like hers, solid and golden.

Without a word, I straddle Matt; leaning down, I put my mouth on his and feel the softness of his tongue. If I dive into pleasure with enough force, maybe my body will momentarily forget that it is broken.

4

A week later, I lie in bed in the dark empty bedroom unable to sleep. Resting hasn't revived me; instead, my body has taken my stillness as permission to give up completely. My mind spins within a lifeless shell.

The doctor didn't tell me that just lying here is hard when my body aches like I've been punched all over. I want to distract myself from the pain that peppers my brain, not bathe in it. Resting should feel peaceful and comfortable, but what I'm doing feels like the opposite. I debate calling the doctor to ask whether resting is meant to make me worse before it makes me better, in case I am doing it wrong. But I can't call her again; she will only label me hysterical.

The phone vibrates against the glass of the bedside table, and I jump. Lifting a leaden arm to pick it up, I squint against the bright light. Jordan's name glows on the screen. Having put her baby boy to sleep, my boss and mentor will be working from her home office. They say new mothers should sleep when their babies do, but Jordan will be ignoring this – she doesn't take directions; she only gives them.

"Just checking in," she says. "How are you doing?"

"Oh, better. Definitely." I clear my throat. "Almost back to normal now."

"Excellent!" Jordan says. "I knew you would bounce back quicker than the doctors said. No limits! So, can you come in tomorrow and join me for the meeting with the prospective clients?"

"Just tell me what time and I'll be there."

"You sure? If you're not up for it, Jas said she's happy to cover for you."

"No, I'm fine – I'll be there."

"Super. Meeting's at nine, so let's convene at eight?"

Without saying goodbye, Jordan hangs up. The room feels too silent. I want to call her back and ask her to stay on the phone. *You don't have to say anything; you could just keep the phone on speaker mode next to you while you work.* Closing my eyes, pain shoots through my head. I haven't showered since my bathtub collapse, and my hair is so greasy that my scalp is itching. The only person I have seen all week is my cleaner, a reserved, middle-aged woman who worked around me, as I told her too many times that I'm sick, desperate to make it clear I am not a snowflake millennial who believes herself entitled to restorative days in bed.

Now, I shuffle to the bathroom on wobbly legs. I peel off my pyjamas, turn on the shower and step into the bathtub. I sit below the warm cascade of water, soaping my body – there are suddenly so many parts to me. I shampoo with aching arms, hating my hair.

Wrapping a towel around me, I walk back to the bedroom, my wet hair dripping onto the floor. I collapse naked into bed, shattered. My hair soaks the pillow. I debate whether to text Jordan saying I can't come tomorrow after all, but maybe another night of sleep will cure me, and by tomorrow morning, my lie that I am fine will have transformed into truth.

By the time Cleopatra was twenty-six, she had ruled Egypt for years, become Caesar's mistress and given birth to his son. She would not have given into a rebelling body – but then she also married her brother and killed herself in the end. *You need a new role model,* Matt said, when I first explained my childhood obsession with Cleopatra to him.

I walk towards the cluster of buildings that stretch towards the sky, my breath visible in the cold morning air. Tightening the belt of my trench coat, I attempt to fall into step with the woman walking ahead of me, but she is moving so fast, like she's walking on an invisible conveyor belt. I trail behind her on autopilot, feeling like I'm wearing my normal self on top of something else. By the time I reach the riverside office, my teeth chatter, and my face gleams with moisture. Sweat glues my dress to my skin. The automatic doors to the foyer sense my presence and slide open, welcoming me to the shiny oasis within.

The warm air caresses my face before I whip around. Retracing my steps, I move against the tide of people flowing out of the dark into the lit-up buildings. *I can't let Jordan see me like this.* I scan the throng. *Please, let them all be strangers.* A blonde woman strides towards me while looking at her phone, her heels clicking against the pavement. Each efficient step is as unique as a fingerprint; in China, they use gait analysis to identify criminal suspects on CCTV. Swerving left, I bury my head in my own phone and stare at the home screen, hoping my newfound sluggish shuffle makes me unrecognisable.

"Grace! Where are you going?"

I shoot my eyebrows up and widen my eyes. "Oh, hi, Jordan! Nice surprise! Good morning!"

"Office is the other way?"

I laugh. "Yes, just grabbing a coffee. You want one?"

She furrows her brows. "Still not feeling great?"

"Oh no, I'm fine." I grin like a terrifying clown. "All back to normal. I'll be there in five."

The six people look small in the cavernous meeting room. Around the elongated table, the suit-clad men sit spaced apart, as if they don't like each other. Jordan and I stand on each side of the large screen that fills the wall, the first slide of our presentation glowing behind us. Cradling a small tablet, I feel out of place. Jordan's assertive voice fills the room, and I concentrate my gaze on her. Her scarlet top pops against the white wall; she's into colour psychology, where red signals force, courage and drive. My black dress clings to my clammy skin, and I'm glad I'm not wearing grey; at least now the sweat is invisible. We've been told to never wear pink at work; compassion is not on brand.

"Seventy-five per cent of business transformation initiatives fail." Jordan points at the slide behind her with a laser pen. "Our analysis of hundreds of transformations shows delayed instigation is the primary cause of failure. Ideally, pre-emptive transformations should be initiated early on."

Half-listening, I go over my talking points in my head. My skull feels compressed, like I am holding my breath underwater.

"Grace will elaborate on what this means for you specifically," Jordan says.

As she turns to me, I glance down at the small screen and see only a blurry soup. Heart pounding, I start speaking, but the sentences fail to connect into a seamless whole. I concentrate to straighten up each word and make it walk in a straight line. I glance at Jordan, but I can't read her face either; she's a smiling mask. I speak louder. When I point the laser pen onto the slide, the red dot trembles.

Turning to Jordan, my eyes beg her to take over. She nods in slow motion. "Thank you, Grace. To add to that..."

Her voice spews out statistics at speed. The tablet in my hands shakes too now; I am at the epicentre of an earthquake. What I am breathing doesn't feel like air, only a poor replication, and I want to rip open the hermetically sealed windows. The caffeine pulses in my body, but I can't access the energy; it dances out of reach. Clinging to my tablet, I dread the moment Jordan will revert to me, but she has decided to turn me into a prop. I wear a half-smile on my burning face, though my body isn't beautiful enough to add value as a decorative object. Shivers shoot up and down my back and legs, as Jordan finally closes off.

"I'll walk you out," she says to the men. Wiping my hands on my trousers, I reach my hand out to each in turn. Once the room is empty, I crave curling up in a ball on the carpeted floor. Leaving my tablet and phone on the table, I disappear to the bathroom.

Sitting on the toilet lid in the corner stall, I lean forward. Placing my spinning head in my hands, I adopt the brace position they tell you to assume during an emergency plane landing, as if it's a universal position applicable in any emergency. My cheeks burn against my palms. I stop desperately paddling to stay afloat and the fatigue submerges me fully. Someone in the stall next to me flushes. The fear claws at me with sharp teeth; I can't tune it out. *Exhaustion at this intensity must be irreversible.*

What will I tell Jordan? I should have stayed home; it's harder to outlive a negative presence than an absence. Blotting my sweaty face with toilet paper, I hope equally that no one will find me and that Jordan will come searching. I picture my phone lying on the conference table. If I had it, I could call Jas, but what would I ask her to do? In the office, we have made a collective decision that the mind is a distinct thing that functions separately from the body. Whether we have the flu or food poisoning or a broken leg, we do not stop. Limits may exist outside the office and for other people, but not for us. The burned-out woman with red lips looks down at me from the poster on the cubicle door. I close my eyes again. *I am fine; I am fine; I am fine.*

The door to the bathroom opens, followed by heels clicking against the tiles.

"Grace?"

"Yes. One second." As I stand up, the room spins and bright spots dance. After flushing for effect, I open the cubicle door. Jordan is standing in the middle of the room, her arms crossed, eyebrows raised.

"What's going on? What happened in there?"

"I'm so sorry." I walk over to the sink and wash my hands with scalding water, searching for a lie that will not make me look weak, but frozen fog fills my brain.

"Well?" Jordan says. She locks eyes with me in the mirror.

"The notes… I couldn't… the words… my brain just…"

Jordan stares at me, her eyes blazing. "I explicitly asked if you were feeling okay."

I turn around to face her. "I wanted to be. You know, fake it till you make it. Like that American woman with that supplement company?"

Jordan frowns. "The woman who is now in jail for fraud because the supplements didn't actually work?"

My face heats up. "Yes, but you said... if she'd had more time before she was caught... she would have turned the lies into truths, and it would have been a success story instead of a scandal."

"Oh, for God's sake!" Jordan's voice echoes against the tiled walls. "I don't mean everything I say. I was joking! That woman was a psychopathic liar." Closing her eyes briefly, Jordan takes a deep breath. "Look. Go home. Just... go home. Come back only when you're actually ready. No faking it."

"Okay. Thank you," I say, my head doing a little bow.

"It's only a liability having you here right now." Jordan walks out of the bathroom, waving over her shoulder, her artificially straight hair bobbing with each step. "Get better soon!"

"Yes! I will!" I inject energetic gratitude into my voice, as if her words were a caring statement rather than a demand. Jordan herself is meant to be on maternity leave, but she took only four days off before she was back on email. I'm surprised she wanted to become a mother at all. Picturing her blowing raspberries on a tiny tummy is impossible, but she has told me she has a work persona and a home persona, so she could be a warm mother, I just wouldn't know. She briefly considered outsourcing her pregnancy to a surrogate – it's an emerging trend in Silicon Valley – and following her out of the bathroom, I desperately yearn for a service that would let me transfer my illness to another body in exchange for payment.

If she can continue working only days after being ripped open by a child, how can I not force my body to pull itself together? If I remain sick, the others will sprint ahead without me, and I will be unable to catch up.

5

Two weeks later, I lean back against the car seat, as I'm driven back to my flat after yet another doctor's appointment. A news presenter's voice fills my dizzy head with stories of carnage in Syria, but I am too consumed with the war between my body and my mind to take in the destruction of others. A relentless hangover has hammered through me ever since my office visit, but the doctor in her uniform of white only repeated the same thing today: *all your tests are clear. Just continue to rest.* I pull my hair loose from its neat bun. I dressed up in case it would nudge the doctor to take me seriously despite the blank tests. She didn't look at me any differently than when I showed up in an oversized cotton sweater over leggings, my greasy hair limp around my bare face.

Closing my eyes, I picture the skeletal body and shiny skull of one of the senior partners in our department, who got diagnosed with pancreatic cancer last summer. When he returned to the office after treatment, supporting his frail limbs on a walking stick, he was greeted as a hero; his fight was futile, but we admired him even more for showing up to a battle he knew he would lose. At the time, I pitied him for his fate, but now I am not sure how I would react if the doctor told me they had discovered something in me after all. Her voice would soften as she conveyed the news of cancerous cells running rogue in my bloodstream, but I would only ask for next steps of action in a strong voice. She would applaud me for my stoicism, and I would pretend I am enlightened, when I am really only desperate for a concrete enemy. I hunger to punch and kick myself free, but I can't fight an invisible, unknown opponent – especially when it's possible that the enemy is my own imagination.

Grabbing my phone, I scan through my own social media posts, stalking my past self for evidence of breakdown.

At the office Christmas party, Jas and I smile against the backdrop of a spacious bar decorated with fairy lights and tinsel, clutching glasses of white wine. We spent the night walking up to senior partners at the consultancy, introducing ourselves and sparking conversations, so that the people with influence would later recall our dedication and put us forward for premature promotions. My body felt heavy, and I got drunk too easily, but it can't have been that bad; Jas and I stayed until closing. Someone called us a dynamic duo, I can't remember who.

At Halloween, a black bodysuit clings to my body like a second layer of skin and a pair of cat ears perch on my head, Matt's arm around my shoulders. When I squeezed my legs and arms into the shiny black outfit, my body complained with a blinding headache and loud whispers: *please, can't we just sleep for days?* I killed off the headache with paracetamol and prosecco, because I wanted Matt to see my body in the best-selling costume the website had marketed as sexy; we had only just had a conversation about exclusivity.

In late September, against a backdrop of office desks, Jas and I throw back shots of espresso, making it look like we're shotting tequila. In my desk drawer, I had stocked up on caffeine pills, but I can't remember when I did that; next to colleagues popping ADHD medication for jolts of artificial concentration, my occasional caffeine pill seemed tame and insignificant.

I continue to scroll, wishing I had marked each photo with an honest caption:

'Looking happy, feeling like death, #fakingit.'

Abandoning my past self, I scroll through new posts. Jas has snapped a selfie in the office. Halfway down my feed, I see a photo from Matt: a huddle of laughing people are standing in the middle of an open-plan office, an exposed brick wall behind them. His whole start-up fits in a single frame. Seeing the post, I remember he was pitching to investors today.

'Congratulations?' I text, even though the photo tells me nothing about whether the pitch went well or not; in his office, they toast success and failure as if they are the same thing. Assuming he closed the deal may border on naivety; it's the fourth start-up he's joined in three years, as one by one, the companies folded like cards.

Cradling my phone and waiting for a reply, I itch to ignore my brittle body and divert my car ride to his office. After lying home alone for weeks, the floor-to-ceiling windows of my flat make me feel like a fish in an aquarium, constrained to a glass space that's too small.

If the doctors say my body is fine, maybe they are right. The heaviness that holds me down could be only an aftermath, like being sore after a workout. My mind could be playing a horrible magic trick on me, making things feel real when they are not. My face burns at the thought of falling for the trick; I would be no better than people wiring money to a stranger after receiving a poorly worded email from a self-proclaimed prince who promises he will 'reward them handsomely' once he receives the mythical inheritance he can only access if they help him first. I ask the driver if I can change my destination.

6

I step out of the car onto a narrow side street. The reception of Matt's co-working space glows through large windows. Prints of bright abstract art adorn the walls. Large potted palm trees and ferns hug the corners of the room. The receptionist asks me to scan a code with my phone to sign in. A pile of dreadlocks rests on her head in an intricate nest.

Stepping out of the lift on the fourth floor, I hear voices and music spill out of a room at the end of the corridor. I walk into the room, expecting everyone to look up, but they are all engrossed in conversations. Matt is perched on top of a desk talking to a woman wearing jeans and hot pink trainers, her grey T-shirt declaring in large yellow letters that Black Lives Matter. I feel out of place in my heeled boots and blouse. I poke Matt on the shoulder.

"Surprise!"

"Hey!" His face breaks up in a grin. "What are you doing here?"

"You were celebrating! I wanted to celebrate with you. Like last time you landed a deal, remember?"

Matt pulls me close and kisses me. "Oh, I remember." He kisses me again, lingering this time, a clear indication that he's drunk. When sober, we are both averse to showing affection in front of other people. "It's nice to see you."

"You too." I'm relieved that he also wants to pretend that everything is fine. While I have refused to see him for weeks as I've been lying in my glass coffin, I have been texting him the things I would like to do to him and him to do to me, creating a healthy electronic avatar full of lust and vitality.

"Blip over," I say. "Congratulations again."

Matt jumps down from the desk. "Let's get you a drink!" He reaches into an ice bucket for an unopened bottle of prosecco.

"Give it to me," I say. I twist the bottle and pull the cork out with a controlled pop and a breath of steam. I fill a plastic glass and cheers it against Matt's bottle. Years ago, after the first week at the consultancy, when I understood I was now surrounded by people who ordered champagne like it was sparkling water, I bought a case of cheap prosecco, and alone in my flat, I practised opening the bottles, spilling foam onto the floor and shooting corks into the ceiling until I could make it seem like I was one of them.

"Let me introduce you to some people," Matt says.

Cradling the cool glass, I hover next to him, as the woman in the activist T-shirt talks about police brutality against Black people.

"People think it only happens in the US," the woman says. "But it's a problem here too."

"Like discrimination against women," I say. "We like to think we've progressed beyond it, but it happens all the time. The gender pay gap is massive."

"Yeah, but at least a gender pay gap isn't fatal, you know? And even then, Black women are hit twice, aren't they?"

As the woman talks about systemic racism, the voices in the room bounce off the air and attack me like icy hail. I am woozy. The noises keep attacking. My brain is on fire. I want to contribute relevant facts, but I can't find them, and my heart pounds.

Ignore it, it's only your mind playing tricks. Splash some water on your face, and snap out of it.

"Hold my drink," I say to Matt. "Bathroom."

I make it halfway down the corridor before I give in to my body's screaming tantrum. Collapsing against the wall, my legs splay out, blocking the corridor. The exhaustion wraps me like a straightjacket. Dense rocks replace the muscle and bone and blood. Fear dances on top of the pains. *We're dying. You will never feel like yourself again.*

"Hey, are you okay?"

I open my eyes. A man is looking down at me. A neat beard sits below concerned eyes.

"Yes, all fine." I smile and wave my phone at him. "Just had to take a call." I pull my legs up towards my chest. "Sorry for blocking your way. You may pass." I bow to him and laugh.

He hesitates. "Alright then."

As he walks off, I want to reach out and cling to his legs.

"Actually, I'm not fine," I mumble. "Not at all."

Crouching beside me, his hand is heavy on my shoulder. I stare down at my phone; looking at his concerned face would be like looking directly into sunlight, the pity would blind me. His trainers are an aggressive combination of turquoise and red.

"I'm okay," I say. "Really. I was only being dramatic."

"No offence, but you look like shit. Can I order you a ride?"

"Oh no, I'm fine. Thank you."

"Lie down. I'll get you some water."

Like an obedient child, I lie down on my side and melt into the floor. My mind floods with a vivid image of a dead woman I read about in the news. They found her face-up on the kitchen floor, her uneaten toast next to her body with the sticky side down, jam oozing onto the laminated wood. Wearing pyjamas and with her hair freshly washed, she hadn't spilled a drop of blood onto the floor as she died, only the raspberry jam. The news referred to her as a woman, but she looked like a girl in the photos. She was smiling with an open mouth, dimples marking her rosy cheeks.

"Actually, can you get Matt for me?" I call out to the back of the man's trainers.

A minute later, Matt strides down the corridor ahead of the bearded man, who's carrying a glass of water. Seeing me, Matt's eyes widen. "Grace! What the fuck?"

"Hey," I say, frantically pushing myself up to sit. Seeing the panic on his face, I wish I had escaped unseen.

"What happened?"

I smile, my teeth chattering. "Never been better."

"Here you go." The stranger hands me the glass. I gulp the lukewarm water like medicine.

"I'll leave her with you then?" The bearded man looks at Matt.

"Yeah." Matt nods then turns to me. "You shouldn't have come. I'm taking you home."

"Oh, no. Please don't. I'll go home, you stay."

"You're not okay. I'm coming with you."

"No, honestly. I'm fine. I came here to make your night better, not to ruin it."

Matt stares at me. Holding his gaze, I intend to convey solid assurance, but the terror must be breaking through,

31

because Matt reaches out and puts his arms around me. His body is warm like a bath.

"We'll get you better," he murmurs into my ear. "But for fuck's sake, you have to stop saying you are fine. You're lying on the floor in an office corridor."

"Okay," I whisper. I want to crawl out of myself and float away, like a lost helium balloon. My throat is burning. I swallow the tears that want to push up and out. A throbbing mass of fear sits in my chest like an inflamed tumour, but I don't want to reveal the extent of my brokenness; it makes us even more incompatible than we already are. *Fun, heard of that?* I close my eyes, driven by that infantile impulse: if I make the world disappear from view, I will disappear too. Matt strokes my back with his fingertips.

"I hate my body," I snap. "Why can't it behave?"

Matt's fingers recoil as if burnt. He extracts his phone and orders a car.

While we wait, I rest my head against the wall.

"Do you remember that woman who died last year?" I say.

"Who?"

"You know, the one they found dead in her kitchen."

"You're not dying," Matt says. "Just because it happened to her doesn't mean it will happen to you."

I pick at a loose thread on the edge of my blouse. "Yes, I know. She had a heart condition or something."

"And a friend of a friend of mine who knew her said she also did a little too much coke. You don't have a secret drug habit, do you?"

We sit in silence, but I can't stand it. When I stop talking, it feels like we're only watching the tragic figure of myself lying on the floor. I don't remember feeling sad when

32

I first saw the article about the dead woman, she only stuck with me because we were the same age. *I've never been this close to death, I can smell it.*

"So, the pitch," I say. "The deal. Tell me."

"Car's almost here, I need to grab my coat."

When Matt disappears down the corridor, I type out a note on my phone, saving Matt's words: *we'll get you better.* I want to remember Matt's voice saying the word 'we', and if I don't write it down it might just fall between the cracks; I don't know if my brain is now as unreliable as the rest of me. I look at the words glowing on the screen before I delete them again. I don't want us to live as a single entity. We are only one plus one, two self-reliant individuals in love. I want him to desire me, not feel obligated to save me.

7

The doorbell's melodious tune wakes me. Afternoon light fills the room. Disoriented, I look at my phone, my body still half asleep. Shuffling over to the beeping intercom, my eyes squinting against the brightness, I rehearse playfully telling Matt off for ignoring my texts where I told him not to come over this weekend, but when I get close enough to see the small screen the face that shows up is my older sister Ellie's.

"Which floor?" she asks in a distorted voice.

Buzzing her in, I propel into the bathroom. Stripping, I lift my naked arm to smell my armpit, worrying I stink like the decaying animal I feel like, but I am odourless, a statue. I pull on jeans that feel tight around my legs; I've been wearing only loose clothing for weeks now. In front of the mirrored wardrobe, I collect my hair in a neat bun, surprised at the discrepancy you can create between the outside and the inside of a body. I paint my lips red, then blot the colour off again. Ellie knocks on the door.

I plaster a smile onto my face, before flinging the door open. Ellie is holding a bulging plastic bag of food in each hand.

"What are you doing here?" I say.

"I would hug you, but..." With a shrug, Ellie indicates the heaviness of the bags she is holding. "Kitchen?"

I point. She walks off, and I trail behind her. A sizeable strip of colourless hair separates her blonde hair from her parting, and I'm pleased with this sign of imperfection on her part, even though I would now trade my body for hers in an instant.

At the counter, she unpacks a net of oranges, wholegrain crackers and carrot soup, then kale, kiwis and shiny green apples that look like they are made of plastic. It's a pile of colourful foods that are meant to create health and vitality. *She must know.*

"Why haven't you told me you're ill?" Ellie says, as she places the vegetables and fruits into the fridge, which is almost empty, except for a whole shelf of coconut water cartons I ordered after Jas sent me an article about the multitude of vitamins and minerals that swim in the white liquid.

"Who told you?" I say.

"Your boyfriend. Who I didn't even know about, by the way."

"Matt called you?"

Ellie pauses to look at the drawing taped to the fridge, a childish doodle of two stick figures holding hands. Large and uneven handwriting runs across the top:

To the best aunt in the world.

"Andrea misses you," Ellie says. "You haven't come to visit in ages."

"Yes, well, I've been poorly," I say.

Closing the fridge, Ellie scans me up and down, like those metal detectors at airports, before sinking into one of the chairs by the glass table. I mirror her, taking in the wrinkles in her white T-shirt and her breasts hanging low. Jordan said you can buy pills to stop your breasts from producing milk, so they don't lose their perkiness.

"Why don't you go back to Mum and Dad for a while?" Ellie asks.

"I'll get better soon."

She raises her eyebrows at me, and I shrink, feeling our nine-year age difference. The gap has always felt vast, but now it elongates back into the insurmountable divide that split us as children. We have spent more time together in the five years since Andrea was born than in all the years before put together. If Andrea didn't exist, we would be estranged.

"Don't tell them," I say.

"Why can't you just go home for a while?"

"I'm not a child."

"You're their daughter. When Andrea becomes an adult, if she gets sick, I would drop everything to take care of her. Even if she's no longer a child, she'll still be my baby."

"Mum and Dad are different."

"No, they're not. They are parents. The eternal nature of parental love is a biological thing."

"It doesn't matter. I don't want you to tell them, okay?"

I picture myself lying across the back seat of my parents' car wrapped in a duvet like a fragile parcel, forced back to the confines of our tiny village where everyone knows everything about everyone else. The only thing worse than never leaving is moving away and then returning. If I moved home, people would whisper.

She is sick.

But what is wrong with her?

No one knows. Big city life, she just couldn't hack it, I guess? All I know is she is back living with her parents.

Escaping into the bathroom with my phone in my hand, I sit down on the toilet lid and call Matt. He doesn't pick up. Calling repeatedly, my anger heats with each beep. On the fifth round, he answers.

"You called my sister without telling me?" I say.

"Yeah."

"Yeah?" I echo. "You had no right to do that."

"Fine. I'm sorry. But why don't you want her to know? I don't get it, you desperately want to convince the doctors that you are sick, but you also want to hide it from everyone else."

"Yes, well, the doctors are meant to find out what's wrong so they can fix it. When anyone else hears I'm sick, all they offer is pity."

"Whether you want it or not, you need help."

"Rich coming from you, you wouldn't even let me carry grocery bags after you broke your arm."

"That was different."

"How?"

"We had just started dating. I wanted to impress you."

"My sister is trying to get me to move back home with our parents. I can't do that."

"Okay, then don't."

As if my hands are acting of their own accord, I pull the phone from my ear and hang up. Anger courses through me like electricity. I count to ten before calling back.

"Sorry, battery died," I say.

"That recharged quickly," Matt says.

"Yes."

"Look, I want to take care of you, but I…" His voice is soft. "You won't let me. And even if you did… when my mom gave me a goldfish as a kid, I only kept it alive for eleven days." His laugh is brittle.

"I have to go, Ellie is calling me," I say and hang up again.

When I shuffle back into the living room, Ellie has moved from the table to the couch. She's holding a cup of tea and looking around the room. When she was my age, framed photos of her and her friends covered every surface in her flat. My shelves only hold a selection of cacti in marble pots.

"Lemon and ginger," Ellie says, indicating another steaming mug on the glass table.

"You're only feeding me things meant for sick people."

Ellie looks at me, opens her mouth, then closes it again. She takes a sip of tea. "I'm not sure you should be living alone right now. What about your boyfriend? Can't you stay at his?"

"No."

"Or he can come stay with you?"

I shake my head. Matt and I have not yet peeled our way anywhere close to the innermost layer of a relationship where being taken care of might feel okay. I can't imagine what that feels like; I don't even know if adults can reach that space at all. Matt and I are not anywhere near the depth where you feel more like yourself when you are with the other person than when you are alone. I don't know if that kind of relationship is even attainable either, it's only what Ellie said in her speech when she married Hector, a Colombian man a decade older than her. They have promised to stay together in good days and bad, but Matt and I haven't promised each other anything. We have not lived through more than tiny shocks together, like him breaking his arm and getting his phone stolen.

"You should really be in a hospital, you know," Ellie says.

I play with my necklace and shake my head. If I insisted they place me in a hospital, they might only allocate me to a mental institution, believing the tests telling them I am physically fine over my testimony that I am not.

"I can handle it," I say.

"Please," Ellie sighs, exasperated. "You're like Andrea, refusing to get help with anything, even things you can't manage at all. That's not strength; that's stupidity."

"I can pay for a nurse to check on me, like old people do. I can get food delivered, and I already have a cleaner. I'm fine."

Shaking her head, Ellie searches in her purse for her phone. Without saying a word, she dials and holds the phone to her ear.

"Who are you calling?" I say.

She holds up a finger. I close my eyes and sink into the cushions.

"Hey, darling," Ellie says. "I'm just at Grace's now, and..." She pauses. Hector's voice booms through the speaker, but I can't catch the words. "Yes, worse than I thought. And I was thinking..." She pauses again. "Exactly what I was going to suggest. Okay. I love you more than anything."

"What?" I say, without opening my eyes.

"You'll come stay at ours for a while."

I take a deep breath and let myself deflate.

8

While Ellie drives, I slump in the passenger seat, facing the window. The queue of cars snakes its way out of the city centre. Ellie switches on the radio, and erratic jazz fills the car.

"Can't we listen to something else?" I say. "This is mess, not music."

Ellie turns up the volume.

Her house is only a few miles from my flat, but it belongs to a different city. We drive into her neighbourhood where married couples and their babies, children and fluffy dogs fill identical terraced houses. Here, people's homes are where their lives unfold, not just the place where they sleep.

"We've cleared out the spare room for you," Ellie says, as she steps through the vibrantly yellow front door. She's carrying my bags, one on each shoulder. Massive flowerpots in teal and tangerine frame the door, but they are empty; Ellie tends to abandon new ideas halfway through. I trail behind her. I will not stay for long; I'm a new project, soon she will want to move on.

Coming from the pristine box of my flat, their house feels both massive and cluttered. Paintings and framed photos cover the walls, mainly of Ellie and Hector at various parties and exotic locations, alongside a sea of photos of Andrea's grinning face. A mosaic of rugs covers the wooden floors and piles of pillows litter the couches. The kitchen extends behind the living room onto a small walled-in garden.

I follow Ellie up the stairs, my legs moving with glacial speed, and step into the small rectangular room that faces the street. I lie down on top of the duvet of the double bed, my feet dangling off the edge. Like a hotel room, there's only a bed, a bedside table and a closet. Only the walls give away that the room wasn't originally intended for me. Colourful cartoon animals dance over light blue paint. A smiling giraffe reaches its head up to a group of monkeys dangling from a tree branch. From another branch, a flock of red birds takes flight. The work of art was created for a baby that never made it all the way out into the world, only almost. I expected they would have painted over it by now; it's been more than a year.

"Dinner's at seven-thirty," Ellie says and strides back out of the room, without a glance at the walls.

Hector's voice booms from the kitchen. When I don't respond, he strides up the stairs and bursts into my room.

"*Gracita*! Come down for dinner. You're never going to feel better if you stay cooped up here all alone." His loud laugh shoots out of his mouth, as if his short and compact body can't contain sounds. Grey specks his hair like confetti.

"I can't," I whisper. "Didn't Ellie explain?"

"Come on! A glass or two of wine, some music…" He shimmies from side to side, but I shake my head. Hector sighs, a dramatic exhalation with his whole body. My desire to follow his instructions hits me like a burst of hunger.

"I won't stay with you for long. A few weeks, tops," I say.

Hector waves his hand. "Stay as long as you need. This is what family is for. But tomorrow I expect you downstairs!" He winks and walks out. I want to be back in my empty flat, eating microwaved meals in bed alone.

I brace myself for his footsteps to return, but it's Andrea that floats into my room on light feet, carrying a tray that looks huge in her grip. A large glass of red wine and a bowl balances on the tray. Inching forward, her tongue peeks out at the edge of her mouth. The tray wobbles, the wine sloshing against the curves of the glass. Sitting up, I hold my arms out and take the tray from her. She holds her tiny hand to my forehead.

"You can be my real-life doll, and I can be your nurse."

I smile. "Thank you."

She looks down at the chicken, rice and plantain in the bowl, then frowns.

"Should I feed you?" Her whisper is loud.

I wave the fork in the air. "I'm fine."

Curtseying, Andrea laughs and skips out of the room. I collapse back onto the pillows. *If our ages were reversed, could I have taken her up on the offer to feed me?* I can't remember if it ever felt comforting to receive care from others. Giving assistance is much easier; the words lie when they imply effort is only expanded by the one who helps.

When Andrea returns a minute later, she's wearing one of Hector's white shirts, a plastic stethoscope draped around her neck. Peeling back the duvet, she presses the plastic onto my chest. She scrunches her face.

"You have fabulous heartbeats," she declares.

Later, when Hector's footsteps come back upstairs and approach my room, I close my eyes and make my breathing heavy. I hear him move to the bedside table, where he picks up the tray with the empty plate and the still-full glass of wine. His footsteps leave the room, then stop at the landing.

"No need to go in, she's sleeping."

"Right," Ellie replies.

"We have to get her out of that room. It's like she's given up."

"She's sick, sweetie. Sick people lie in bed."

"Yes, sure, but not for weeks and weeks, no? Without even getting up to have a proper meal with other people?"

"She claims it's not depression."

Hector snorts. "Well… let's say it's not. She should be out there, getting treatments."

"She says they won't give her any. They can't even find out what's wrong with her."

"*Claro*, but they are just doctors! There are a million other options – acupuncture, massage, osteopathy – you know, when I had my shoulder, the acupuncture fixed it like that!" He snaps his fingers.

"Shh, let's talk downstairs; you'll wake her."

I sink deeper into the mattress. I want to shout out that I have followed instructions; I have rested, slept, cut out alcohol and caffeine and sugar. I have forced my aching head to scan the internet for treatments that promise to throw a blanket of health over any possible ailment. I could sweat in infrared saunas or float in sensory deprivation tanks, inject myself with vitamins or let an osteopath manipulate my muscles and bones. I could go vegan or paleo, eat only fats or no fats, or live exclusively on juice. I don't know how I am meant to do any of these things when I can barely drag my dead body to the doctor's office – and even if I could, fear whispers: *but what if experimenting with any of those things makes you worse instead of better? Imagine what worse looks like: being unable to go to the bathroom on your own and relying on Andrea to feed you. You could remain a horizontal doll for the rest of your life.*

My throat and chest burn again. *You have fabulous heartbeats. You have fabulous heartbeats. You have fabulous heartbeats.* I repeat Andrea's words like an affirmation until the pressure eases, her statement somehow more comforting than what any of the real doctors have said so far.

Part 2

1

Hector walks into my room holding a cake, its frosted surface covered in a forest of flaming candles. I push myself up to sit, as Ellie places a paper crown on my head and drapes a pink feathered boa around my neck.

"Come on, make your wish!" Andrea demands.

I blow at the candles, extinguishing the flames in one. Silver glitter rains down on me, as Ellie extracts handfuls of it from her dressing gown pockets. Andrea climbs into my bed and burrows her warm body against mine.

"What did you wish for?"

"It won't come true if I tell you."

"You can whisper it just to me. I'm good at secrets."

When I lean down, she vibrates with expectation. I breathe into her tiny ear: "I'm not telling you."

"Hey!" Pulling away, she looks up at me, sulking, but I only shake my head. I have become the kind of crazy person who clings to the minuscule possibility that birthday wishes have magical powers, if only I don't say them out loud.

"Are you okay to walk downstairs?" Ellie asks.

In my dressing gown and fluffy slippers, I lead a slow procession down the stairs. Balloons cover the living room floor, like an oversized ball pit. A banner with my name on it hangs across the window. I wade through the sea of silver and gold, the balloons bouncing off my legs. The extravagance of the decorations feels wrong when I haven't achieved anything in the past year, beyond staying alive. Instead of aging, I have regressed to the helplessness of childhood. As I reach the island of the couch and collapse into the cushions, I hear familiar voices outside the house; they are dancing in an endless conversation I have listened to since I was born.

I sit up. "You invited Mum and Dad?"

"Of course!" Ellie smiles. "And Matt's coming too."

I glare at her. "But they've never met!"

"Really?"

"You knew that!"

"Did I?" She winks at me. Seeing my face, her eyebrows shoot up. "Come on! Smile! It's your birthday!" Reaching into the pocket of her dressing gown again, she showers me with more glitter. "Jas said she would also try to make it."

"How did you—"

"I stole your phone while you were sleeping." Ellie grins.

Stepping into the room, my parents distribute hugs. My mother kisses my forehead, and my dad places a sparkly pink gift bag in my lap, even though I stopped liking pink before I turned four. They sit down on the other couch, so close to each other that their bodies touch. They haven't spent a single night away from each other in their four decades together. Andrea is on the carpet at their feet, temporarily still. Ellie lounges in the armchair, while Hector distributes mimosas in champagne flutes.

"What's a mimosa?" my mother asks.

"Prosecco and orange juice," Ellie says.

"Oh, fancy." My mother observes her glass.

"I hear you got an early birthday present," my father says to me.

"I did?"

"A diagnosis!" Grinning, my father delivers the word with more joy than it's meant to hold. The same day his own father died abruptly, he went ahead with hosting the dinner party they had planned for that evening. He papered over his sadness with cheap wine, jokes and music. When Ellie lost her baby, he told her to look on the bright side: at least now she wouldn't have to worry about sleep deprivation.

When I only nod, my father frowns. "Isn't a diagnosis what you've wanted for the past year?"

I play with the ribbon on the gift bag. "I didn't get a good one."

"You can't pick and choose them," my mother says. "At least it's not cancer."

"People recover, don't they? You will fight your way through," my father says. "You always had grit." He turns to my mother. "Didn't she?"

"Let's have cake!" Ellie says, glancing at me.

"Matt isn't here," Hector points out.

"Let's have cake!" I echo.

As Hector cuts the cake and Andrea chatters like a bird, I pull at Ellie's arm.

"Did you not explain it to them?" I hiss.

"I did!" Ellie whispers back. "But it's a hard thing to grasp, isn't it? You look fine, on the outside. And it's true that some people recover, right?"

The doorbell rings, and Ellie jumps up. I push myself to sit. Matt steps through the door with his hands in his pockets and rain in his hair.

"Hey, Matt!" Hector booms.

"Happy birthday!" Matt says, his eyes on me. "Nice crown." He waves at my parents, who grin and nod at him in unison, like synchronised swimmers.

"Aren't you going to give Grace a birthday kiss?" Hector says, placing his hand on Matt's shoulder. "No need to be shy!"

Matt leans down and pecks my lips. Hector laughs, grabs Ellie and dips her down in a wedding day kiss. Emerging back up, he grins and raises his eyebrows at Matt.

"Stop it," Ellie laughs. "You're embarrassing them."

Matt leans back down and frames my face with both hands, before placing his warm mouth on mine with hard determination, his lips parted. After several seconds, I pull back, my cheeks warm. I stare at him. His eyes belong to a boy playing a game. The room is a sea of laughter. I want to swim in it, but my body is sinking again. *Come on, not already*. Matt leans down and murmurs: "I didn't want to come across like I'm not invested."

Warmth glows in my chest, even though I know Matt mainly wanted to please Hector. For months now, whenever Matt comes to visit me, he doesn't seem to mind too much that I can only chat to him for ten minutes before I have to rest again; as soon as I close my eyes, he rushes downstairs to join Ellie and Hector for dinner or drinks. I remind myself that him leaving the room makes him less likely to leave me altogether: I offer a package deal now, three for the price of one. Hector hands me a plate with a huge slab of cake.

My father shares stories from the school where both my parents teach, and my mother eats her cake in rushed bites.

For my father, the endless supply of anecdotes is the main perk of being a teacher, even more so than the long holidays. My mother scrapes the last bit of icing from her plate before she pecks at my father's remaining cake with her fork. He hands her the whole plate.

"Let's go into the kitchen," Ellie says.

"Why?" My mother frowns. "We're all settled."

"Grace needs to rest."

"What do you mean she needs rest? She's already lying down."

"I just need to close my eyes for a bit," I say.

"Go ahead then, just close them."

"She needs quiet," Ellie says.

"We're only talking."

Hector gets to his feet and holds his hand out to my mother, as if he's asking her to dance. "May I escort you?"

Laughing, my mother grabs his hand. Hector leads her into the kitchen. Andrea bounces after them, and my father trails behind carrying the pile of empty plates. I feel my mother's thoughts: *why is Grace being so difficult? Why can't she pull herself together?* Reaching out, Matt steals the paper crown off my head and places it on his own. He kisses my head before following the others.

Closing my eyes, I try to float on the cloud of their humming voices, while my body submerges me in aching exhaustion and guilt. I should be able to deliver a happy, grateful persona; my parents have driven hours, and I have only given them minutes in return. I want to make them understand that while some people do recover, my diagnosis doesn't come with a cure – I do not know if there's a pattern to who gets better and who remains stuck in this half-life for decades. I feel drugged. The heavy fog in my head laughs at me. Like my parents, I'm clinging to the belief that I will be one of the people who recover, but I don't know if that should be applauded as positive thinking or written off as denial.

The year I turned eight, my parents decided they had no energy left for hosting birthday parties for me; Ellie had used up their parental energy before I was even born. Hearing their announcement, teenaged Ellie herself decided to play host for my party. She invited everyone in my year group and transformed the house into a carnival-themed wonderland, while also transforming me into the person she thought I should be. Dressing me in a purple tutu, she showered me with glitter and told me I was now the Birthday Girl, an imaginary character with qualities I didn't normally possess. *Today, you are bubbly, sweet and fun, okay? I command you.*

In the living room, Ellie had hung a yellow sun-shaped piñata from the ceiling. She handed me a baseball bat and tied a blindfold around my head. My small hands gripping the bat, I smashed at the air. All the other kids watched, and we were meant to take turns batting, but when Ellie said it was time for someone else to have a go, I shooed her away, shouting that I could do it alone.

I kept smashing at the yellow circle, enraged that I couldn't burst it. The other kids moved to the other side of the room to play charades, while I pounded at the sun, until it finally shattered and showered me with sweets. Jolted out of my trance, I ripped the blindfold off to find myself in a sea of shiny wrappers, but I wasn't surrounded by smiling faces and applause like I'd expected. When I found myself standing there alone, I felt deeply lost, like I'd misunderstood something. Aching, I watched the other kids play without me, until I yelled the word sweets as loud as I could.

I wish I could bribe my health to come back too, but it doesn't respond to anything I yell out.

"You don't want to come back and stay with us again, do you?" my mother asks. She's standing over me, my father hovering next to her. Matt is lounging on the other couch, watching us like we are a TV show. We've just had lunch, but my parents are already leaving; they will rather drive the four hours back to their own familiar beds than spend the night. They claim they can't sleep here; the traffic and sirens keep them awake. For Christmas, they transported me home for two weeks. I lay on the couch in the living room, feeling left out of something as they both hummed along to Christmas songs and spoke amongst themselves in low voices.

I shake my head, as I bite into a chocolate. Caramel oozes onto my tongue.

"Didn't think so," my mother says. "You wouldn't want to be that far away from Matt." She winks at him before bending down to kiss my forehead. Her lips are soft, unlike the rest of her.

"Get better soon!" my father says, patting my blanket-covered leg.

They blow me kisses that fly through the air like twin doves. By the door, they exchange loud hugs with Ellie. Soap bubbles dance in the air around me, as Andrea blows a stream of them into the room, her face creasing in concentration. The door slams shut. I stop smiling, my cheeks sore. Leaning back, I close my eyes and sink further into the pillows.

"Are your parents actually happily married, or are they putting on a show?" Matt says.

"As happily married as they come," I say without opening my eyes.

"Really?"

"Yup."

My phone vibrates, and I look down, glad to escape the conversation. Matt's parents broke up before he was even born, then got back together on and off, until his father left when Matt was six. We had been together for months before I saw a photo of his family, and that was only after I stalked his social media; I scrolled years back in time until I found a photo his mother had tagged him in. A twenty-year-old version of Matt stood rigid next to two identical girls who were only four or five. The bulky man standing next to Matt had his arm around Matt's shoulders. Matt looked like he wanted to throw his stepfather's arm off and sprint out of the frame. His mother stood smiling on the other side of the two small children, her hair hiked up in a cheerful ponytail. She captioned the photo: 'One happy family!'

I have never met any of them, not even virtually. I suspect my parents love each other more than they love me and Ellie, but maybe that is still better than having parents who do not love each other at all.

I open the message from Jas. She wishes me a happy birthday and says she can't make it today – 'work is crazy' – but she will come visit tomorrow instead. I want to reply that I am busy with exciting plans, but I have made the same joke too many times by now, and it was never a particularly funny one in the first place.

2

The next morning, I open the door to Jas. Cold winter air rushes into the room. Since the last time I saw her, months ago now, she has cut her hair; it's too short to stay in her ponytail, and half of it frames her face. The black running tights cling to her slender legs. Behind her, cartoon clouds dance across the sky. Jas has been running for over an hour, and I've only walked down the stairs, but my wobbly body seems to think it's the other way around.

"Marathon training is such a commitment!" Jas declares, as she steps into the house. "I can't stay long – I don't want my muscles to cool, it will be impossible to start again."

"Trying to look like Jordan, are you?" I say, indicating her short hair.

"Ha! You're the one who's obsessed with her, not me. I only want to look older. You know, authoritative."

I nod. At work, Jas wears glasses she doesn't need, claiming studies have shown people automatically assume those wearing glasses are more intelligent. She believes in playing the game more than changing the rules.

She follows me through the living room. Stepping into the empty kitchen, the smell of coffee hits us. I pull open the fridge, which is full of cartons of unfamiliar juices that Hector buys in bulk from Colombian speciality stores. I grab a pink carton at random. With glasses of juice, Jas and I sit down across from each other at the table.

"So, how are you?" Jas takes a huge gulp from her glass and wipes her mouth with the sleeve of her running top.

"Oh, fine." I cling to my glass with both hands, as if the glass is an anchor that can stop my head from spinning. "I don't seem to be getting worse anymore at least."

Jas studies me. "You look great."

"Thanks." I smile, covering up smouldering embers of annoyance. I have told her so many times that my outer shell is an irrelevant illusion. *Most days I can't even hold myself up for long enough to shower or bathe. I smell fresh only because I clean myself with baby wipes I found in a drawer in the bathroom. I spray so much dry shampoo in my hair that it becomes grey.*

Jas looks around the room. "I can't imagine being confined to a house. It's like a reality TV show."

"Minus the cash prize at the end," I say, even though the house is not my prison, my body is. If I could roam the whole house, I would feel free. I could place an exercise bike in my room and join spin classes on my phone, sweat dripping off me. If my brain functioned like it used to, I could glue myself to my laptop all day, working and accessing the world remotely. The online world is meant to operate independently from the limitations of our physical bodies, but it doesn't work that way if the body is faulty like mine.

"How was last night?" I say.

"I feel horrible today. Drank too much. Running on a hangover, it's the worst. I never learn."

I want to grip her arms so tight that it hurts, dig my nails into her skin and create red half-moon marks on her smooth surface. *Don't you know it's rude, showing off your health like this? You have so much of it that you voluntarily throw it away on a hangover?* I breathe deeply. I was the one who demanded Jas doesn't treat me differently, but I wish she could do that while also recognising that something's changed.

"*Eee ooo, eee ooo,*" I say half-heartedly.

Jas laughs. "You're right. No complaining." She stretches her neck to the side, and it cracks. "Even Jordan came out. Well, she didn't drink, of course."

"Why not?"

"Oh, you don't know? She's pregnant again."

Jas's phone buzzes in her hand, and she looks down. Lifting my glass to drink, I reveal a watermark blooming on the wooden table, adding to the mosaic of marks already there. For Jordan's first pregnancy, I was the one who shared the news with Jas.

"I miss drinking," I say.

Jas's face snaps up from her phone. "What? You can't drink? At all? You never said that! Fuck, that sucks." She puts her phone down on the table, as Ellie walks into the kitchen wearing a dressing gown, her feet bare.

"Don't mind me," Ellie says. "Just grabbing coffee." Opening one of the cupboards, she extracts two mismatched mugs. She spoons ground coffee into a cafetiere.

"Jas is training for the marathon," I say, desperate to insert Ellie into the conversation in my place, so I can just watch the two of them talk about something other than the state of my body.

"Really? You couldn't pay me to do that," Ellie says, turning to face Jas while the kettle hums behind her. "Are you doing it for charity?"

"Yes," Jas says. "I've raised almost four thousand. If you want to donate, let me know."

"But you don't believe in charity donations?" I frown at Jas.

Jas laughs. "It's a competition, in the office. Jordan said she will double the donations of whoever raises the most."

"I didn't realise the marathon was an office thing."

"Oh yeah, a bunch of people are running. Jordan too."

"Can she do that when she's pregnant?"

"Sure. No limits, right?"

"No limits," I echo.

"Well, I'll leave you two to it." Ellie lifts a tray off the counter. I want her to stay, but she disappears into the living room. The stairs creak as she walks back upstairs. For a moment, Jas and I sit in silence.

"So, I googled your diagnosis," Jas says.

Taking another sip of juice, my heart pounds.

"It's such a stupid name," I say. "It makes it sound like I'm just tired."

"The official medical term is such a tongue twister though. Try saying it three times fast."

"Try living with it," I say, but it comes out bitter instead of witty.

"But you might not have to for much longer." Jas leans forward, her gaze intense. "That's what I wanted to tell you. An ex-boyfriend of my sister's had the same thing; I had just completely forgotten."

"What do you mean he 'had' it?" I lean forward too, anticipation fluttering in my stomach.

"Well," Jas says, twirling her glass of juice. Her apprehension is unusual, and my heart pounds harder.

"He went to see a psychologist." The words tumble out of her.

My face goes hot, and my pulse rises.

"Apparently he recovered almost instantly after that," Jas adds, shooting words at me like bullets. "My sister didn't know all the details; they broke up before he discovered the shrink. But apparently, he lives in the countryside now and runs his own little gardening business, doing landscaping for rich people. He's completely healthy and happy as a clam."

"He can't have had the same thing as me then," I say. "It's not all in my head. The doctors say a virus knocked me out, and then I just never recovered."

"But why? *Why* didn't you recover?"

"It's a real thing. A physical illness."

"Okay. Fine. Forget it then," Jas says.

"I'm on a waiting list," I say. "To get the diagnosis confirmed by an expert."

"Great."

The silent air sits heavy between us. Jas escapes into her phone, staring at the screen. My brain whirs. *Psychologist, psychologist, psychologist.* It's not my mind that's faulty, or if it has broken too, it's only a result of the torture of spending over a year in solitary confinement and pain. I have clung to this belief for months, but now uncertainty creeps back in; maybe all of this originated from a defunct mind.

"Did you see the latest from Syria?" I say. "All those ancient temples. Gone, just like that."

Gaze snapping back up, Jas jumps on the bait. She takes over the conversation, and I let her, feeling relieved to discuss bombings and flows of refugees bobbing across the sea in tiny boats. I still check the news on my phone several times a day, as if knowledge of atrocities that aren't mine will be enough to make me feel like I am still part of the same broken world as everyone else.

I watch her mouth move. The vast discrepancy between my reality and what Jas thinks it feels like bothers me almost as much as my failure to get better. My secluded existence may become bearable if she would think I am strong for enduring it instead of weak for it happening in the first place. The pain in my head has hardened, and I can barely follow what she is saying. My depleted body needs her to leave, but I am starved of human interactions, and I want her to stay.

"I should go," Jas eventually says, draining her glass. Stretching her legs, she grimaces.

I shuffle behind her through the living room to the front door. She bends down to tighten the laces on her neon green shoes. My teeth are chattering, the nausea surging.

"I want to finish the marathon in three hours forty-five," Jas says.

"If that's your goal, you'll make it happen," I say to the top of her head, even though the version of me who believed life was order, not chaos, feels like a pixelated hologram. "I'll watch online, see if I can spot you."

I hover by the door as Jas runs off up the road. Crossing the finish line of a marathon under numbers that proclaim you ran faster than average must sit so high up on the hierarchy of needs that it's floating somewhere above it.

When I visited my grandfather in the nursing home before he died, I felt relief when the visit was over, and I got to escape the building of the sick and the dying. Will Jas feel that same relief now, as her legs propel her into the park, her body free to take her wherever she wants to go? Months ago, I decided that our slogan of no limits was ridiculous, and I shouldn't be surprised it didn't work out, but limitless living still works for both Jas and Jordan, just not for me.

I drag my body back upstairs and collapse into bed. Forcing my trembling hands to pick up my phone, I scroll through Jas's sister's photos, searching for her ex who may or may not have had the same thing as me.

3

Jas's sister fills her page with photos at least once a day. The faces squeezed into the frame alongside hers keep changing; she is clearly more sociably minded than Jas, who mainly hangs out with the same group of colleagues. Searching amongst the mosaic of faces, I click on every photo with a man in the frame, while trying to evaluate from the composition of his face against hers whether they are a couple or only friends.

The hangover that hits me after every exertion is already pounding, and my body begs for dark silence, but the itching in my mind is violent.

On the screen, in a shot from last May, Jas's sister is wearing sunglasses, kissing a man on the cheek, as he's squinting against the sun, smiling and holding a takeaway coffee cup. She's written underneath:

'Finally, a day out with bae, #blessed.'

I study the man's content expression, knowing that it's pointless to look for clues in his face as to whether he is the sick one, since the illness I want to find is invisible. I want to know whether Jas's sister broke up with him because he was sick, or if they would have ended anyway. If she did leave him because of his illness, which part of him did she not want anymore, the outside, the inside or both?

I click through to his profile. Selfies sit next to plants and hedges and trees. I should send Matt the link and tell him this man is proof that recovery is possible, but then he also proves that leaving a sick person is an option. My phone vibrates.

'Don't dismiss the psychologist' Jas says, her words overlaying the photo of her sister's ex cradling a plant in each arm like twin babies.

'Wouldn't you rather admit that this might be a mental thing and get help? Emotions can create involuntary physical responses.'

Her text includes a link to an article about a woman who started having seizures after her wife was in a traumatic car accident; she had no control over the attacks, they were completely involuntary, but they did not have a physical cause. When she started going to therapy, the seizures disappeared.

I throw my phone as hard as I can across the room, but my arms barely have any muscles left in them, and the phone only hits the wall with a soft thud.

I close my eyes and try to rest, but the exhaustion strangles me now. I crave distraction even more from this rougher pain, but I can't give in; ignoring the pain is futile. Avoiding pain might always have been an act of postponing instead of eliminating, but I am only seeing that connection now that the time between running away from it and tripping over it again can be counted in minutes.

Don't dismiss the psychologist.

When I was a toddler, whenever I got angry or scared, I automatically held my breath for up to a minute. Several times I deprived myself of air for so long that I fainted, terrifying my parents. But the woman with the seizures had experienced trauma, and I don't have a knot of suppressed emotions that would shout at my body to shut down; I have never experienced anything that can count as traumatic. Growing up, it only felt like I was waiting for something, like adulthood was going to be my time.

At the end of the first year working at the consultancy, our group of colleagues from the graduate scheme went on holiday to Portugal. While we waited to board at the airport gate, ridiculously early so we could make the most of our days off, Jas circulated an itinerary for the week via email.

'7am: morning run by the beach. 8.30am: breakfast. 11am: beach volleyball tournament. 1pm: lunch. 4pm: swimming competition. 7pm: dinner and drinking games.'

At the bottom of the email, she outlined the room allocation in the rented villa; the two of us were sharing. No one mocked the overly structured days; all of us equated planning with optimisation rather than rigidity.

As soon as we stepped into the sun-lit villa, cooled by air conditioning turned on by unseen owners, Jas extracted a whiteboard from her bag, scribbled *scoreboard* across the top and placed it on the kitchen counter, balancing it against the wall. She announced the first activity would start in fifteen minutes – water polo in the pool glittering outside the patio doors – and everyone rushed upstairs to unpack and change, giddy with the promise of competition. No one wanted to float listlessly in the pool on inflatable animals.

When I stepped out onto the hot flagstones of the patio, Jas was already sitting on the edge of the pool, dangling her feet in the water while pushing air into inflatable plastic goal posts. Without pausing, she handed me the remaining flaccid plastic tube. I sat down next to her, and our lungs worked in tandem, until the others came out to join us.

In the cool water, we split into teams. Jas blew a whistle to start the game. Muscular arms hurled the ball and we propelled through the water, crashing into each other in the too-small pool. I threw the ball towards Jas, but Viktor jumped up and intercepted the shot, then flung the ball between our goalposts. Jas shouted at me to concentrate; her frustration showered onto me with a spray of water. I felt like she had hugged me; she was revealing the kind of sharp edges I had always been told I should cover up with bubble wrap. When she failed to catch my throw to her, I swore at her, and she laughed, as if fuck was an affectionate word.

Last summer, they all went back to the same villa on what they dubbed a 'reunion' trip, and I watched the photos online. Like last time, they held an actual ceremony on the final night to mark the winner of the week; Jas stepped onto a chair serving as a makeshift podium, and Viktor handed her the small golden trophy she had bought, probably in the knowledge that she would be the one to win it. In a video clip, Jas grabs the handle of the little golden cup, then roars and lifts her arms up.

I click onto my own social media profile. The last photo remains the rooftop photo from my birthday last year, where Jas is occupying my place in the centre. Most of the people in the photo I have not seen since it was taken. Some have texted regularly, but most only sent one or two messages when I first disappeared from the office. No one has called or visited, except for Jas.

My phone is still abandoned on the floor when Ellie brings me dinner in bed. I prop my inert body up on pillows, as she hands me a bowl of vegan risotto filled with mushrooms, peas and green swirls of spinach. Hector has long ago stopped attempting to entice me downstairs for dinner, but he cooks me meals filled with vegetables, claiming health starts in the gut. Every morning, on a small table outside my room, one of them leaves a bowl of porridge drizzled with honey and berries next to lunch packed in one of Andrea's lunch boxes. Picking up the food after they've gone off to work, I pretend that I'm on an endless holiday in a luxury hotel, living on room service. On bad days, my mind only tells me the feeding system is proof that I'm as incapable as a pet, but I override it: *luxury hotel, luxury hotel, you're living in a luxury hotel.*

My phone vibrates with another text, and Ellie turns her head towards the sound.

"What is your phone doing on the floor?" Picking it up, she hands it to me.

'Free tomorrow?' Matt says. He still phrases it like this, rather than asking how I'm feeling, either to make me feel better or pretend to himself; busy is attractive – we all want to be in demand.

"Nice of Jas to come visit," Ellie says, hovering by the door. "I never stay in touch with colleagues when I don't work with them anymore." She leans against the door frame, crossing her arms. "Work friends... it's such a strange thing. You see them every single day for years, and then they disappear, never to be seen again."

"She thinks I'm making it up."

"Making up what?"

"This." I indicate my horizontal body. "She said I should see a psychologist."

"That's not the same as saying you're making it up."

66

"It's not all in my head."

"No, of course not," Ellie says.

"And I know lots of people who are still close with people they used to work with," I say.

"You do?"

"Yes."

Ellie sits down at the foot of the bed. "You have to stop ordering us bottles of wine, by the way. The cupboard is full. Hector drinks too much as it is; you shouldn't encourage it."

"But you won't let me pay rent. I can't just scrounge off you forever."

"If you're absolutely going to insist on buying us presents, wine is a little insulting, you know. It's so generic; it's what you give to acquaintances when they invite you to a dinner party."

"But isn't that what we've always been? Acquaintances related by blood?"

Ellie's hand shoots to her chest. "Ouch."

"I didn't mean…"

"I'm just being silly. I know you adore me."

I take a bite of the risotto and it burns my tongue. Ellie watches me eat. We have had this conversation before. She tells me family relationships aren't transactional, but I wish they were – I would rather pay her in money than guilt.

"You know what Andrea said last night?" Ellie says. "She asked me if it makes her a bad person that she likes that you are sick because it means you are here all the time, and she can see you whenever she wants."

"I can read to her later," I say, ignoring my pounding head and leaden limbs, because I crave Andrea curling up next to me and showering me with praise. *You have the best voice.* Her hair, damp from her bath, smells of strawberries. *When you read to me, it tickles my brain and my stomach.*

When Ellie first had Andrea, the repetitiveness of motherhood shocked me. I loved Andrea more than I had ever loved anyone or anything, but the relentless rotation of feeding, nappies and sleep seemed simultaneously demanding and dull, like working on an assembly line. Watching her breastfeed, I told Ellie that if everyone has children, it's like a pyramid scheme, because parents sacrifice for their children so they can have the best possible lives, but by the time those children are grown up and realising those dreams, they are meant to have children of their own, and in the end, no one gets to live out their visions. I asked her if she didn't think having a baby was similar to foot-binding in how it contained women, but she only laughed without looking up from Andrea's tiny face and said a certain degree of containment was good for her, without it she would just float away.

"At least I can offer you free babysitting services," I say to Ellie now, even though I need Andrea more than she needs me. A disproportionate number of people die in the first year after they retire because without a purpose to their days, they only float around aimlessly until they disappear. As a law student, I could read eight hundred words per minute, and it felt as easy as inhaling air. Now, my brain will only lift each word slowly off the page, like it's a fragile object, but Andrea doesn't seem to mind that it takes forever to get through each story. I like that all of Andrea's dreams may still come true; they aren't even formed yet.

4

The next morning, I potter into Ellie and Hector's empty bedroom and lie down widthways across their cloudlike mattress, relishing in its softness. The aftermath of my visit from Jas is still pulsing through my body. I'm holding my phone in my hand, waiting for a daily text that has usually arrived by now. When I'm home alone during the day, I take turns between this bed and Andrea's because being confined by a different set of walls counts as novelty. I can go days without touching the ground; the stairs remain too mountainous. *You're like a princess locked in a tower*, Andrea says. *Even your hair is growing long, soon you can braid a rope from it.* The cool metal of the phone comes to life, vibrating in my grip.

'How are you today?' Lara says.

For a while, I only stare at the screen, then my fingers dance across it. Lara was only a friend of a friend until I fell off the face of the earth, someone I saw occasionally on nights out with Matt and our mutual friend Oliver, but now we text every day.

I want my extreme loneliness to attach itself to the electronic words and disappear into the air, like an exorcism. *It shouldn't be possible to feel lonely already in the moments after waking.* Deleting the loneliness instead of sending it, I reply with a repetitive charade:

'I'm fine. You?'

'Are you home?'

'Where else would I be?'

Lara sends me a photo of herself holding a takeaway cup and smiling.

'I'm just around the corner! Free coffee! Full stamp card! And the sun is out. What a day! I'll pop by in twenty.'

If Lara's personality was a colour, she would be yellow, all cheerfulness and childlike elation. She isn't just a half-full instead of half-empty kind of person; if there was even a droplet at the bottom of an empty glass, she would exclaim and point: *wow, look at that tiny bead of water.* I used to call Lara's way of viewing the world delusional, but now I crave her like a drug.

I open the door before Lara has even rung the bell. The sunlight hits her as she walks up the short garden path. She is holding a bouquet of sunflowers that looks huge against her petite body. They are not wrapped in anything, as if she has simply picked them from a field. She holds the flowers out to me. They are heavy like a baby.

"Aren't they just gorgeous?" she gushes, and I nod.

"Do you want to come in?" I say.

"Oh no, I can't stay, not today. Just wanted to give you these." Smiling, Lara points at the flowers. "Beauty is medicine."

I look down at the flowers. "Yes, all cured now."

"If we didn't need beauty, why would people have invested in making art for thousands of years?"

"I don't know." I shrug. "The art didn't save them, though, did it? Everyone died young until science came along."

Darkness flashes in Lara's eyes, and I chide myself for mentioning premature death in front of her.

"Thank you though," I say quickly, giving the bouquet a little wave, painting over my previous comment.

"Hang in there, okay?" Lara's intense gaze is hypnotic.

I nod. *Hug me, hug me, hug me.*

As if I am the hypnotist, she steps forward and wraps her slender arms around me, transferring heat to my cold body. Her hair smells of coconuts. After only an instant, my mind squirms.

"I think we have the same shampoo," I say.

Lara wraps me tighter, whispering into my ear: "Shhh, just stay."

"Some snakes wrap their prey until they can't breathe."

Laughing, Lara releases me. Reaching out, she grabs my face with both hands and looks into my eyes. "It will all be okay."

My legs pulse with pain, and I sink down onto the cool cement of the front step. Lara sits down next to me.

"Hey," she says. "I've been thinking, have you thought about joining a support group?"

"Sick people rounded up and put in one place? Like a leper colony? No, thank you."

"I joined one when David died – it was super helpful."

My head whips around to face her. "Shit, sorry."

Lara laughs. "It's not for you, that's fine." Picking up a piece of gravel, she plays with it, moving it from hand to hand. "I mean, it was really a group for widows and widowers; I shouldn't have been there. But they said it didn't matter that we weren't married."

"My grandmother is telling me to leave London and come home to be cured by seaside air," I say. "But I have a specialist appointment soon." Copying Lara, I pick up a sharp pebble and press the edge into my palm.

Whenever I think of David, it's like the only thing he did in life was die. Sitting next to Lara, Oliver and Matt in the cold church at the funeral, I felt like a trespasser; I had only recently become part of their group through Oliver, and even that link was tenuous. Oliver and I were incompatible, one of those unlikely friendships made in the first weeks of university, when you form relationships based on who you happen to sit next to in a lecture more than anything else. I'd only met David a few times before the accident. Looking at his coffin covered by bright flowers, I cried mainly because I could taste the others' grief. Lara's tears did not stop all day; it felt impossible that her body could have held all that liquid. Oliver and Lara had known David since school, and he and Lara thought they would spend the rest of their lives together, which, in a way, is what they did.

After she lost him, Lara couldn't sleep; she became even smaller than normal. Her collarbones poked out. She filled the windowsill of her bedroom with crystals that promised to bring clarity and peace, and I held back what burned on my tongue: *this is ridiculous, as irrational as praying to an invisible man in the sky.* Now I can see why she bought the crystals; I almost want to ask if I can borrow them.

"I know what you need." Lara grins. "Get a puppy! They're the best company. Unconditional love on tap."

"I'm not really a pet person."

She rolls her eyes. "Everyone loves puppies."

Lara taps on my phone screen and leans in close to show me a video. A litter of golden puppies run around on a scorched lawn. I don't need puppies, not in their full form or electronic shadows. I need someone who is two steps ahead of me who can drag me with them. Attaching myself to others who have what I want is how I've always lived.

One of the puppies trips and tumbles. I smile. Lara nudges me. "See! Told you it would help!"

"Don't tell anyone I've become the kind of person who finds happiness in animal videos," I say. "It's sad."

"You're ridiculous. How can it be sad if it makes you happy?"

Putting her phone in her pocket, Lara pushes herself to her feet. She reaches her arms out, and I stretch mine towards hers, letting her pull me up like a ragdoll.

"Hang in there." She kisses me on the cheek.

I watch her walk effortlessly down the garden path. Halfway down the pavement, she turns and walks backwards, waving at me.

"The cells that make up your body now will have been replaced with new ones in a few years!" she yells. "You will be fully renewed!"

I clutch the thick stems of the sunflowers.

"The universe has your back!" Lara yells, from halfway down the pavement. Shutting the door, I wish I believed an external benevolent force was puppeteering my life. I have asked my grandmother, who goes to church every week and prays every evening, how she can lean so confidently on something unseen, but she said she just knows we are part of something bigger. I can no longer explain my atheism by saying I refuse to believe in something that can't be scientifically proven to exist; my body has shattered this line of argument.

Shuffling my aching body over to the couch, I lie down and open my social media feed. The first photo that pops up shows Matt, Lara and Oliver crammed into a pub booth, the table a forest of empty glasses, as if my phone knows Lara was just here.

'Are you still coming over tonight?' I text Matt. 'Also, I didn't know you met up with Oliver and Lara yesterday. Why didn't you say?'

'No point, is there? We all know you can't come.' The phone vibrates again. 'And we went to a comedy show, you would have hated it.'

'The group is falling apart. First David, now me' I reply, then watch the words on the screen in horror, my stomach dropping. My fingers fly over the keys. 'Don't know why I said that. It's not the same at all.'

'No.'

Anger radiates from the hard-edged word. Watching Matt continue to type, I text rapidly that I am sorry.

'I shouldn't have said it.'

I wait for a reply, but Matt isn't typing anymore. I want to keep spewing out apologies. I'm not dying, but if I keep this up, our relationship could be. How long can the irrational love independent of qualities and actions last when the rational parts of what you used to love about the other person are gone? Desperate to compensate for my failing body and behaviour, over the last year I have sent Matt an excessive flurry of gift cards for different unusual experiences – axe throwing, a magic show, dinner cooked and served by prisoners in an actual jail – but no matter how exotic the experiences I'm giving him, it can't compensate for the state I am in. Being the perfect patient is the only room I have left to play in; I can't become unlikable on top of everything else.

5

"You look like a dog joyriding a car," Matt says, as he walks into my bedroom. I'm sitting by the open window on a chair sticking my head out. I crave fresh air, but my legs can't handle the stairs again. "All that's missing is wind whipping your hair," Matt adds. "Want me to grab a hairdryer so you can pretend?"

My shoulders relax; his anger at my earlier texts has evaporated. Bouncing onto the bed, he spreads plastic containers of takeaway food across the duvet. I force myself out of the chair and lie down on the bed next to the food.

"I got Ghanaian," Matt says. "I've never tried it before, have you?"

"Chinese would have been more appropriate," I say.

"Why?"

"Isn't that where the martial arts festival is? You know, the documentary you suggested?"

"Oh, right. The festival. Yes, it is."

My face heats up, as I fill my plate with a spicy meat stew and a rice dish that resembles paella. *Don't talk about virtual experiences as if they are real.* Matt only watches other people's stories on the side of his life, like normal people; I'm the only one who treats electronic replications of other people's lives like they matter.

"We can watch something else, whatever," I say.

Matt reaches for one of the chilli peppers sprinkled on top of the stew and bites into it. He positions the laptop in the middle of the bed, before shuffling back up to lean against the headboard next to me.

"There's a prisoner of war documentary that Hector said is really good." Matt shoves food into his mouth, like he's the prisoner.

"Did you not eat today?"

"No time," he mumbles. "Lots of meetings and induction stuff with the new Israeli guy."

"Oh, yes! How is he? Tell me."

As Matt talks, I nod, playing the part of engaged audience member. The first months after being forced to abandon the consultancy, I inundated Matt and Jas with questions so I could live in the world of work through them, but now I only feel like they speak a different language.

"Tel Aviv has crazy nightlife, apparently," Matt says. "Even when they were shooting rockets from Gaza a few years ago, people continued to go out. When I said it's surprising people party so close to conflict and death, he said that closeness is exactly *why* people party. Amazing, huh?"

I want to add facts about the conflict to have something to contribute, but I can't remember any.

"Hey, are you ever going to unpack those boxes?" Matt says, indicating the neat tower stacked against the wall.

Already last summer, Matt and Hector packed up my flat and moved the boxes here. I protested and said I could pay someone to do it, but they insisted. They came back laughing, like a father and son in a commercial.

"I should."

"But you probably won't."

"No. I've become one of those people who believes they will find peace if they own only twenty-three things," I say.

"Minimalism, I like it."

"Lara came by with flowers today."

"Little saint Lara. She loves trying to save people, doesn't she?"

"She does?"

Matt looks at me. "How have you not noticed that? She always did, but it got so much worse after David died. She's got such a saviour's complex." Matt indicates the plastic container on my lap. "Are you not going to finish that?"

Distracted, I pass him the box. The sunflowers on my nightstand morph from real to plastic, as I picture Lara going door to door handing out identical copies to everyone she knows.

"Shall we watch?" Matt says.

Pushing his toe onto the space bar on the laptop, Matt starts the documentary. On the screen, a deep male voice talks about his solitary confinement as a prisoner of war.

"I was alone in the tiny cell. I didn't see a human face for three years. I saw the guards, but their faces were covered. The man in the cell next to mine though, he'd somehow gotten hold of a book. We had figured out a code we knocked on the walls to talk – you know, one knock for A, two for B – so my neighbour spelt out the whole book. Anna Karenina. Two million letters in that book. Two million! That's dedication, man. He'd wrap his shirt around his knuckles because they would bleed from hitting the wall so many times."

I move over to lie on Matt's chest. Listening to his thudding heartbeats, I pretend I'm horizontal simply because it feels good to have my body resting against his. On the screen, the man's voice trembles.

"He saved my sanity. But I never saw him. I don't know if he died in there."

Lara dances in my mind. I tell myself it doesn't matter why she wants to help me, it only matters that she does.

"Humans can adapt to anything if we know why and for how long we have to endure it," the soldier says. "Not knowing how long... that was the hardest thing."

I open my eyes. On the screen, the soldier is now a civilian with slicked-back hair. He rolls up the sleeves of his crisp mint shirt, as he explains he spent most of his time in the cell immersed in an imagined reality of what his life would be like when he was freed.

"I lived through my wedding day to my fiancée again and again," he says.

Reaching out my foot, I press the space bar to pause the show.

"Do you think he actually got married, when he came out?" I say.

"After three years? Who would wait that long for someone? She must have assumed he was dead." Matt bends down and rummages in his backpack. "Chocolate?" He smiles, pulling out a purple bar from the front pocket.

Breaking the bar in two, Matt hands me the bigger half, and I smile, pretending his words didn't sting. He brings a different type of chocolate every time he comes over, like an advent calendar without an end point.

On our anniversary last summer, Matt stepped into my

bedroom wearing the same T-shirt he wore at the music festival where we met. Music blasting from his phone, he tied an orange cotton band around my wrist. With a make-up kit borrowed from Ellie, he painted blue glitter onto my cheekbones, before placing a pink plastic flower behind my ear. He wanted to recreate the first photo of us together, where I am sitting close to him in a field filled with people, leaning my head on his shoulder, purple glitter on my cheeks and a tipsy grin on my face, both of us clutching plastic cups of cider. I didn't tell him the loud music felt like it was punching my tender brain.

After we had taken the copy photo, he asked if he was allowed to say he misses that version of me. I pretended to smile because the festival version of me was never the real one; festivals are not where your truest self is unleashed – they are only extended fancy dress parties for personality. I had only gone to the festival in the first place because everyone at work had been talking about it for weeks, and I didn't want to be left out.

Biting into the chocolate now, the pieces of sweets baked into the chocolate crackle like fireworks on my tongue.

"Why?" I burst out. "Why has someone spent time figuring out how to make a chocolate that pops in your mouth? It's such a waste of limited scientific resources."

"Can I have the rest of your share then?"

Matt reaches out, but I swoop my hand away. Biting into the chocolate again, I chew aggressively, explosions filling my mouth.

Matt pulls me down to lie on his chest. "Come on, lighten up. Why would you even want to be cured, what would there really be to live for, if we couldn't have things like chocolate that crackles?"

Hearing his smile, I force my mouth to copy his.

"Don't you have another appointment soon?" Matt says. "With that specialist?"

"Yes, next week. Friday."

"I would come, but I've got a wedding. So rude, getting married on a weekday and forcing people to waste a day of holiday."

"Whose wedding?"

"Michelle's."

Sitting bolt upright, I stare at him. "You're invited to your ex's wedding? The ex that you cheated on?"

"I told you, we're friends."

"You slept with someone else behind her back for months, and now she wants you at her *wedding*? Is she crazy or does she have no other friends?"

"She knows it wasn't personal, just an experiment."

"A ridiculous experiment."

"I know that!" Matt snaps. I jolt, and he sighs. "Look, I told you ages ago that I regretted it after." Looking down at his fingers, he pulls at them, cracking the joints one by one. "Can we just go to sleep?"

"Just letting you know, if you have an affair, I'm not inviting you to my wedding." I smile, but my stomach is a tangled knot. My freshly washed hair smells of citrus, and I'm wearing delicate red underwear, but I have no desire to sleep with him now, even if my body would surge with an unprecedented burst of energy.

"Your wedding? You don't even believe in marriage."

"That's the part of this hypothetical scenario you focus on?"

Matt laughs and kisses me.

6

I light up the screen of my phone. The glowing numbers claim it is only just past midnight. I am wide awake in my dead body, wishing for morning. Sleep is like humans, repelled by visible desperation. Watching Matt sleep next to me, his back rising and falling, I move close and kiss his naked back. He doesn't stir. I kiss the skin repeatedly, but he remains still.

"Hey," I whisper into his ear.

He mumbles. "What?"

"Why haven't you left?"

His heavy breath indicates sleep again. I shake him awake. He grumbles. "What do you want?"

"What do *you* want?" I say. "Is this still what you want?"

"I just want to sleep."

I should shake his shoulders until he sits up. *You don't need to stay out of obligation. I'm not holding you hostage.* Before Matt, I used to call myself self-partnered: single implied something was missing, and I had no gaps in my life. Now I am made of gaps.

Hearing Matt's deep breaths, I want to inhale his exhales, as if I can swallow sleep itself like a pill. I refuse to let actual sleeping pills carry me into oblivion, having read too many articles about the thousands of people in the US dying from opioid overdoses; their addictions also began with a desire for temporary, effortless relief. I don't know what my body is capable of anymore.

Forcing my body up, I wrap myself in my dressing gown and sneak out of the room. On leaden legs, I descend the stairs. Tackling them twice in one day is like slamming four tequila shots in a row down my throat; it burns now, and I will pay for it later too, but it lets me feel temporarily free. Shuffling through the kitchen, I step barefooted into the darkness of the back garden.

My naked feet meet the soft spikes of the fake grass. Sinking down into the outline of a deckchair, I wrap myself in a woollen blanket. I listen out for sounds from the neighbouring garden, out of sight on the other side of a tall brick wall, but no one is there; not yet.

I slip deeper into the chair. I can't imagine ever summoning the energy to get back up.

On one of our first dates, Matt and I walked along the river at dusk. Tipsiness made us light; we had spent the afternoon in a rooftop bar, the sun toasting our skin. I asked Matt what his biggest regret was, and he told me about Michelle. I felt relieved then, because I already knew about his bizarre cheating experiment and the question was a test; Oliver had told me, even though he had sworn Matt he wouldn't. Oliver couldn't ever keep a secret; he loves the easy connections gossip can build.

Hands in his pockets, Matt explained he just wanted to know what it felt like to cheat on someone. *So many people have affairs, and I was curious what cheating would feel like – I just wanted to experience the fullest possible life, right?* I only laughed, because Oliver hadn't relayed this information, and the fact that it was calculated rather than impulsive made it feel better somehow.

Matt visibly relaxed then, and he said he only chose to do it to Michelle because she seemed like someone who would punch him in the face when she found out, rather than someone who would get upset.

We sat down on a bench overlooking the river and the cityscape on the other side. On the tiny beach below us, exposed by low tide, a middle-aged woman with long grey hair and rolled-up jeans was building an elaborate sand sculpture of a mermaid.

Matt said he planned for Michelle to find out eventually, that had to be part of the experiment; he left his phone screen open in front of her with sultry messages until she finally one day glanced at the screen. *She threw her glass of diet coke over me and the phone; it was sticky for days.* He smiled and shook his head slowly.

I told him it didn't sound like he regretted it, but he shook his head again, vigorously. *I have never felt so low in my life*, he said, his voice serious. *I thought it made it better that I was doing it as an experiment, but it made it worse because I wasn't even pulled by uncontrollable feelings.* Okay, I said, nodding, feeling more comforted by the honesty than I felt appalled by the infidelity itself.

A door sliding open breaks the silence. My head snaps around towards the sound of the neighbour's footsteps. The invisible man sits down in a creaking chair. I sit as still as

I can, suddenly conscious of the sound of my breath, as if the neighbour is a wild animal. *Breathe too loudly, and the lion will tear you to pieces.* A faint breeze of music hits me. As usual, the classical notes are only leftovers streaming out of headphones turned up too loud. The energetic sounds border on aggressive.

My bare feet sting with cold and my skin prickles all over, but I don't move. The neighbour sighs. He must think he is alone; I have never made a sound when we are out here together. During the days, I have spotted him when I'm sat by the open bedroom window gulping fresh air, as he wheels his road bike up the garden path, his trousers bunched up into his socks. He wears a helmet strapped tight and a high-vis vest, even on bright summer afternoons when everything is already visible. I have never seen or heard anyone else enter his house, but the neighbour is a hermit by choice – we are not the same.

Every evening, he sits down to play the piano in a room that borders mine, the sounds seeping through the wall. I imagine that he watches the evening news, then rushes upstairs, as if long streams of music can counteract school shootings and market bombings; *I will drown the horror in beauty.*

Peeling myself out of the chair, I walk over to the wall. Reaching out a hand, I rap my knuckles against the cold brick. *Once for A, twice for B.* I stop, vibrating with alertness, but all I hear is the same faint music from his headphones.

"Hello?" I whisper.

Experimentally, I reach my arm up and wave it slowly, like I'm at a concert holding a lighter in the air.

I remain standing by the wall on aching legs, until the neighbour gets up from his chair and strolls back inside. The door closing after him is like a gunshot.

Sinking down to the ground, I lean against the cold wall and pull my phone out of the pocket of my dressing gown. Online, I hunt for people like me. We could make up several metropolises, if we were all rounded up in the same place, like animals in a zoo. *We are twenty million globally, but there are only four thousand tigers left in the wild.* I click on the link to a message board titled chronic warriors.

'I can't get out of bed, my husband has to wash my hair, and even that I can only handle once every few weeks. I can't bear bright lights, I'm always lying here in the dark behind an eye mask, and...'

I close the window. The stranger is piling rocks onto my chest, pinning me down with her words. She is reaching out through the screen and grabbing onto my arms, begging me to hold her up, but I'm barely afloat myself, I can't handle her weight too.

Where are the happy survivors? I don't want to find people exactly like me, I want to find those who used to be like me, but who have come out on the other side. *Why are they so hard to find? Because they don't exist or because they are busy leading full and vibrant lives, pretending this never happened to them?*

Ambling back to bed, I count the days until my specialist appointment.

7

The receptionist seems too young for all the tattoos scattered across her neck and arms; I have no idea how she can possibly have lived long enough for all those stories on her skin to mean something. Her fingers attack the keyboard of her computer, inputting my name and date of birth with forceful speed. She must have a contest with herself for how quickly she can check someone in, like those train drivers in Spain who competed in speeding around a particular bend in the track, until one of the trains derailed, killing scores of people.

"Take a seat." She doesn't hand out affectionate words.

I step into a small windowless waiting room. Empty rows of chairs line the walls. Their worn upholstery in burnt-orange belongs to the seventies. *Where did all the people go who were ahead of me on the waiting list?* A framed print of a fierce red sunset hangs on the wall. Sitting down underneath it, I close my eyes against the glare of the fluorescent lights. Maybe the lack of windows is an intentional policy; maybe patients like me are considered liable to jump in an unguarded moment.

"Sorry I'm late!" Lara bursts into the room. Out of breath, she drops into the chair next to me, then reaches out and touches my arm. "You ready? Do you have the papers they asked for?"

I lift them out of my bag and hand them to her. Leafing through them, she seems like a lawyer, even though I am the one who studied law and she never went to university at all. She completed the classic gap-year trail instead, swimming in tropical waters with David and taking photos of temples. When she first offered to come with me to this appointment, I said no, before spending ages typing, deleting and retyping texts asking if the offer still stood.

"Grace?"

A balding man steps into the room, a clipboard resting in his hands. A pair of glasses perch on top of his head, and he's chewing gum. In Singapore they banned gum for years because they considered it anti-utopian, a messy thing inconsistent with the orderly and prosperous society they wanted. It wasn't the gum-chewing itself they found problematic, only that people would dispose of their used gum on subway doors and pavements, but the way this doctor is chewing, I can see why even the activity itself would be frowned upon.

I follow him into a tiny office. Bright lighting beams down on us, like it's an interrogation room. He introduces himself as a psychiatrist, and I want to get up and leave. *Jas is wrong and I am right.* He reads out my symptoms and lists off the latest test results. I'm perching on the chair with the alertness of a child playing musical chairs, ready to get up and run when the right sound is played.

"Do you have any family history of mental illness?"

"No," I say. "None."

I want to flood the room with negation until he stops this line of investigation, but I hold back, in case he will jot it down as denial, or a sign that I'm hiding something. If it's one in four, like they say, mental illness must exist somewhere in my expansive family tree. My cousin's wife has agoraphobia, but she's not related.

He asks me to tell him about my work; how I would classify my relationships; whether Matt is a supportive partner; whether I am close to my family. I tell him what I think he wants to hear. *Work is non-existent now, but I used to love my job. I have excellent relationships, even now. I couldn't feel more supported, and I am so grateful to everyone, for everything.* My head feels crammed, pushed to its limits. The psychiatrist looks up from the pad where he's been ticking off boxes and jotting down notes.

"Okay, Grace."

He must have read that squeezing people's names into conversation builds trust artificially fast, but he can't manipulate me; I know the tricks.

"I believe your diagnosis is the correct one."

"Oh, okay." Confusion floods me. I had expected that he would collect more from me than just words. *Where are the cutting-edge blood tests or scans? How is he a specialist if he can't provide a solution?*

"So, we have to get you to pay less attention to your symptoms." The psychiatrist points at a piece of paper, where a stick figure is first lying in a two-dimensional bed, then standing up next to the bed.

"You lie in bed, then you decondition. Then, when you try to do something, say going for a walk, it feels hard because your body isn't used to exerting itself, yeah? And so, you feel tired and uncomfortable, and then you think walking is bad for you, and you go back to lying down in bed again – but that only makes your body decondition further. You see?"

His pen draws arrows between the two stick men so they are stuck in a tiny cycle.

"You experience some symptoms from activities now because you have been lying in bed for too long doing nothing. The symptoms are trying to protect you, but you don't have to listen to them, okay? Then you will just be stuck in this cycle."

He circles his pen above the paper faster and faster.

"But I used to ignore my symptoms," I say. "I tried that, so many times, but every time it just made me worse."

"Yes, of course, because your body is weak now. You have been lying in bed for months now, yeah? You see the logic?"

"Yes, but... what made me have to lie down in the first place then?"

Sweating, I feel shaky. *Did you know I constantly topped the leader board in my spin class? I wasn't weak, initially.* It seems impossible for my body to break down every single day, if I am actually healthy now, just weakened.

Lara's hand touches my arm gently. "Do you need a rest break?"

Against the wall, an examination bench is covered with crinkly sanitary paper. I am desperate to be horizontal, but I can't lie down now, when this man has just told me I shouldn't be listening to my body's fake shouts.

"No, no, I'm fine."

The psychiatrist opens his mouth, but Lara speaks first: "Don't you think it's arrogant to think we know nothing is physically wrong just because the tests can't find anything?

Don't you think the body is more complex than that?" She cocks her head. "Medicine hasn't understood fully how the body functions, not yet. Didn't you see the latest study?"

In a light voice, Lara lists details of physical anomalies that scientists have found in patients like me; we have immune system malfunctions, inflammation chemicals in our blood, and our cells fail to turn fatty amino acids into energy like they're meant to. Lara knows all these facts that I should know.

In the car home, I rest my head against the window. The driver has headphones in, and when we stop at a red light, he drums his hands against the steering wheel. Lara leans forward between the seats to talk to him; reluctantly, he takes one headphone out. The disappointment crushes me into the seat, as the words I should have said to the psychiatrist flood my mind.

The psychiatrist referred me to another therapist who will help me 'manage my condition', which sounds like they only intend to cup my head in their hands and hold my mouth and nose above the surface, so I can breathe. *What kind of life is that?* I need to be lifted out of the water onto solid ground.

As we stop at another red light, a woman jogs past us, her face set. Her T-shirt declares she ran a half-marathon to raise money for cancer care. One in two now, the T-shirt warns in bright purple letters. I can't remember when Jas is running the marathon. I don't even know what she's raising money for, but she will surely also have chosen cancer; everyone loves cancer – they pump research funding into solving even the rarest forms. Closing my eyes, I zone out.

Suddenly, I am pushed against the back of the seat, like we are a plane taking off. My eyes spring open to see the light flip from orange to red as we zoom into the wide crossing. Several cars honk as we fly forward. Once we're on the other side, the car slows, but Lara punches the back seat in front of her with a closed fist.

"No! Don't you dare!" Her sharp voice cuts the air, her eyes wild. "You can't drive like that!"

"It's okay, it's okay." The driver waves his hand.

"It's *not* okay!" Her eyes shoot fire, and a droplet of spit flies out with the words. "We'll get out right here. I mean it. I will report you!"

The driver glances in the mirror. "Okay, sorry. Sorry, miss."

He slows the car. Leaning back, Lara puts her head on the headrest and closes her eyes. She is gripping her left wrist with her right. On her inner left wrist, a small tattoo, the letter D with a tiny heart next to it, is etched into her skin. The driver keeps glancing at her in the mirror.

When we arrive at Ellie's, the driver jumps out of the car and opens the door for Lara. I follow her into the fresh air.

"Thank you." She smiles at the driver, like nothing happened. We walk up the garden path, and I unlock the door to the house with a shaking hand.

"Are you okay? Let's get you to bed," Lara says.

"Are *you* okay?" I say. Every word is heavy in my mouth.

I curl up on the bed with my jacket still on. Sitting down next to me on top of the duvet, Lara opens her laptop. Her rapid typing fills the room, and I close my eyes. The sound of her typing is calming, like raindrops. She's supposed to be working from home today; her boss believes in flexible working. She works at a small jewellery company that makes lab-grown diamonds. After her gap-year, she started as an administrative assistant, and now she works in their customer care team and says she will never leave. I'm drifting off, when without warning, Lara slams the laptop shut, and my eyes snap open.

"I just wish I had been in the car with him," Lara says abruptly, her voice hot. "I wish I would have slammed my hand into the seat and demanded that they stop racing against that other car."

Lifting a trembling hand to her mouth, her teeth attack her nails.

"But... even if I had been there, next to him... I wouldn't have done that." Her biting is primal. "I want to think I would have, but... I would have thought it was a fun game too. I would have laughed. The racing could even have been my idea."

"But it wasn't your idea. You weren't there." I reach out and squeeze her hand, but she pulls it away and continues to bite her nails.

The photos were on the news. The metal front of the car was crushed, crumpled like a ball of paper. A witness said they'd seen an arm dangling lifelessly out of the open passenger side window. When I read that line, I ran to the bathroom and threw up. Until that day, I assumed that London traffic moves so slowly that a crash wouldn't cause much damage, but in the middle of the night, when the roads are empty, it turns out you can drive absurdly fast.

Looking down at her wrist, Lara is pushing her thumb over the skin, pulling at the tattoo, as if David is a genie in a bottle she can conjure if she rubs at her skin hard enough.

"People aren't really dead until they're forgotten," I say.

Lara snaps her head up. "Dead people are dead. It doesn't matter if I think about him every moment of every day until I'm dead too, he's still gone."

"Sorry, I was just..."

"Trying to fix it?" Lara sighs. "I know."

"It will get better," Lara says to the screen. She doesn't start typing, she only stares at the stationary image of her chaotic email inbox; she has over four hundred unread emails.

On the first anniversary of David's death, we all went to his grave together late at night and sat in a semi-circle facing his gravestone like it was a bonfire. Lara placed candles in glass jars all around the grave. We drank David's favourite beer straight from the bottles, and Lara drank for both herself and him, lining up the empty bottles by the gravestone like an offering. For a while, she shared funny anecdotes, and it felt like a celebration of life instead of a mourning of death, but then she got soppy drunk and started bawling.

When Oliver leaned in to prevent her from toppling over, she clung to him and kissed him on the mouth with a desperate hunger, drowning his lips in salty tears. I don't know if she chose Oliver because he was sitting next to her, or because he had a boyfriend at the time and therefore seemed like the most neutral territory to pour her leftover love into; she might not have been thinking at all. The rest of us sat there watching her kiss him without comment, until Oliver gently pulled his face away from hers and wrapped her up, resting her head against his chest. He stroked her hair while she cried so hard her breaths came in wild rasps.

Later, when we suggested it was time to leave, Lara insisted she wanted to sleep there, and she curled herself around the gravestone. Exchanging looks with Oliver, Matt was the one who walked over, put his hand on her shoulder and murmured in her ear, until Lara pushed herself back up and grabbed his outstretched hand. All the way to the bus, she walked unsteadily between Matt and Oliver like a child, her hands in theirs.

"Matt went to his ex's wedding today," I say now.

Lara looks up, disoriented. "What?" Focusing her eyes, she lets go of her wrist. "Oh, Michelle's? She invited everyone she's ever met. I was invited too, and I think I met her maybe three times, ever." Her voice is normal again.

"But why would he go? Matt doesn't even like weddings. He doesn't believe in marriage."

"Really? At Oliver's brother's wedding, Matt definitely teared up during the speeches, he sat next to me."

"Do you have her on social media? Michelle, I mean."

"Oh, maybe." Lara turns her gaze back to her laptop and begins typing again, but she doesn't say anything more. Glancing over, I see her finishing off an email. I have checked Matt's profile repeatedly, and he hasn't posted any photos, but my jealousy feels petty now, when it's lined up next to death.

8

In the warm bubble of my room, I lie in bed watching a massive stream of runners move across the laptop screen. Through a misty drizzle, I search the throng for Jas and Jordan, an impossible dynamic version of spotting the red-and-white-striped shirt of Wally in picture books with Andrea.

Two men are jogging along dressed in banana costumes, their faces red with heat. Grinning, they wave at the cameras while remaining in motion. A flabby middle-aged woman overtakes them, her legs strong under the layers of fat. Watching all these people at liberty to run several hours without stopping, on top of working and raising children and doing whatever else they do in their daily lives, I want to siphon up their surplus energy, tap it into a bottle and use it for myself. Energy should be donated and transfused like blood.

"Look! Wow! That's a pregnant woman running," the commentator says.

Scanning the screen, I look for Jordan; surely it must be her, not many will share her ideas of what is appropriate to do while you're growing a baby. The camera zooms in, and she fills the screen, turquoise Lycra stretching across her round belly, her slim legs flowing. She makes it look effortless moving herself and her unborn baby forwards. Her short blonde ponytail bobs with each step.

I search the screen for Jas; I would have expected her latched onto Jordan, wanting the experience to bond them. *Remember that side ache you had at mile sixteen? Remember that man who twisted his ankle and fell at mile nineteen?*

I only complete two miles of watching them run before snapping the laptop shut. Pushing myself up, I cross the room and rip open the nearest cardboard box. Discarding the neat stack of shoeboxes inside, I tear the brown tape off another box, rummaging through the T-shirts inside like an animal searching for food. In the fourth box, I finally find a pair of workout tights and a sports bra. Diving back into the first box, I open the shoeboxes until I find my black running shoes. Their soles are still white, having only ever touched sanitised treadmills.

Squeezing my soft body into the Lycra, I walk downstairs. *The pain isn't solid, remember. It's flimsy as a hologram.* The psychiatrist would approve of me ignoring my body's screams; I can see him nodding his bald head while chewing an old piece of gum.

I step through the front door, and so much air surrounds me, as if each molecule of air is more expansive here than in the garden. Hovering on the front step, I close my eyes and insert myself next to Jas and Jordan.

Jas told me about the mantras and visualisations she borrows from elite runners to optimise her athletic performance. *You have to trick your mind. Make it believe that your body has already achieved what you want it to. Your body can't tell the difference between what you visualise and what's real. Your brain is really a blind blob in a bucket – it senses only what you feed it.* Clapping and cheering surrounds me, thousands of feet pound the asphalt like a vast communal drum. The sweet smell of sweat fills the air. Sore feet throb in moist shoes.

I push myself into a slow jog, my lungs burning, my legs on fire. I make it five metres, ten, fifteen, twenty, before I bend over and place my hands on my shaking knees, gasping. I kneel down on the rough pavement, resting my hands on the uneven surface. I pant and tremble. Pushing myself back up, I trail back to Ellie's house, knowing I will pay for this experiment, like I have paid for all the others before it.

Back in my bed, I am pinned to the mattress by strong hands. My impossibly heavy body belongs to death. Terror grips my mind. *You are drowning now. You will never resurface.* I talk to the fear, reassuring like a parent: *it will pass. You are safe. We have been here before, remember? We have been here so many times, and it always passes.*

My phone vibrates against my leaden leg, and I leap at the distraction. Jas has sent me a photo of herself in the marathon finishing area, a medal draped around her neck. Holding up the golden circle, she bites at it. I open her social media, where she's posted the same photo for everyone to see.

'Finished in four hours twenty, right on target.'

'Congrats' I text her. 'Shame you missed your goal time.'

I should let her pretend she ran exactly as fast as she wanted. Her caption is a harmless micro-lie, and she will be full of hot disappointment already. Her sweaty running gear still sticking to her skin, she will have decided she has to run it again next year and train even harder, because she still believes insufficient effort remains the only explanation for not achieving your goals.

In the next photo, Jas stands next to Jordan with her arm around her shoulder. The two of them are surrounded by a group of people from the office, who all have identical medals around their necks. Jordan's gold circle rests on top of her protruding belly, like it's the baby's achievement.

'Raised five thousand pounds' Jas writes in the caption. 'Bet you regret offering to double it now, Jordan.'

I click on the profile Jas has tagged and see a closed profile with Jordan's face smiling next to a toddler's chubby cheeks. Jordan always refused to share her private social media accounts with colleagues. Clearly, she's made an exception for Jas or changed her policy. Longing expands in my chest. My throat burns. *Why Jas? You don't even like her that much.* Long before I got sick, Jordan drunkenly confided one evening at the bar that there was just something about Jas she couldn't stand. *I don't know what it is. Her voice is grating, maybe that's it? She talks too much.*

I don't know if Jas has changed her behaviour or whether Jordan simply likes having someone next to her looking up, someone she can mould into another version of herself, regardless of whether she likes them or not.

'Did you see the donation total?' Jas texts me.

I type on autopilot. 'So good! You must have won?'

Under the photo of her and Jordan, Jas has written that there's still time to make a last-minute donation. I want to donate an absurdly large sum to each of them, insert myself into their experience and make them talk about me.

I click through the link, and as the page materialises, my throat constricts. I stare at the screen. I feel like I have swallowed a hot water bottle.

The name of my illness runs across the top of the page in aggressive capital letters. *Try saying that three times fast.* I scan the text Jas has written. My name isn't mentioned. The money will go to scientific research, not me as an individual; this isn't America, where last year, a high school friend of Matt's begged friends and family for money to afford cancer surgery. But I see my name slathered all over the page in invisible ink. Familiar names jump out from the long list of donors. A parade of my colleagues is cheering me on. I am crowd-surfing, held up by their hands. I want to wrap my arms around Jas and squeeze her with abandon, the way I only do with Andrea.

I send a screenshot to Jas. 'Why didn't you tell me?'

'Is that your way of saying thank you? If so, you're welcome.'

'Can I see you soon?'

'Work is mad, I don't know when I'll be able to make it all the way to yours.'

'I can come to you!'

'Can you?'

'Yes.'

In the drawer of my bedside table, I find a pile of neon green sticky notes. If I am carried along by all these virtual hands, I can surely go anywhere. On a string of notes, I write it down, as if making the words solid and visible will help:

I believe in recovery. I believe. I believe.

Spreading the papers out on my bed, I am lying in a field of bright green flowers.

9

I look up at the tall glass building, the office that felt like my home before. The sun warms my face. I'm sweating in a scarf and hat. Unbuttoning the coat, I search for Jas. A group of children are playing in the hidden fountains that spew water out of the ground, as if it's already summer.

'Here' I text.

'Come upstairs.'

My stomach drops, as my phone buzzes again: 'The others want to say hello.'

'Why did you tell them?' I reply.

'If you wanted our meeting to be secret, you should have told me that – I'm not a mind reader.'

The glass doors glide apart, and I step into the lobby. Walking across the shiny floor towards the turnstiles, I expect the immaculate man at reception to stop me, as if it would be obvious that I don't belong here anymore. Tentatively, I put my old employee card on the scanner on the barrier, praying it will still work, even though it shouldn't. The glass gate slides open soundlessly. Even as I walk over to the lifts, I wait for the receptionist to call after me.

As the lift ascends, I look in the mirror. I am trembling. Seeing myself in a blazer and pristine white shirt, and seeing that image of me in this place, feels more like looking at an old photo than a live reflection. I look like no time has passed at all, and I momentarily imagine a parallel life where I never stopped working here. I want the lift to continue upwards and shoot through the roof. I picture myself flying into space; I have read too many children's books to Andrea.

When the lift opens, I try to let myself be carried by habit. Ten thousand hours is supposed to be the amount of time it takes to master something, and I have spent way more in this building. I step into memories: in the foyer, I met Jas for the first time, when we were here for our interviews; in meeting rooms, I've buzzed with the elation of a presentation well delivered; on my desk, I've felt the satisfaction of completing a final report for the client. *I belong here. My body just needs to remember it.* But my body needs to remember a lot of things, and it has so far failed to recall any of the things I want it to.

I walk down the corridor towards the open-plan office space. The walls of the corridor are covered in plants and moss of different shades of green; before, they were cream-coloured and blank. Reaching out my hand, I touch the green wall quickly, as if I'm breaking a rule. The soft moss isn't even fake; it's moist and soft.

Already, my feet hurt, even though I'm wearing a pair of heels that used to be comfortable. In my hand, I am clutching my phone as a disguised emergency button in case my body falls apart; to anyone else, I only look like I'm someone who needs to be constantly available. Ahead of me, a woman enters the narrow corridor from the bathroom. She's walking on her high heels as if they were a natural extension of her feet.

"Jas!" I yell out.

The woman spins around with elegance, and it looks like a dance move; growing up, Jas took ballet for a decade.

"Hey." She smiles.

I reach the point where she is standing, and she leans in to kiss the air close to my cheek.

"Being here feels like time-travelling," I say. "It feels so strange, I…"

"Sorry, sorry, it's really nice to see you," Jas interrupts. "But we have to hurry if we're going to have time for lunch; I have a meeting in thirty." She clicks on the side of her phone, and the screen lights up in the palm of her hand.

"Let's go then," I say. "I don't have to see everyone else; I'm here to see you."

"They all donated; they want to see you."

"Just need to pop to the bathroom," I say. "I'll be quick."

In the empty bathroom, I splash water on my face and rub off my make-up with a paper towel. *I owe them something; they want to see what their money is going towards.* I wish I had stage make-up, so I could paint sickness onto my face. I should have asked Jas to push me in a wheelchair. If I look healthy, they will feel tricked. I wish I could turn my body inside out like a sweater.

I walk into the open office, expecting it to feel familiar, but it's not how I remembered it. On rows of white desks, people are sitting measured distances apart staring at identical screens. The effect is eerie; instead of a buzzing hub of excellence and drive, it looks like a factory production line manned by robots.

I see Jordan at the same time as she spots me. She is talking into headphones while typing on her laptop, her fingers flying across the keys with the ease of a professional pianist. Pausing her typing, she motions me over to her desk.

"Two minutes," she mimes, holding up two fingers with manicured red nails.

Her belly is huge, but the rest of her body looks unchanged, like she's an actress in a film wearing a fake bump. On her desk sits a framed photo of the two kids she already has, a toddler and a girl a few years younger than Andrea. I hover, until Jordan pulls out her headphones and smiles at me.

Others flock around us. I do a round of handshakes and smiles, hurrying to ask what projects they are on now, without listening to their answers. I'm spewing out energy I don't have. As soon as I'm out of the building again, I will collapse, and they will feel cheated: *she seemed fine – why did we donate all that cash?*

Jordan talks about a pitch meeting they just had, saying she thinks their chances of winning the bid are good. She details the timeline and budget, and I keep nodding. My legs throb with exertion.

"Can I have a chair?" I interrupt. "I can't stand for very long."

In a flurry of movement, too many people search for chairs. A soft office chair is wheeled forward, and I sink down into it. My cheeks are on fire; I'm brimming over with heat.

"Do you normally use a wheelchair then?" Viktor asks.

"Oh no, I can't really leave the house, so… well, I can, for super short periods of time, but it just makes me worse for weeks after, so I try not to."

"Even if you have a wheelchair?"

"Yes. I'm a medical mystery. I could be wheeled around in a bed and still crash."

"I have to steal her now," Jas says, pulling at my arm. I stand up in slow motion.

"Good to see you," Jordan says. "I'll give you a call soon, check in."

I return her smile. She hasn't called since last year.

Shuffling into the mossy corridor, I wave to the rest of the group, who are all watching us. It feels like I have been here for hours.

"You know, I saw Jordan in the shop the other day," Jas says, once we are standing in the descending lift. "On the weekend. She was with her kids, and one of them was throwing a proper tantrum, lying flat on the floor, beating its little hands against the tiles and screaming, and the other one was bawling. Jordan looked horrible, no make-up, greasy hair and the darkest circles under her eyes I've ever seen. She looked close to crying too. She saw me see her, and now it's just awkward. Yesterday when I saw her look her normal pristine self in the office, I couldn't look at her. I feel like I've walked in on her naked."

"Awkward," I say, unsure if Jas is holding up this story as yet another proof point that she is now the one who knows Jordan. It seems irrelevant; Jas can have this world if she wants it; it's all hers.

We sit next to each other on a bench facing the river. I drink in the outside air like a parched animal. Ginger juice burns my throat as I spear salad leaves with a cardboard fork. Jas takes huge bites of a rustic sandwich, flour dust gathering on her black trousers. The children are still playing in the fountain. Their happy shouts attack me. Office workers buzz around us.

Jas sips her coffee. "So, do you think you'll ever come back?"

"Don't know. Maybe."

"Maybe always means no."

I watch the river flowing past. "I'm too far behind you now. Even if I recover..."

"*When* you recover."

"Even if I can get back to where I used to be... you haven't just stood still, you have sprinted way ahead. I won't ever catch up."

Jas nods. "Yeah... I get that." She drinks her orange juice. "It's not the same without you."

"Better or worse?" I smile, but she only looks at me, shakes her head, a repetitive motion interrupted by her phone vibrating in her pocket.

"Fuck! I'm late." Shoving the rest of her sandwich into her mouth, she jumps to her feet. Walking faster than I have in years, I follow her back to the front doors.

"Bye then," Jas says, as the doors glide open. Suddenly, she leans in and gives me a quick, hard hug, before turning around and striding through the reception to the lifts, her heels reverberating against the hard floor. Watching her walk away is like being at an airport, seeing off someone with a one-way ticket. We've only ever hugged when drunk.

I walk a few steps towards the river. Glancing around me, I hold my phone up and snap a series of selfies, capturing myself and the shining surface of the office, before I turn around and take a shot of the whole building stretching up to the sky. All these hundreds of days in silent pain should have burned off my desperate desire to outshine. I should be content if I am ever able to live independently and hold down a menial job. Excelling shouldn't matter anymore.

'Never coming back here' I text Matt, attaching the photo.

He sends me an animation of a champagne bottle popping, foam spilling out. In an infinite loop, the bottle reseals itself and pops, as Matt says he will bring the real thing over tomorrow, so we can celebrate my escape from the clutches of the corporate world.

10

When I open the door to Matt in the evening, he is wearing a suit. I mock gasp and widen my eyes.

"Have you been to another ex-girlfriend's wedding today?"

He frowns. "I told you, didn't I?" Seeing my blank face, he adds: "We had the final acquisition meeting today."

"Sorry, I forgot. How did it go?"

"Smashed it. The contracts will be signed by the end of the week."

"Didn't you want to stay and celebrate with everyone?"

Grinning, Matt takes his backpack off and extracts a bottle of prosecco, the condensation dripping off it in the warm evening air.

"You're free!" he says. "That's a more important thing to celebrate! Now, once you're better, you can do *anything*."

As if he's the one who lives here, he crosses the living room with the bottle dangling from his hand, and I follow. I sit down by the kitchen table, while Matt opens the cupboard to find glasses. I play with the baby monitor I'm holding; Hector and Ellie are out for drinks, and I am watching Andrea.

You can do anything. It doesn't feel alluring; I only feel like I am plummeting from the sky in a dream, my stomach lurching as I freefall into blank static.

Matt pulls two champagne flutes out of the cupboard and waves them at me. Popping the bottle, he pours out two full glasses of fizzle and foam. I trace watermark patterns on the wooden table with my finger.

"I was free," I say. "Before. I didn't *escape* anything. I lost it."

"I think you've forgotten what it was like. Didn't you work until midnight on Christmas Eve?"

"I wanted to work on Christmas Eve. And I wasn't there alone, I was with Jas. It was probably my favourite Christmas ever."

"You missed all of Andrea's birthday parties."

I reach out for the glass Matt offers. "They hosted the parties at four in the afternoon! And I always came the weekend after with a tower of presents. She was too tiny to know the difference anyway."

"Well…"

"Oh, I'm sorry, do you have kids? Are you a father? You didn't even…" I stop.

"Do you want me to leave?" Matt snaps back, anger radiating from him. "You keep biting my head off."

I look at him, startled. "But… I've always bitten your head off. We were always like this. You know, challenging each other."

"This isn't the same and you know it."

"You started it." I paper over my shame with a sip of

bubbles. "Anyway, I don't get why you're complaining that I used to work too much when you work all hours now too."

"That's different – I'm not a cog in a machine; we're creating something new. I'm not replaceable."

I jolt. Matt grimaces. "Sorry. I didn't mean that." He puts his palm over his eyes and breathes deeply. Looking at me again, he sighs. "I came here to cheer you up, and now... why do we do this all the time? Attack each other?"

Our glasses hover in the air. With force, I clink my glass against his. I want it to shatter in his hand.

"Well, now that you've been acquired you don't work for a start-up anymore," I say. "Now you are also replaceable."

"Really," Matt says. "I shouldn't have said that. I'm sure they miss you."

I take a sip, barely noticing the fruity bubbles on my tongue. Matt has already drunk half of his glass.

"You can go celebrate with your colleagues, if you want," I say.

"If that's what I wanted, I wouldn't have come here, would I?" His voice is softer now, and I soften too.

"So, will you leave now then?" I say.

"Leave?"

"The start-up that's no longer a start-up. Will you join a new struggling venture and try to make that one a unicorn?"

"Yeah, maybe. I don't know. I like the people though; I don't want to leave just yet."

"You do look good in a suit."

Holding my gaze, Matt loosens his tie and removes it. He unbuttons his shirt and takes that off too.

"What are you doing?"

"Told you, I hate wearing this."

Wearing only boxers now, Matt drapes the suit over a chair. "I'll go borrow some of Hector's clothes, he won't mind."

"They won't fit you."

Matt shrugs. "Anything's better than that." He points at the crumpled suit.

"Here." I hold my glass out to Matt, so he can drink the rest of my prosecco, but as he reaches out, I pull it back and down the whole glass. The aftertaste of the drink lingers on my tongue. Matt laughs.

"Be right back." He strides out of the room. I shuffle after him.

When I reach Ellie and Hector's room, Matt is standing in front of their open wardrobe, pulling on a pair of washed-out jeans that expose his ankles and lower calves. When I sink onto the bed, he turns and looks at me with hungry eyes.

I shake my head. "Nope."

"They're not home."

"Come on, it would be weird."

"Only now that you've said it's weird."

"She's my sister. And you think of Hector like a surrogate dad."

His face reddens. "No, I don't."

"I don't mind that you do. And he clearly doesn't either. What do you talk about when you have drinks with them?"

His back to me, Matt rummages through a pile of T-shirts. "What am I meant to do when you have to rest? Just sit there next to you and watch you like a creep?"

I look at his hands. On our first date, I accidentally knocked my glass of red wine so that it flooded the table and my top. The liquid dripped down onto the floor like blood. Without saying anything, Matt knocked over his beer too, while grinning at me, and my embarrassment transformed into mutual laughter, as Matt asked a waiter for extra napkins. *We're both a bit clumsy, you see.*

"Remember that?" I say, relaying the memory.

"When you're better, we can go to that restaurant where you eat in complete darkness," Matt says. "If you knock your glass down, no one will see."

"At least I am unpredictable," I say, as Matt pulls on a grey sweater. "You would have never guessed this would happen, having a girlfriend who can't leave the house. If you had to choose between abnormal suffering or boring normality, which would you pick?"

Matt laughs and leans down to kiss me.

"When is your first therapist appointment again?" he says.

"Next week. But if he is anything like the psychiatrist, I will run."

"Okay." Matt nods his head towards the hallway. "Let's go back downstairs?"

"In a minute," I say. "Need to rest my legs."

Alone in the room, I roll over to my side and stare at the small silver frame holding the macabre portrait of Ellie's old ultrasound. Suddenly, I understand why Ellie grieved as if that baby had actually lived and died; losing a future you were sure belonged to you feels like losing something you already have. *But look at Ellie now. She's fine, even happy.*

Matt laughs from my bedroom. "Come in here!" he yells. Pushing myself up, I straighten out the bed covers and fluff the pillows, removing every trace of my presence while wondering whether the pillow now smells like me. I shuffle across the landing and into my room.

"What is this?" Matt indicates a collection of items spread on top of the bed. A cardboard fork. A skinny birthday candle, the wick burnt. A pile of orange and green sticky notes. A red lacy thong. An empty shoebox balances on the edge of the bedside table.

"Are you going through my stuff now?" I say.

"I was looking for a phone charger. So, what is this?" Matt says, plopping down on the bed.

I place the lid on the box and lie down next to it. "They're just... reminders."

"Of what?"

"I don't know. That I'm not... that this isn't... you know how people save cinema tickets from their first dates and that kind of stuff."

Matt screws up his face. "That's the underwear you wore the first time you..."

"No! It's just a symbol. That my body isn't just sick, it's also... never mind." Reaching out, I sweep it all into a pile and throw it into the box, my face burning. "I'm trying to convince myself this is also some sort of life."

Matt nods, suddenly serious.

"You know," he says, "you shouldn't hide it in the drawer if you want it to remind you. You should put it in a big display case, like the ones they have in museums. It's modern art, really, isn't it?"

I envisage the motley collection of items exhibited in the centre of a vast white hall, people crowding around it, snapping photos, their voices echoing off the walls, and suddenly I see what he sees, and I am laughing so hard I am gasping for air. My abs ache. Matt laughs too, and we ride the waves of it together, until Andrea emerges in the hallway, clutching a plush green dragon in one hand and rubbing sleep out of her eyes with the other, demanding to know what's so funny. I wish I could bottle our laugh and cram it into the box too.

11

In the dilapidated waiting room, I slump in a chair, staring at my phone, where I have typed out a list of the things I should have said to the psychiatrist last time I was here, alongside generic reminders to stand my ground. *Do not be cowed by authority! You are here as the client; they should respond to your demands, not the other way around!* Like last time, I sit alone in the room, wondering where all the others like me are hiding.

Hearing footsteps, I look up, just as the man in the doorway calls out my name. He looks too young to be a legitimate therapist; he must be an intern allocated as a cost-cutting measure. His handsome face looks friendly: long, soft lashes frame his eyes like a cartoon Bambi. The extreme youthfulness cancels out the unexpected beauty; he is too young for me to admire the features of his face.

Extending a hand, he introduces himself. I shake his hand but instantly forget his name; I am concentrating on remembering my list of defensive arguments. *I am not simply deconditioned! I can't tune out my body's screaming protests!*

The therapist leads me along a linoleum-floored corridor to a cramped room. Two chairs sit next to a table with an old desktop computer. Bright fluorescent light beams down on me. The single narrow window looks straight into a grey wall. Sitting down in the chair the therapist indicates, I take off my coat. My shirt clings to my back, moist with sweat. The window is cracked open, but the air remains stale and hot, as if it has filtered through many sick bodies already. The computer fan hyperventilates.

The therapist smiles, showing off teeth from a dentist commercial. His skin is an unblemished ice rink.

"So, I want to make one thing clear right away. Me being a therapist and you seeing me does not mean that your illness is psychological. We still don't know what causes your illness, but the research increasingly shows that it's a serious physical condition."

His prodigal lips keep moving, telling me what I've craved since the beginning. *You are not crazy. I believe you.* Every cell of my body lets go, and I float on his words. Straightening up in my seat, I push my chest out slightly and raise my chin.

"But the psychiatrist said I shouldn't listen to my symptoms," I say.

The therapist nods slowly, then leans closer.

"I shouldn't say this, but he doesn't know what he is talking about." He puts a finger against his lips. "Shhh, don't tell anyone I said that."

Reflecting his smile, I nod, and suddenly my chest tightens and my throat burns. I bite my lip to zip myself up.

"So, I'm not making it up." I inject lightness into my voice.

114

He furrows his brows. "Who told you—"

"No one. Never mind."

The therapist straightens. "The absolutely most important thing is that you stop pushing your body beyond what it's capable of right now. Only very slowly, over time, can we hope to increase how much you can do."

"Stop pushing myself. Got it."

"Exactly." The therapist scribbles in a notebook on his lap. I breathe deeply. *Keep it together. Don't give him any reason to rescind his words that it's not in your head; he needs to think you are as emotionally sturdy as a mountain.*

He reaches into a desk drawer and extracts a pile of silver spoons.

"Here." He holds them out to me like a bouquet of flowers. Confused, I grab the cool metal.

"Every morning, you wake up with a given amount of energy, here represented by a set number of spoons." The therapist indicates my hand. "Now, you have to carefully choose what you spend your spoons on. Getting out of bed may require one spoon." He reaches out and extracts one of the spoons from my grip. "Walking to the bathroom may be another." He takes another spoon from me, and I cling harder to the remaining ones.

"Showering... that might take two spoons." He yanks them from me.

"Getting dressed would be one spoon."

"Making and eating breakfast... three spoons."

"My sister prepares breakfast for me," I say, as he reaches for the spoons.

"Okay, only two then. But say you scroll on your phone for a while – that's another two spoons. And then someone wants to have a conversation with you for a few minutes." As he grabs onto the final spoon, a fierceness surges in me, and

I want to wrestle him for the spoon. *I could take you, I used to beat my cousin when we arm wrestled as kids.*

My empty hands feel lost in my lap. "Now what?"

"Game over. When you don't have any spoons left, you have to lie in bed. No phone, no music, no TV. Or..."

"Or?"

"Or I can give you some of the spoons you were meant to have tomorrow."

"Yes please." I hold out my hand. He offers them up, and I grab them.

"But it's like a payday loan; it comes with high interest. And so, tomorrow, you will start off with much fewer spoons, as you try to pay the loan back."

"And how do I get more spoons?"

"Sleep and meditation, mainly. Do you meditate?"

"Yes," I say automatically.

"Brilliant!" He beams at me, and I glow back, like a moon.

"I know the spoons are a bit silly, but a lot of people find it helpful. As a healthy person, I have pretty much an unlimited number of spoons."

"Show-off," I blurt out. He laughs.

"That's the goal for you too, but I have to tell you that I can't make any promises. I do have a good track record. Lots of my patients have recovered now. But I don't want to oversell myself. Basically, we'll use sleep and meditation and diet and stress management to create a bubble of healing for your body. And a big part of what we need to do is working with your mind."

I tense. "No, that's not—"

"I'm not saying your *symptoms* are in your mind," the therapist interrupts. "Your pain is physical and very real. I'm only saying that the body and mind are super

116

interconnected. We all think tens of thousands of thoughts every day. The content of those thoughts has an effect on your whole system. So, if your mind is stressed, your body will stress out too, and then it can't repair itself."

I nod, but my muscles stay alert.

"We don't need the spoons anymore now." The therapist nods to my hand, where I'm still grasping five of them, as if the spoons are energy itself. I hand them back.

He indicates the floor. "Before we continue, why don't you have a bit of a rest? You can lie down, if you like. Create a spoon or two." He winks and steps out of the room, shutting the door behind him. Bending down, I touch the pale green linoleum floor and feel its stickiness, but I lie down anyway.

In the car on the way home, my body melts into the seat, soft with relief. My mind buoyant, I call Matt. The therapist's voice cradles me. *Lots of my patients have recovered now. I have a good track record.* When Matt doesn't pick up, I call Ellie. She doesn't answer either, and I find myself texting Hector, the first time I've sent him anything other than a cursory happy birthday text.

His response is instant. '*Gracita*! That's so wonderful! We will celebrate, tonight. I will cook; we'll have wine; it will be *fantastic*.'

Underneath my excitement, my crumpled body begs to lie down in cool silent darkness.

'Tomorrow?'

'Of course! This is just the best news.'

He acts as if I have already been fully cured, but I override my impulse to pierce the bubble; instead, I let it envelop me too.

On my phone, I search for the meditation app I downloaded years ago but never used. A woman in a productivity workshop in the office promised our team that meditating every morning would improve our performance, but meditation only felt like a fancy word for idleness. Now, I plug my headphones in, before closing my eyes and leaning back in the seat. A soft male voice fills my ears.

"Take a deep breath in… a deep breath out… feel your body push down against the surface you are sitting or lying on… now, notice your breath flowing in through your nose… flowing out… you don't have to control the breath, just feel it move. Flowing in… flowing out…"

I only realise I've fallen asleep when the driver wakes me up outside of Ellie's house.

12

"Our guest of honour!" Jumping up, Hector strides over and envelops me, lifting me off the ground. Getting halfway to his feet, Matt hovers, then sits back down. Ellie takes a large sip of her red wine. Candlelight dances on their faces. Sitting down next to Matt, I watch the three of them, my chest warm.

"Here." Matt hands me a wine glass filled with water and ice cubes.

"To Grace!" Glasses clink together.

"So, tell us!" Hector's eyes are large. "What did the doctor say?"

"Therapist, not doctor," Matt says.

Ignoring him, I relay my new instructions and meditation regime. The words bubble out of me like fizzing champagne. Elation swaddles my exhausted body and holds it up.

"Rest *more?*" Matt interrupts. "How is that even

possible?" Slumping in his chair, he drains his glass of wine. I grab the spoons and forks and knives from the table and clutch them in my hand.

"So, it's like, I have only a limited number of spoons when I wake up every morning."

"And forks and knives?" Matt says.

"Pretend they are spoons. And everything I do requires a spoon…" I copy the therapist's explanation, placing each piece of cutlery down on the table in turn.

"I don't want to run out of spoons," I say.

"And this will help you recover how?"

"It'll give my body space to heal itself," I say.

"Heal itself? What kind of hippy-dippy bullshit is that?" Matt reaches out for the wine bottle and fills his glass to the brim.

"I'll track the number of minutes I spend on an activity in a spreadsheet, so I can figure out how much my body can handle."

"Only you could sound this excited about a spreadsheet," Matt says. He turns to face Hector. "When we officially merge with the big corporate, we will have to track our time at work too. In ten-minute increments! It fucking sucks."

"I used to do six," I say.

"In the office now, we—"

"Excuse me, isn't tonight about me?" I say, raising my eyebrows.

"Yes, of course." Matt is smiling, but his face has hard edges.

"I was only joking," I say.

"Tracking every minute of your working day… madness!" Hector says, his voice too loud.

"We shouldn't talk more about work, Grace will get

120

upset," Matt says. He glances at me with cool eyes and an exaggerated smile.

"I really didn't mean…" I say.

"Cheers!" Hector says. All our glasses dance together again. Annoyance and guilt bubbles in me side by side. I look at Matt.

"If you can make yourself better now, doesn't that mean you would have made yourself sick too?" Matt says. His words balloon, swallowing up the air.

"This song!" Ellie exclaims, as if she lives in a bubble tension can't penetrate. "Come." She holds out her hands to Hector, who grabs them and trails her into the middle of the room, where they dance. Matt and I stay frozen in our seats, watching them swaying across the tiled floor instead of looking at each other.

Did he say I made myself sick because he believes it's true or because he knew it would hurt? *Even if he only wanted to push where it hurts doesn't mean it can't be true.* It didn't even occur to me to ask the therapist whether power also implies responsibility, but now it seems obvious that it does. I feel wobbly.

"Why are you two still just sitting there? Come on!" Hector says.

Matt only smiles. I shake my head, irritation oozing now, blending with the discomfort. *Why couldn't you just let me have tonight?*

"Come on!" Ellie echoes, shimming her shoulders and beckoning with both her hands in rhythm to the song.

I get to my feet and hold my palm out to Matt, conveying a truce. *You shouldn't have said that, but I also shouldn't constantly dictate the terms of our time together – it's just that I don't know how else to survive; it takes everything I have just to stay afloat.*

He accepts my hand and gets to his feet. I place one hand on his shoulder and the other in his hand. We dance too, but our bodies remain separate, like we are at a school disco. We are still watching Ellie and Hector more than each other, like we need them to instruct us, as if slow dancing is something more than simply swaying in rhythm.

"Did the therapist really not give you a timeline?" Matt says.

"No, he said it varies too much from person to person. He says I need to create the space for my body to heal, and that's all I can do."

Matt stops swaying. Raw sadness flows out of his eyes. "This can't be permanent."

"It's not. Hey." Squeezing his hand, I want his argumentative tipsiness back. "It might just take a while, that's all."

An upbeat song comes on, and Ellie and Hector squeal with elation. Singing along while moving to the rhythm, they are all rolling hips and arms. They are fireworks set off inside, light and colour bouncing off the walls. In their synchronicity, they remind me of my parents. My legs burn. Exhaustion fills me.

"I have to sit," I say.

Sinking back into a chair, I expect the new sad version of Matt to copy me, but he releases my hand, and when Hector and Ellie open a space between them, he slots into their small circle, grinning. Watching them dance, jealousy tugs at me to get back up and join in, but I remain in the chair.

At Ellie and Hector's wedding, I stood next to the dance floor, tipsy on champagne I was too young to drink, and watched them spin slowly under a spotlight for their first dance, the light bouncing off the beads on Ellie's dress.

Feeling Ellie and Hector's love radiate out from their intertwined shape, I wondered when I might have that with someone too. I sat on a chair next to my grandmother most of the night, evaluating couples on the dancefloor. My grandmother was ruthless; she would nod towards a couple and announce they could not last long. *Just look at how her eyes are roaming. See, his hand is gripping hers too tightly. That man, he's too drunk – you only drink like that if you are unhappy.*

I watch Matt. *If I could dance now, would I feel like I had found what I wanted? Or would I still feel like I am searching, regardless of the state of my body?* I pick up my phone and capture him in a video, as if watching a replay later will help me decide.

13

Weeks later, sitting next to me in bed, Matt shows me pictures on his phone from his day out biking. We huddle together over the screen. Rain drums against the window. The dark grey sky holds the daylight hostage. A draft blows cool air into the room.

My own phone lies face up next to us, the electronic stopwatch on the screen accumulating minutes and seconds that I will later put into my activity spreadsheet. I am still searching for the magic limit the therapist told me should leave me feeling no worse than I do when I wake in the mornings. Most days, I crash halfway through the afternoon, then recharge in silent darkness for hours before I deplete myself again in the evenings. I can't hold myself back as much as I need to. You can't put on your own straight-jacket; someone else has to do it for you.

Matt scrolls. On the side of a houseboat, graffiti screams 'TIME TO LEAVE' next to a painted blue rectangle and yellow stars of the EU flag.

"What's your prediction? In or out?" I say, pointing.

"In," Matt says. "It has to be."

"You think? The latest poll shows—"

Matt waves his hand. "Theatrical. People never rebel as much as they say they will."

He clicks onto the next photo. A black-and-white mural shows a woman sprinting on a treadmill in spiked stilettos and a trouser suit, a briefcase clutched in her hand. She's staring desperately at a point far ahead, her long hair trailing out behind her. Behind the treadmill, copies of the same woman lie crumpled in a heap on the ground.

"Don't they arrest people for doing street art?" I ask.

In the next photo, Matt is captured in profile bent low over the handlebars in front of a mural that depicts a young man biking along in the same direction in the same position.

"Spot the difference," Matt says.

"Well, he's wearing a helmet. Why don't you want to protect your brain?"

He shrugs. "Drivers are more reckless around cyclists with helmets, so the protection pretty much cancels out."

The present, live version of Matt has already clicked onto the next shot when it occurs to me.

"Who took that picture?"

"I did."

"No, not that one, the one before. Scroll back. Yes, that one. You on the bike."

"Oh, that one. Jaya. She ended up coming with me today, didn't I tell you?"

"No, you didn't. Who's Jaya?"

"I've told you about her, we work together?"

Clicking onto the next photo, Matt continues to commentate. I pretend that I am still listening.

125

In another photo, Matt and Jaya's faces are squashed close together to fit into the frame. Energy shoots out of their bright eyes, hers dark brown next to his. A round upturned nose sits above cheeks that pop out like a chipmunk's when she smiles, but her eyes are playful and spirited, framed by dark long lashes. A wave of jealousy knocks me over. My chest tightens. I want to move, get out, run away.

"I need to rest," I say.

"Can I use your laptop? I'll stream the football."

"Can you go downstairs? I'll rest better alone."

"Sure, I'll see if Hector wants to watch the game." Matt gets up from the bed. Leaving the room, he closes the door behind him. My minds bursts into activity.

I don't think Matt and Jaya found a grimy bathroom in a canal-side bar. I don't think they frantically stripped down so he could push her roughly against the wall, while their bikes were locked outside in another tight embrace. I don't picture her small sharp nails digging into Matt's back. I can't hear her unrestrained moaning.

Calm down – Matt claims he hated cheating, remember?

But that could have changed. We think we know how our future selves will behave, but it's an illusion – we have no idea who we will become.

Stop it. He would have told you. All they did was ride their bikes together, like children, like siblings.

Sharp envy still penetrates my chest. They were out in the world together, experiencing something worthy of a photo. Matt and I were never constantly out in the world together before either, but a symmetry existed then; we were each out in the world separately; we could meet and compare notes.

I pick up my phone from the duvet to search for Jaya's name online. Immediately, her grinning face pops up, as the algorithms lift her effortlessly out of the internet crowd of others with the same first name through her connection to Matt.

On her page, the photo of her and Matt from today's bike ride is the first thing I see. He must have sent it to her. I can hear her whispering into his ear. *Share it with me.* Tense, I scroll through her other photos. She is wearing the same uninhibited smile in all of them. Matt is in several of the shots. There are many of just the two of them and some where they are in a bigger group. I have scrolled months back into her life before I force myself to open the meditation app instead. My head is a solid brick, as the male voice fills the room.

"Take a deep breath in… a deep breath out… feel your body push down against the surface you are sitting or lying on…"

Breathing in. *Jaya.* Breathing out. *Matt.* Breathing in. *Jaya.* Breathing out. *Matt.*

Back when I could, I only came biking with Matt once. On a rented bike, I latched onto him, as we navigated multi-lane roundabouts and sneaked past buses stuck in gridlocked traffic, ignoring the stickers that warn cyclists from passing on the inside. Terrified, I gripped the handlebars so tightly that my arms ached. We weren't biking anywhere in particular; we were just *exploring.* We had only gone for thirty minutes before I shouted at him that I wanted to stop. I couldn't have known I should have grabbed every experience possible with both hands, even the ones I didn't enjoy.

Giving up on the meditation, I reach for my laptop and open my spreadsheet. I type in an empty cell:

'Talking to Matt: fifteen minutes.'

I colour the number red to signal the activity has escalated my exhaustion and pain. The sheet is a red sea, and I feel defeated. Even these unsustainably large numbers look so small.

'Walking to the kitchen and bathroom: four minutes. Sitting upright: twenty minutes. Scrolling on my phone: seven minutes.'

When Matt walks back into the room, I start undressing.

"Lock the door," I say, as I peel off my top and discard it on the floor. Throwing the duvet to the side, I strip off my leggings and lacy underwear. I spread my leaden legs.

"Where is this coming from?" Matt says, leaning down onto me.

As he enters me, I bite into the pillow in the same way that Jas bit into her marathon medal.

14

I wake up into stuffy warm air. The morning sun beams at the rolled-down blackout blinds, heating the bedroom. Half-asleep, I reach out for my phone. A flurry of texts fills the screen. The old group chat with Matt, Lara and Oliver has been dormant for so long that I thought it was dead. They will have their own group chat now, one I am not part of.

'What the fuck' Matt says. 'London voted remain. Can we declare independence from the rest of this stupid country and just stay?'

'I can't believe we are leaving' Lara says.

'Come on, it's not really that surprising' Oliver says.

'I didn't see it coming' Lara replies.

'I know, but you were always naive.'

'Better to be gullible than cynical.'

Sadness leaks out of the texts, but I feel only a feeble echo of their emotions. The vote will make our country an isolated island, but momentarily, it connects me to other people: now that they want to talk about the political instead of the personal, I can be an active contributor, not just someone who listens and nods because I have no stories of my own anymore.

Pulling on a large sweater over my pyjamas, I walk down to the kitchen on bare feet, pleasure drowning my melancholy. Hector strides back and forth across the kitchen floor like a caged lion, talking loudly into his phone.

"We will march! Protest!"

Andrea circles around him, chanting: "EU! EU!"

"This just shouldn't be happening." Hector's voice breaks. He sinks into a chair.

Walking over to the fridge, I extract a carton of mango juice and pour myself a glass of deep yellow. I want to hurry out of the room and away from Hector's despair. Seeing his shiny eyes, guilt hums at the edges of my mind.

I carry the cold glass of juice back up to my room and collapse into bed, my legs aching. Leaning back on pillows, I drink absentmindedly while scrolling through articles on my laptop. My phone vibrates with more texts from Lara and Oliver. They remain upset, and I fill with guilty exhaustion.

Yesterday, I drove with Ellie to the polling station to vote, but once I stood inside the little cubicle on aching legs with the pen in my clammy hand, I looked down at the piece of paper, and I couldn't bring myself to tick either box; it felt as if I was being asked to vote in the election of another country. Ellie's house is a desert island, where elections do not exist. A blank ballot was a pointless mutiny: no one else would understand what I was communicating.

I abandon the repetitive news articles and open my social media. Next to a pristine pool, Jas is lying on a sunbed in an orange bikini; she is on holiday in Ibiza with the others from the office. Usually, her photos are paired with minimalistic captions that always end in an exclamation mark – 'Drinks! Work hard, play hard! Run, baby, run!' – but this time, she has written an essay:

'Shocked. People say this is democracy, but democracy really shouldn't allow the collective to make decisions on topics they don't fully understand. Benevolent dictatorships are underrated. People have voted on the basis of simplistic, false headlines put forward by biased campaigners. People voted this way because they are angry with the current state of things, and they assume that any change is good change. But change isn't always for the better.'

Jas's hot anger bounces off me. *If Jas can post like this, where the caption has nothing to do with the picture of her toned body, are others using this platform like that too?* Could I find someone like me here, a stranger whose phone carries more of their connection to the world than technology was ever intended to hold? Exiting Jas's post, I type my illness into the search box, anticipation expanding in my stomach like a balloon.

15

On a narrow balcony, a dark-haired young woman sits on a wooden chair. Her head is haloed by masses of colourful helium balloons anchored to the chair's armrests and back. A wide grin reaches her dark eyes. Her gaze grabs me. Her elegant face belongs in ads for expensive perfume. Behind the chair, a blonde woman, equally young, peeks out between the balloons, a messy bun balancing on the top of her head. She's laughing, showing off slightly uneven teeth.

'Today, Ina recreated a snippet of my favourite film simply because she knew it would make me smile, and it did. I love her so much.'

Below the caption, hundreds of people envelop the two women in a cocoon of adoration.

'I love you guys.'

'You give me so much hope.'

Clicking onto her full profile page, I find the name of the woman sitting in the chair: Ailyn. I scroll back through months of daily photos and texts and piece together a person.

Ailyn is lying in bed with her eyes closed, her hair spreading like tentacles over the white pillowcase.

Sitting in the same bed, Ailyn is hunched over a drawing pad, where a cartoon strip runs across the white page, half of it coloured in vivid primary colours.

'I want to become an animator one day. I am more obsessed with cartoons than a small child. My brother makes fun and calls me childish, but I can't help it, I love them, they let me escape. Everyone needs to escape, and people like us need it even more.'

On a cobblestoned street in the tiny Swedish town where she lives, Ailyn sits in a wheelchair clutching a green smoothie, sucking on a plastic straw. The symmetrical beauty of her face makes me instinctually envy her life, even though the wheelchair suggests she is as physically broken as I am, and she writes that she's been sick like this for almost a decade.

'But I believe I can recover. I have improved, and I will continue to improve, I know it.'

Sitting on the tiny balcony, she's wrapped in a blanket under an overcast sky.

'When we visited my mother's family in Turkey when I was little, we went to this rocky desert, and at sunrise, we floated up, up, up in a red balloon, like the rising sun. It's my favourite childhood memory, but I'm not any less happy now than I was then. You can create happiness wherever and whenever.'

My head pounds now, but I can't stop scrolling; I want to dive into Ailyn's posts and sit next to her serenity. It doesn't matter that she lives in a different country, or that I can't draw anything more elaborate than stickmen, or that she does yoga poses in bed every morning and meditates religiously, while I still hate the meditation app and only went to yoga once with Jas, years ago, hoping to cleanse myself of toxins on a hungover morning. My one big similarity with Ailyn trumps all the differences.

In a few of Ailyn's posts, the blonde girl, Ina, is photographed alone. In each of these shots, she is hanging from a trapeze. She's dangling from her arms, then she's hanging upside down with her legs hooked over the bar, before she is flying through the air. She throws herself from one trapeze to another, as if gravity doesn't exist, as if she has been allotted the strength that Ailyn should have had.

Their intricately intertwined lives are almost like a single life instead of two separate ones. In one of the photos, Ailyn and Ina are snuggled together under a white duvet in a wide double bed. Ailyn's shoulders are bare; she looks naked. How did they meet when Ailyn barely leaves the house? Online? Who pushed Ailyn around in her wheelchair before she met Ina? I never wanted a merged life, but looking at Ailyn and Ina, it suddenly seems enviable.

Would it be easier if I had met Matt when I was already sick? Being sick would have been a fundamental premise of our relationship then, instead of an unwelcome surprise, but I can't imagine impressing Matt if I had been my current self on our first date.

I stop scrolling, my head pounding. Submerged in a screen-induced hangover, I lie in the dark room, picturing Ina's and Ailyn's faces lying close together in a bed far away. I try to sink into the bed's softness instead of wishing desperately I could be somewhere else. The soft male voice plays from my phone. "Focus on the feeling of your body against the ground... feel the air flowing in through your nose... feel it filling your chest, your belly. Count your breaths... in... count one... out... count two..."

I feel like I'm sitting still with a swarm of bees humming inches from my skin.

In the evening, I pick up my phone again. Scrolling through a sea of people, I scan the faces, feet and bodies of strangers, before clicking on a random selection. I want to find others like Ailyn; I want to tether myself to a whole group of them, so they can pull me up with them.

A young mother posts pictures of her newborn baby. He's chubby with fat rolls, like a seal pup enveloped by protective blubber. Absentmindedly, I press on my upper arm and feel the hard implant that still spews hormones into my body, even though I am probably temporarily infertile now anyway; surely the body is intelligent enough to know I have no capacity to grow a baby. Below the photos of the gurgling boy, another woman has commented that the new mother is brave for choosing to layer the exhaustion of motherhood on top of her current state:

'Love over fear!'

Another woman in her late thirties has several chronic illness labels piled on top of each other like a Jenga tower. Every morning, she drinks a pint of celery juice, dry brushes her skin and swirls coconut oil in her mouth for fifteen minutes, claiming it pulls bacteria from her mouth and body.

'I have to believe it will help – I *do* believe it will – but I'm so exhausted from the long list of things I have to do each day to heal myself.'

A teenage girl posts images of anonymous body parts: feet, legs, her silhouette from the back. In her captions, she declares that she does not know if she can go on. She has marked the post with only two tags: 'suicidal', 'depression'. I click away from her at speed, as if her thoughts are contagious and can latch onto me if I stay with them for too long.

I scroll back to where I left Ailyn and Ina last summer, together in bed, seemingly naked, and click on a photo I haven't seen yet, of two small children wearing pyjamas. A dark-haired child is smiling serenely with closed lips next to a blonde grinning widely with her front teeth missing. Her expression is closer to a grimace than a smile, and she reminds me of Andrea.

'I love Ina more than I have ever loved anyone, but that does not make it a romantic love. We aren't a couple. Ina and I grew up together; we have known each other since primary school. She's the only person, except my family, who's known me since before I got sick.'

Opening up my old texts, I look for Jas and see we haven't texted since the marathon in April. Even before I graduated from university, I had lost touch with the girls I grew up with. *If you keep experiencing the same thing, you are the common denominator.*

'How's Ibiza?' I text Jas.

She replies with a series of photos. In a pool, she is floating on the same inflatable pink swan we both mocked when we were in Portugal with the others from work. Viktor is standing on a paddleboard in a turquoise bay, wearing sunglasses, a white patch of sunscreen covering his nose. The whole group of them sit around a restaurant table laughing, glasses of foamy beer in their hands, the sun dipping down into the water behind them. It feels more like watching a reality TV show than seeing photos of people I know.

'You should have brought a cardboard cut-out of me' I text. *I miss you; I miss you; I miss you.*

When I fall asleep, in my vivid dreams, I am lying next to Ailyn and Ina in a field looking up at a sea of balloons drifting across a clear blue sky.

16

'You're missing London's hottest day ever' I text Matt. Sweltering and dense, the afternoon heat belongs to a different country. Lying on the couch, my long pale legs stick out of cotton shorts, and I've rolled up my strap top so my stomach can breathe. A fan spins and whirs like a buzzing insect, but it only cools a tiny zone of air around my head. Sweat seeps out of body parts that I didn't even know had the necessary glands.

Four days ago, Matt flew to Chicago to see his mother and the family he still says isn't his. He hasn't accepted his stepfather even now, but he isn't as indifferent towards his half-sisters as he claims; for a while, a photo of his mum with the twins filled the background image on his phone's home screen. Hunting for cooler air, I step into the garden. The heat sits still and heavy between the brick walls. Sinking into the deckchair, the sun caresses my bare skin, but within minutes, the gentle fingertips become too insistent; the rays are groping my body.

My phone pings in my hand. The sun glares on the screen. Shielding it with my other hand, I see an alert that Ailyn has posted a photo of herself sitting in the sun on her balcony. Her face is tilted upwards, like a plant stretching towards the light.

'I'm pretending the sun's light is like an energy transfusion. Beyond grateful to be able to leave the confinement of the flat, even if just for a moment.'

Closing my eyes, I insert her thoughts into my own head. Momentarily, an echo of Ailyn's ease fills me up – *this garden is an oasis* – but then it's gone. *I'm still in a cage, just outside.*

I don't know whether Ailyn's thoughts are naturally infused with positivity, or whether she forces herself to create text that fits the persona of an inspiring influencer. In every shot, she radiates contentment, and if she's telling the truth in her lengthy captions, she has accepted her new body. Instead of comparing herself against those hypothetical bodies glowing with boundless health, she tells herself that having her painful body is better than having no body at all. The healthy body she had before, and the healthy body she could have had right now, are irrelevant constructs that never belonged to her. I have lost a functioning body, but Ailyn has gained a sick body. I should be able to copy her now that she's shared her trick, but my mind won't fall for it. Maybe I am not made for serenity.

My phone vibrates. Shielding the screen again, I watch a short video of Matt rollerblading. He zooms along a bike path against the backdrop of a beach. I know the water is a lake, but it is vast like an ocean. A woman's voice whoops as he zips between a formation of traffic cones.

I'm typing a reply when the phone vibrates with an incoming video call. Picking up, a pixelated version of Matt's face materialises next to his mother.

"There she is! I can't believe I finally get to meet you!" Matt's mother grins at me, her voice crackling. Her blonde hair swirls in the wind, and she brushes loose strands off her face.

I plaster on a smile. "You too!"

"I might never let you have him back," she says. "It's so good having him home. I haven't rollerbladed in forever! When he was little, it was our thing."

"Okay, that's all you get." Matt laughs at his mother while grabbing the phone from her, nudging her face out of the frame. "You've met now."

His mother squeezes half her face back into the screen. "Barely!"

They seem tipsy, but maybe they are just happy. He's told me his mother has an exuberant personality; she was a cheerleader in high school and worked as an aerobics instructor for years when Matt was little. Matt sat in the corner of the studio during the classes because she didn't have the money for a babysitter. I had so many things I wanted to ask her about Matt, but now my mind is blank. They seem more like friends than mother and son. I pictured their relationship as cool and cordial, but none of Matt's resentment towards her is visible.

"Okay, we have to go," Matt says. "How's everything, you good?"

I made a friend. I want to tell him Ailyn has taken the edge of my loneliness, but I can't share that without also revealing the loneliness itself – and social media should only be a mindless distraction. Ailyn is a virtual echo, not a real person.

"Yes, all good," I say. "I have been going up and down the stairs almost every day, sometimes twice a day."

As I say it, I hear only how it must sound to him – he has been to a hundred countries, the ground floor isn't a destination.

When Matt hangs up, I want to call him back. I want to stay on the phone while he continues rollerblading alongside his mother.

I'm dozing in the deckchair in the stifling afternoon heat, when Ellie, Hector and Andrea spill into the house in a cocktail of voices. They rush upstairs, before they emerge into the garden only minutes later wearing swimsuits. I sit in the shade of the brick wall watching as Ellie sprays Andrea and Hector down with ice-cold water from the hose. Hector's abrupt bursts of laughter explode into the stillness. Andrea emits high-pitched screams every time the water hits her. Ellie moves effortlessly on her cellulite-covered legs, and I want to trade the smooth aesthetics of mine for the function of hers.

Hector attempts a cartwheel, emerging with a flushed face.

"People wondered why I wanted to marry an old man like you, but they don't know that you aren't old at all," Ellie laughs.

"The transformational power of love!" Hector grins. "Immature becomes young at heart! Annoyingly loud… or full of life! Chaotic… or never boring." He moves over to kiss Ellie. "Your eyes see me as I want to be seen."

Hector grabs Ellie's hand and twirls her.

Watching them dance without music, I realise they haven't hosted any full-blown parties since I moved in. I picture the framed ultrasound on Ellie's bedside table. She always lived for extravagant celebrations; I used to think of her life as a string of festive events interspersed with days of waiting for the next occasion. If that is how she sees herself too, then she is also waiting to get her life back.

"Want some water on you?" Andrea is standing in front of me with the hose in her hand, a jet of water shooting out of it.

140

"Okay." I hold my feet out, flinching as the coldness hits. Momentarily, my mind is still, and all I feel is the water.

"Not just the legs," I say. "Hose me down."

Andrea's eyes expand. "But you're wearing clothes!"

I bat the words away. "Just do it!"

Wide-eyed, she points the hose at me like a gun. The icy water shocks my hot skin, and I gasp, while Andrea laughs hysterically at my drenched clothes. She drowns me, before redirecting the jet of water straight into the air like a fountain. *This is what Ailyn would have chosen. This is what she would have taken a photo of.* Andrea points the hose at me again.

"Wait! Stop! My phone!"

Fishing my forgotten phone out of my wet shorts, I wipe the droplets off the screen, which still glows bright. I hold it out to Ellie.

"Take a photo!"

I want to fill the empty camera roll so I can shove the screen in my illness's face: *see! You can zap my energy, fill my muscles with pain and my brain with fog, but I am still here; this is also some sort of life.*

In bed, my wet hair makes the pillow damp. My drained body sinks into the mattress, but my mind floats above my corpse like an ascending soul. Piano music streams through the wall from the neighbour. On my phone, I'm looking at Ailyn's old posts with my exhausted eyes, when Ellie comes into my room with dinner.

"This is how celebrities maintain flawless bodies," I say, pointing at the bowl of quinoa salad topped with smiling moons of avocado. "No need for self-control."

"Your personal chef, at your service." Ellie bows her head, her eyes bright. Her lips are stained from red wine. Handing me the bowl, she perches at the foot of the bed.

I poke at the food. "I wish you would let me pay you for staying here."

"Oh, not this again. I was only joking. Don't feel guilty. I don't ever cook either – it's all Hector."

"That just makes me feel worse. Hector's not even family."

"Don't let him hear you say that! He thinks of you as his baby sister just as much as I do."

"I could go stay with Mum and Dad." The words hover in the air like a jet stream tailing a plane.

"Oh, don't worry! Having you here is kind of like having that second child we always wanted." Ellie laughs. "My friend with three children says that having one and two kids feels pretty much the same. It's only when you have three that you really notice the difference and it becomes exhausting. Good thing I still can't get pregnant!" Ellie laughs again, but the sound evaporates quickly. She picks at a tiny hole in the duvet cover, then looks up, a wide smile glued to her face.

"Missing Matt, huh?"

"What?"

"You're more attached to that phone than I was to the baby monitor when Andrea was a newborn." Ellie points at my left hand, where I'm still cradling the phone. I pierce an avocado moon with the fork.

"Yes," I say.

"How are things with you two then?"

"Who?"

She stares at me. "You and Matt."

"Oh, right. Pretty good." My voice comes out high-pitched.

"It must be hard for him, this whole thing."

"It's hard for me too."

"Oh, of course it is. But everyone knows that it's hard for you." Ellie tucks her hair behind her ear. "I'm glad he's sticking around though. We like him."

"Sticking around?"

Ellie looks flustered. "Oh, I didn't mean…"

Shaking my head, I spear a piece of tomato. "No, I'm glad he's sticking around too."

"I should get downstairs," Ellie said. "They'll be wondering what's taking me so long." Walking out of the room, she turns around. "We should repaint this," she says, indicating the cartoon animals on the walls.

In the hot room, I'm half-asleep when my phone rings. Matt's face fills the screen again. He's striding down a city street, his head bobbing erratically on the screen.

"I've fucked up." His hard voice is drunk.

I feel sick. *Jaya.* "What did you do?"

"It's so stupid. Months ago, when my mom was pestering me to come home and asking why I never come back to visit like other kids do – you know, asking if she hadn't been a good mom to me, that kind of stuff – I finally told her that I felt like she'd replaced me when she had the twins. I thought she knew that already anyway, it was so insanely obvious, but—"

"Even I knew that." I sink into the pillows, relieved. *His family is broken, but we are fine.*

"I don't remember exactly what I told her, but she somehow thought I meant I would only come visit her if the twins and Patrick were out of the picture, and so she told them she needed to leave them."

"She *left* them?"

"Not permanently. But she rented a flat for the weeks that I am here, so it could be just us. I'm almost thirty fucking years old, and the twins are only kids." He clears his throat. "If she can't be both theirs and mine at the same time, then she should be theirs." He sighs. "I'll stay until tomorrow, then I'll go off road-tripping, so she can move back home."

"I'm sorry."

He sighs again. "It's fine. I just shouldn't have said anything to her in the first place."

"Who will you go with?"

"No one. I just need to get out of here. I might try to tick off a few states I've never been to."

If he called Jaya, would she jump on the first flight out to drive across the country with him? I watch them zoom down wide-open roads with the windows down, singing along to blaring music.

"I can't wait for you to come home," I say, even though missing implies an ugly emptiness.

"It's only a few weeks."

"Yes, I know. Barely any time at all. I love you."

"Love you too."

Two words instead of three removes his from the sentence. The detached love floats in the air.

17

At night, my duvet embraces me like a human body, actively emitting heat instead of just containing mine. Matt must be hovering somewhere above the Atlantic. I don't know when he's landing, but he said it would be too late to come over. I resisted the impulse to request his flight number and exact landing time.

I reach out for my phone on the nightstand and flood my eyes with the blue light that tells my body it's morning. Over the last week I have collected black numbers in my spreadsheet every day. By restraining myself, I have amassed a tiny reserve of energy. The therapist would tell me I should set that aside for healing, but I want to release it all in a bright burst when I see Matt – I will initiate intense sex, then we will swim together in the inflatable pool that Hector bought last weekend, before I hose Matt down with icy water until our laughs and screams bounce between the garden walls.

I scroll on my phone, but Ailyn hasn't posted anything new. She will be sleeping under pristine white bedsheets next to Ina, artificial wind from a fan stroking their peaceful faces; all of Europe is enveloped in this endless heatwave.

'And people don't believe in climate change' I text Jas.

She responds with a flurry of sentences:

'The vast majority of people believe in it.'

'The problem is not lack of fear.'

'The problem is too much of it, which only leads to people shutting down, like children closing their eyes and ears, singing "la la la".'

Moving on from Ailyn's social media page to Jas's, I see she has posted, just hours ago, a selfie of her with her boyfriend, Sergio, who she started going out with just before I got sick. Jas is smiling below fake eyelashes next to his narrow face and thin lips. Sergio also works at the consultancy. I imagine they are now sitting in bed next to each other in silence, each absorbed by their laptop screen but finding connection in that.

Scrolling away from Jas, I move past photos of acquaintances and celebrities, until Matt's face is on the screen in the midst of a small group of people. I sit bolt upright; Jaya is the one who posted the photo. They are standing in a bar. Matt's tanned face splits in a grin. I can hear his loud and uncontrollable laugh, which I only rarely provoke.

'Surprise welcome home celebrations for this one' Jaya has written in the caption.

Jaya's words, Jaya's picture, Matt's face. My heart pounds.

Jaya has posted a whole series of pictures. In one of them, she is at the airport, holding up a sign with a photo of Matt pulling a silly face. I click through all of them until I come back to the first one. Looping through them a second time, I stop again at the picture of Jaya and Matt alone. *Who goes to meet their friend at the airport when they've only been gone for a couple of weeks?*

I open the latest text Matt sent me to see whether I misunderstood.

'Landing too late to come over. I'll see you tomorrow.'

My mind spins with the intensity of a washing machine at the end of its cycle. I should have replied that it wasn't too late at all. *I will remain awake for you.* Jaya must have known when he was coming back too, but unlike me, she was unwilling to wait. Showing up at the airport wouldn't have occurred to me even if I wasn't held prisoner by my body.

I am desperate to move, as if it's possible to run away from my frenzied thoughts. I slip out of my room and into the silent house, down the stairs and through the kitchen. On bare feet, I escape into the dark garden. The air is still warm against my skin. Tension wraps my body. My chest constricts. I walk over to the inflatable pool. The edges press against the brick walls on either side of the garden. If the pool was pumped to its full capacity, it would push against the walls and burst through them like a live creature, bricks flying everywhere. With trembling fingertips, I touch the lukewarm water, rippling the surface. In my right hand, I'm clutching my phone, where the picture of Matt and Jaya glows like an ad for a successful relationship.

What happened off-screen? Matt would have hugged her and shared a funny anecdote from the plane. He hasn't even texted me to say he's landed.

Holding the phone over the pool, I release my grip. The round plop of the phone hitting the surface is immensely satisfying. My tension releases. Watching the phone sink into the water, unexpected exhilaration bubbles in me.

Through the blurry lens of the water, I look down at the black screen resting on the floor of the pool. I should lean over the edge, dunk my arm into the water and pick the phone up again, but instead, I strip out of my pyjamas and slip my naked body into the water. Light still colours the edges of the sky. I attempt to float on my back, but as soon as I exhale, I sink. I inhale to buoy myself upwards again. I exaggerate my inhales and shallow my exhales, until I float.

Love you too.

Hector and Ellie declare their love out loud several times a day. I asked Ellie if the words don't lose their power, but she just looked confused. *Of course not, that's not how love works.* Then her confusion transformed to pity. *You do know you can't use up love, right? It is endless.*

If I was in Matt's position, would I have gone to his flat to sit next to him like a nurse while he slept? *No.* If he was the one who had spent his days inert in bed for a year and a half, I wouldn't even be contemplating the choice between going out with my friends or rushing to see him; I would have left him a long time ago, like the climbers on Everest walking away from other dying climbers to save themselves.

Flipping over, I dive under the lukewarm water. I am compressed, held together momentarily. I override the lungs' hunger for air. Adrenaline floods my body. When I break the surface, my throat is burning.

18

"I found your phone in the pool! Why was your phone in the pool?" Andrea yells when I enter the kitchen the next morning. She's sitting at the table spooning cereal into her mouth, wearing only a swimsuit, her messy hair damp. The sun streams into the room. I had hoped I could get the phone out of the water before anyone spotted it, but my alarm clock was lying dead in the water.

"I don't know if it's rescuable," Ellie says.

"Why was your phone in the pool?" Andrea repeats.

"Where is it?" I say.

Ellie points to a bowl on the counter. "Google said I should put it in a bowl of dry rice, supposedly it extracts the moisture."

"But why was your phone in the water?" Andrea persists.

"I dropped it."

"But why did you just leave it there?"

I hover by the bowl of rice, my hand itching to dig out

the phone. As soon as I woke, I regretted drowning it; I want to see if Jaya has posted more photos of her and Matt together. Following them online is the only control lever I have left.

The doorbell rings. Leaving the kitchen, I cross the living room, open the door and step towards Matt. I barely see him before my arms wrap him. I pull him towards me with force, as if I want my body to merge with his. I inhale the musky smell of his sweat. His T-shirt is damp. He tries to pull away, but I only cling harder.

Words about Jaya swirl in my head, but I focus on his arms on my back, my stomach against his, my cheek against his jaw. Images of Matt with Jaya fill my head; they move erratically like an old film. I simultaneously want to cling to Matt and push him hard.

Pulling away, Matt looks down at me, his hands on my shoulders. A layer of stubble covers his jaw, and the sun has brightened his hair. He is wearing glasses instead of lenses, meaning he is exhausted or hungover.

I kiss him, opening his mouth with mine. I trail my fingers across his back, wanting to pass off my clinging embrace as something less desperate than what it was.

"Why aren't you answering your phone?" Matt says. "I called and called, and it went to voicemail every time." Each word is round and fat, his American accent more pronounced than I have ever heard it.

"I dropped it in the pool."

"Since when do you have a pool? And why would you bring your phone?"

"There was a heatwave." I shrug.

We walk through the house and into the kitchen, where Ellie and Andrea both hug Matt.

"Did you bring me any presents?" Andrea asks.

150

Matt laughs. "Nice to see you too."

"Come on, let's go outside," I say.

Dragging Matt by the hand, I step out into the garden, inhaling cool air as if I have been holding my breath. Sitting down on the fake grass, Matt leans against the brick wall. I sit between his legs, leaning back against him.

"Did you have fun last night then?" I say. "Some pictures popped up online."

My heart is pounding. I wish I could see his face, but I'm glad he can't see mine.

"Oh, you saw. Yeah, it was great, they'd organised a surprise welcome home thing. I didn't get home until four."

"Fun." Leaning my head back, I close my eyes. "You said you were arriving too late to come over."

"Yeah, it was past your bedtime."

"I thought you meant you were arriving in the middle of the night. I wouldn't have minded if you came over. It wasn't that late."

"How was I meant to know that you all of a sudden aren't religiously obsessed with the minutes in your spreadsheet and going to bed at nine?"

I want to disappear to the solitary safety of my bedroom.

Did Matt send Jaya photos from his travels too? And if he did, did he send her the same ones he sent to me or different ones captured especially for her? Which would be worse? I should ask him out loud so I can remove the words from my mind, but I don't want to hear my own jealousy solidified.

"Did you talk to your mum?" I say. "After you left?"

"Kind of. Not really. She pretended she didn't understand when I tried to explain; she likes to live in a make-believe world where everything is always fine."

Twisting my body around, I look at him. His smile is flat and his eyes vacant.

"If we pour salt in the water, do you think we could float as easily as in the sea?" I point at the pool.

"Is that how you dropped your phone? You tried to recreate the Dead Sea?"

"Shouldn't that work? With the salt?"

Matt shrugs and holds up his phone. "Want to see photos from the road trip?"

He layers narration over the same photos he already sent me. We scroll through the camera roll until the photo on the screen is the one of him and Jaya from last night.

"I have to go rest," I say. "Want to stay out here? I'll be back down in a bit."

I rush into the house and up the stairs. Diving into my bed, I pull the duvet over my head and curl up, but it's like trying to sleep in the middle of a dance floor in a club; my loud thoughts pump into every corner of me. All the things I think but do not say, do traces of them remain somewhere in the depths of my subconscious, creating a mess because I didn't let them out? Sitting up, I reach for my laptop and wrench it open. Ailyn has posted a photo of herself lying on her wooden balcony wearing a bikini, her eyes closed.

'Let's say you get to the end of your life without having recovered, and you couldn't have changed that no matter what. Would you want to have spent your whole life feeling miserable and hopeless, but at the end, you got to say you knew all along you could never get better? Or would you rather live in hope and then be proven wrong? When we don't know what the truth is, wouldn't you just want to choose to believe the version that would make you feel better right now?'

I look at Ailyn's tranquil face. I would choose her naïve optimism instead of my own cynicism if it could make me feel as content as she looks, but I can't seem to force my mind into new grooves. I shuffle back downstairs, my body exhausted by my hyped-up mind.

"Okay, I'm back!" I say as I enter the warm garden, but it's empty. I double back on myself and search the kitchen for a note. On the counter, Ellie has left a scribble on a scrap of paper saying she has gone to the park with Andrea and Hector, but Matt hasn't left a trace. I pick up my phone from the bowl of rice, but the screen refuses to be revived.

I lie down on the couch, waiting. My mind spins. Has he gone out to get a coffee? Did he just leave without telling me? I attempt to meditate without the calming guidance of the male voice from the app, but I can't remember the instructions. I inhale counting to five, then exhale counting to seven; my therapist says extended exhales help calm my frayed nervous system.

How long has Matt been gone for? My laptop is the only source of time now that my phone is dead, and I can't move my aching legs up the stairs again. Time expands and slows.

When the front door opens, I pop up from the couch like a newly wound jack-in-the-box. Matt walks into the room carrying a huge white sack, his body bending with the weight of it. Relief floods me; my muscles melt.

"Where have you been?"

"Turns out you need ridiculous amounts of salt if you want to float in fresh water. I have two more of these outside. Come on." Matt strides into the kitchen. I push through the wall of exhaustion, get up and shuffle after him.

In the garden, he stops next to the pool and rips open the bag, before lifting it up to the edge. Tilting it, he releases a waterfall of salt into the water. I sink down onto the ground, watching.

Once the contents of all three sacks of salt are swirling in the water, he pulls me up to stand. We both strip down to

153

our underwear, leaving our clothes in piles on the ground. Water splashes onto the grass as we step in. Our bodies elevate the water until it nips at the edge of the pool. We lie on our backs – Matt's feet by my head, my feet by his neck – and we float.

Sounds disappear. We are weightless. I reach out for Matt's hand and our fingers touch. He's saying something, but I can't hear. I have to drown my jealousy the way I drowned my phone, kill off its supply of oxygen.

I need to be serene like Ailyn. This floating is the kind of thing she would love; if I had been her, Ina would have taken a photo of me from above, and the shot of a woman's body floating in a starfish formation would cover millions of small screens. Admitting to jealousy would be more damaging to my relationship with Matt than Jaya herself.

As I step dripping out of the pool, a flash of bright green streaks through the air above and zooms straight into the upstairs window of the house, hitting the glass at full speed with a loud thud. Somehow the bird stays airborne. Its vivid green colour is a tropical shade that doesn't belong here. Screeching and flapping its wings, the bird flies back in the direction it came from. Joining a flock of others like it, the bird disappears behind the rooftops. I feel like I have witnessed something that shouldn't exist, a miracle that proves anything is possible.

"Did you see that?" I whip my head around to look at Matt. "It looked like a parrot!"

"Why do you sound so surprised?" Drying his hair with the towel, Matt shakes his head at me. "Where have you been? There are parakeets everywhere in London, literally thousands. They're classified as a pest, actually. There are so many of those birds that if they are on your property and they are bothering you, you are allowed to shoot them."

In the early evening, I lie in bed, listening to the piano music from next door. My mind replays the conversations with Matt in the garden, searching for signs that he wants out. He just left now, claiming he needed to sleep at his own place to recover from last night. Relieved, I kissed him goodbye; I have expended way more energy than I had saved up. I will need to repay my depleted body with several days of nothingness.

Lifting my heavy arm, I grab Hector's old phone from the nightstand, an ancient thing Ellie found in a drawer. Even with a new SIM card, it feels like an organ donation, strangely intimate. I text Jas.

'Do you still believe jealousy can be a good thing?'

Keeping the phone in my hand, I wait for her reply. On her first date with Sergio, he openly declared over dessert that he was a jealous guy. He was working on it, he said, but it had caused problems in the past, so he wanted to flag it upfront. When Jas relayed his confessions, I pulled a face, but Jas laughed and said she didn't mind the jealousy; she found it flattering, a sign of devotion.

Even on weekends, Jas's phone is a bionic limb, but no reply comes. After staring at the screen for too long, I hide it in the nightstand, but I can still feel the phone's presence. Thinking I hear it vibrate, I open the drawer again, but I have no new texts. I close the drawer, lie down, then give up and extract the phone.

'Stop ignoring me.'

I don't know whether demanding a reply makes me look assertive or anxious, but it works:

'Who's jealous? You or him?' Jas says.

'What would he have to be jealous of?'

'Come on, just stop chasing him. Let him chase you.'

'I'm stationary – I can't be chased. And we have been together for too long to play games.'

'You should never stop playing games.'

I want to ask if that's what she's doing with me, when she doesn't reply as quickly as she used to.

19

The next evening, I'm lying on the couch, while Hector and Ellie are in the kitchen cooking with Andrea. The sounds of an ongoing argument between Ellie and Andrea seep out to me. I listen to their mundane interactions like it's a TV show; a few days ago, Ailyn challenged her followers to spend more time with real people instead of online, and I'm trying to obey. I don't know if what I'm doing counts as spending time with real people, but I have already expended my allowance for cognitive activity for the afternoon by scrolling on my laptop, and lying here absorbing their sounds is as close as my body will let me go.

When the doorbell rings, Ellie yells out: "Don't move – I'll get it!"

Emerging from the kitchen, she jogs across the living room on bare feet. She opens the door. Cold air drifts in alongside the sounds of raindrops hitting the ground; it has poured down relentlessly all day.

"I'm so sorry to disturb." The male voice is deep and rasping. "I live next door? So silly of me, but I have locked myself out."

I sit up and crane my neck so I can see half of the drenched man standing outside the door.

"I must have left the keys on the kitchen counter this morning, and the door locks automatically, and now my phone is out of battery too, so I can't call a locksmith, and—"

"Don't worry," Ellie interrupts. "Come on in! Let me take your coat."

The man peels off a dripping jacket. His soaked grey suit trousers cling to his short legs. He can't stop shaking, as he pulls a charger out of his backpack and a phone out of his pocket. His rough voice doesn't suit his delicate features and the gentle fluidity of his movements; his form and sounds are disconnected like a badly dubbed film.

"Really, I can't tell you how sorry I am, barging in on you like this."

"I didn't catch your name?" Ellie says.

"Oh, I'm sorry. George."

Ellie points him to the closest socket, where he plugs in the charger. Immediately, he tries to turn the phone back on, but nothing happens. Every few seconds, he jabs the button that should bring the phone back to life with the desperation of someone giving CPR to an unconscious child. When the screen finally lights up, he makes a call in a faint voice that borders on whispering. He has to repeat himself to the person on the other end several times. As he gets off the phone, he turns to Ellie.

"Thank you so much. I'll just be on my way then." Unplugging the phone, he moves to put his backpack back on.

"You're not telling me you want to go outside to wait?" Ellie laughs. "It's miserable out there."

"Dinner's ready!" Hector calls from the kitchen.

"Why don't you join us?" Ellie asks George.

"Oh no, really." He shakes his head. "I don't want to interrupt." His face is red.

"It's not interrupting when we're inviting you."

George shakes his head again so hard that his neck cracks. "No, honestly. Thank you, but I'm not hungry."

"Okay, fine. You win," Ellie says. "But at least wait here instead of outside." She indicates the couch where I am sitting, then walks towards the kitchen. "Grace, you joining dinner?"

As George walks over to the couch, I move to get up. Without introducing himself to me, he takes the blanket curled up in the corner of the couch and spreads it out, before perching at the edge of it. He crosses one leg over the other, then places both feet on the floor. His socks are covered in large rainbow-coloured polka dots. He looks older than I expected, closer to Hector's age than Ellie's.

"It's you playing, right?" I say as I stand up. "The piano, I mean." I point over my shoulder towards his house. "I hear it through the wall."

"You hear it?" Leaning forward, his eyes light up, and his anxiety evaporates. "Which songs have you heard? Do you have any favourites?"

He starts humming different tunes and saying their names, his whole being eager. As he keeps talking, lightness fills me. *He doesn't know I am sick.* He knows nothing about me, except that I am sometimes home in the evenings to hear him play. *He will assume that I am normal.*

"You should come over and have a proper listen sometime," George says. "Next week maybe? I mean, only if you want, of course." His voice falters. "No pressure, you might not fancy it. I just thought... you can't hear it

159

properly through a wall, and if you enjoy it, you might find it fun, but… it's a silly idea, I—"

"No, that sounds great," I say, ignoring my fear roaring at me that I can't possibly leave the house. *If you do, you know what happens; you will crash, then burn for weeks. You will never get better if you keep pushing it. Stay here, alone, it's safer that way.* The therapist keeps reminding me that expanding my limits is like blowing a soap bubble, I have to do it slowly or the bubble will just burst.

20

Lara and I walk over to George's house through a wall of rain. Water pounds against the pavement so hard that the drops bounce back into the air. With wet hair and big splotches of water dotting our jeans, we huddle together under the tiny roof that sticks out over George's door. My tight mind is whirring. I pinch my palm with my nails. *You mocked your cousin's wife's agoraphobia and look at you now. You need a chaperone to go next door.*

I ring the bell. A snippet of piano music plays inside the house. *It is not irrational to be terrified when my body has fallen to pieces so many times before.* The door opens, and we fall through into the living room.

"I brought Lara," I say.

"Hello, hello." George waves at us.

He wipes his hands on his rust-coloured corduroy trousers. A white shirt is tucked into them. His socks are bright purple with black stripes. The living room is wide open like a dance floor; there's no furniture at all.

"Wine?" George asks.

He walks through to the kitchen, and we follow. At the counter, he pours two glasses of white wine to the brim. When he hands me a glass, tiny pieces of cork float in the pale liquid. Following him and Lara up the stairs, I spill wine on my jeans.

We step into a single large room that contains a shiny grand piano and a kitchen chair. The surface of the piano is like a mirror; he must have polished it especially.

"The acoustic is better downstairs," George says. "But I didn't really have anything else to use upstairs for." He wrings his hands. "Oh, we need another chair!" He disappears from the room.

"He's sweet, isn't he?" Lara whispers. "Socially awkward but adorable."

Emerging back upstairs, George hands Lara the chair without looking at her. He hurries over to the piano and sits down. He declares the name of a piece, then places his fingers on the keys – and the air becomes music. The notes dance inside my skull, belly, chest and bones, replacing the internal broken structures of my body.

I want to pull my phone from my pocket to record it. It seems wasteful that this music will be gone as soon as George stops playing. I don't know anything about classical music, but I can taste the excellence in the air, and I want to swallow it. If I were him, I would record everything I played, upload it online and wait for electronic applause from strangers.

He plays piece after piece. I want him to play forever. I can't feel my body; I am floating.

When he finishes, I clap until my palms sting. He gets up from the piano chair and takes a little bow. Lara wolf-

162

whistles. My aching body returns. I want to sit on the chair and never move. I don't know how I will be able to walk back down the stairs, across to Ellie's house, and back up to my bedroom. I wish I could leave my body behind so I could just seep through the wall that separates this room from mine, like a ghost.

"You're so good! Do you ever play public concerts?" Lara asks.

George blushes. "Oh no, I'm not a professional. I just dabble. Did you have a favourite piece?"

They talk about the music. I remain seated in silence. I want the music inside me again. Lara asks George when and why he started playing. I clear my throat. George starts talking about his lonely childhood. I get up.

"I need to get going," I say.

We walk back downstairs. On a small table by the front door, a picture frame holds a photo of two boys of Andrea's age. Weeks ago, one evening the piano sounds that entered my room were only noise, and it sounded like a child slamming their tiny hands onto the keys, but Ellie said the neighbour definitely didn't have a child, unless he was one of those crazies who had kidnapped a kid and kept them locked up in the basement.

Lara is also looking at the photo. "Oh, they are adorable!"

"Nephews," George says.

"I assumed you were divorced," I say, my face immediately burning as I hear the words come out. I have forgotten how to socialise like a normal person. He may not know I am ill, but now he will know I am not normal.

George laughs nervously. "Oh no, it's just me. No children or ex-wife." He clears his throat. "Well, thank you both for coming!"

He stretches out his hand, and Lara laughs.

"Don't be silly!" Stepping forward, she hugs him. Following her lead, George hugs me too, but our embrace is prescribed and awkward; we barely touch.

Outside, the rain is still hammering down. I shuffle towards Ellie's house, but halfway between the houses, Lara stops, leans her head back and lets the rain shower her face. I hover next to her, crossing my arms. I look at my phone. I've been out of bed for a full hour. I feel horrendous, but I am still standing. Hope expands in my chest. *Maybe this is it. Finally, I can exist outside the house.* Lara is still facing the sky, her eyes closed.

"I'll see you at Matt's birthday next week?" I say.

Facing me, Lara grins and claps her hands. "Yes! I didn't want to mention it; I wasn't sure if you'd be up for it. Oh, it will be so great. All of us together again."

I smile, the fear that I won't make it fluttering amidst hope.

21

Lying across my bed, his feet dangling off the edge, Matt is lost in the world of his phone. I'm sitting on the floor in front of the mirror holding a make-up brush. The room smells of citrus and flowers; I've sprayed my wrist and hair with excessive amounts of perfume.

"Are you sure you want to come?" Matt says, without looking up from the screen. "You know it's fine if you can't?"

I turn to look at him with one eye made up, the other one still bare. "It's your birthday; I don't want to miss it again."

"If you're sure."

Returning to the mirror, I make up my other eye. I want to lie back down in bed, but when I asked who was coming from his office, he said 'everyone'. My polished face glows in the mirror, but the insides of my body are crumbling.

"Ready?" Matt says, getting up from the bed. "We're late."

"Why don't you go ahead without me." I look at my phone screen. "Just need a quick lie down; I'll come along in a bit." The words feel too familiar.

"You sure? No pressure if you don't feel up for it in the end."

I push myself up to standing, put my arms around Matt and kiss him insistently, before pulling away again, my eyes steady on his. "I'll be there." I say this as if I can control what my body will and will not do.

At the restaurant, a waiter tells me to take the stairs down to the basement. The cocktail of voices and loud music hits me like a gust of hot air. Scanning the room, I barely recognise anyone, and I can't recall the names of most of the people who do look familiar. I might not even have met them in person before at all; I could recognise them only from photos posted on Matt's social media. I spot him standing in the far corner. People are flocking around him.

"You came!"

Oliver appears from the crowd and hugs me. He holds me for a long time. I feel special until he lets me go and hugs another woman in exactly the same prolonged way. I have not seen Oliver since last summer, the one and only time he came to visit me at Ellie's.

"Sit with me," I say, grabbing his arm. We find two seats in the middle of the table, and I feel momentarily electric. The room is a furnace of energy and voices and music, and I am part of the fire. I inundate Oliver with questions. As he tells me about his new girlfriend and her baby daughter – his boyfriend broke up with him in the spring – he is looking over my shoulder, scanning the room. I had forgotten that annoying habit of his, like he's constantly debating whether to remain in the conversation or move on.

"Is Lara not coming?" I say.

"No, she's having a bad day."

"Yes, I know," I say quickly. "I just thought she would want to come anyway."

"She didn't tell me what happened," I add. "Did she tell you?"

Oliver shrugs, taking a sip of his drink. "You know what she's like – the tiniest things either make her ecstatic or heartbroken. She feels all the feelings, instead of just suppressing them like a normal person." Oliver laughs.

A man I haven't met pokes Oliver's shoulder. When Oliver turns around, I am left in silence, embarrassed that I was oblivious to Lara's bad day; she holds me, but I don't hold her. *Every relationship I have is asymmetrical.*

The vitality is already draining from me, like I have a leak somewhere. Oliver pushes his chair back so we sit in a half-circle. He introduces me to his friend, who acknowledges my presence with a sharp handshake. He presents an anecdote about a pest control visit that I can't follow. His loud voice feels exaggerated, like a stand-up comedian. When he pauses in the story, they both erupt into laughter, and I laugh too. I didn't even hear the joke, but my laugh is only false for an instant before it becomes real – if a photo were taken of the three of us in that moment, I would look like a young person should.

A skinny woman sits down on the other side of me. I beam at her.

"Hi, I'm Grace."

"Aziza."

"I went to primary school with a girl called Aziza."

She wrinkles her eyebrows and laughs. "Cool."

I can't tell if her laugh is mocking or kind.

"So, what do you do?" I say.

"I'm a social media manager. You?"

"Oh, I'm… between things."

"Oh, cool." She's swivelling back towards the friend she arrived with.

"I'm an event manager," I say, plastering my own face onto Ellie's life on an impulse. I haven't got the imagination to make something up, but if I sit here in silence my body will take up too much space in my mind.

"Really?" Aziza looks at me again. "Have you done any celebrity ones?"

"Mainly corporate events," I say.

Aziza nods, then turns away to face her friend. My ability to interact with strangers has disappeared with lack of use, just like the muscles in my legs and arms. I am not even a moon reflecting other people's energy; I'm a dead rock that doesn't glow at all. I should have just told her that being sick is my current full-time job.

Matt erupts in a fit of laughter at the other end of the table. Jaya is sitting next to him, and she is laughing too. I purposely didn't sit next to Matt – I didn't want to cling – but seeing Jaya there now, I regret not claiming the chair next to him.

"Wine?" Oliver is holding up a bottle.

"Yes please." I hold out my glass to him. "Large."

"Cheers." He clinks his full glass against mine, and I take a sip. In a blind test of liquids, I would find it sour rather than pleasant, but I take another deep drink. *You love wine, remember?* When my bowl of pasta arrives, I hear Hector's voice in my head, shouting that I should have ordered a dish filled with colourful vegetables to boost my intake of micronutrients, but I don't want to think about my immune system right now. I repeat the affirmations the therapist has prescribed me. *I am healthy. I am strong.*

Oliver is still talking to the man sitting next to him, leaving me in an empty space between conversations.

Spinning the thick ribbons of pasta around my fork, I chew while counting to twenty in my head; I don't want to run out of food and sit purposelessly in front of an empty plate. Taking another gulp of wine, I feel the first inklings of tipsiness, the nauseous kind that forced me to give up alcohol in the first place. It must be a placebo effect.

I pull my phone out and text Lara.

'Are you okay? Wish you were here – we miss you.'

While chewing, I momentarily lock eyes with Jaya on the other side of the table. Immediately, I avert my gaze, but she yells out: "Grace! How are you feeling down there?"

We have never met. How does she know that I am Grace? Has she seen my social media too? Has Matt shown her pictures while talking about our relationship?

Her shout stops all the clusters of conversations. Everyone turns to look at me. I turn on a smile.

"I'm great! All good! Wonderful!" I lift my wine glass up. "Cheers!"

"Cheers!" Jaya yells, and everyone follows.

Around the table, the conversations resume, but Aziza turns to me. "So, Matt never mentioned, what are you recovering from?"

Only then does it occur to me that everyone around the table will know that I am sick. I hate the idea – tonight I wanted to be someone else – but if Matt hadn't told them about me at all that would be worse.

I hesitate. Once I share my diagnosis, I will only become someone who broke too easily, but I let the words out anyway.

"I've got myalgic encephalomyelitis."

"Oh. I've never heard of that."

"Chronic fatigue syndrome?"

The concern evaporates from her eyes. "Oh, right. Sucks being exhausted, doesn't it?"

"I initially got sick because of a rare heart disease." I hear the words as if it's someone else saying them. "But I've had an operation, so they think I can recover now."

My heart thumps in my chest, protesting my lie. Aziza's eyebrows jump up again. I nod sombrely.

"Oh!" Aziza repeats, the warm sympathy refilling her eyes. "I'm so sorry."

"Yeah, it's been hard, but it makes you appreciate life," I say, like a self-help book. Seeing her expression, the heart disease doesn't feel like a lie; the look on her face now is a more accurate reflection of my experience than her expression when I told the truth.

As if my apparent vulnerability has released something in her, Aziza confesses she had an eating disorder when she was in school: "I was at an all-girls boarding school; it was a horrible place." Words spill out of her until our plates are empty, and people start looking at dessert menus. I'm trembling, and my limbs are heavy like metal. This must be how it feels to be poisoned, every part of me attacked from the inside.

"Excuse me, I have to leave," I say.

"Good luck with recovery," Aziza says.

"Thanks. You too, with yours. I mean, if you're still…"

She nods. I nod back, then prod Oliver's shoulder. He turns around to face me.

"I have to go."

"Yeah?"

He doesn't push further, he only gets up and hugs me again.

As I walk over to where Matt is sitting with his back turned to me, Jaya sees me and smiles.

"Hey, Matt," I say. The sound of his name coming from my mouth feels strange; I can't remember the last time we called each other by name.

170

He turns his chair around and pulls me down onto his lap. When I lean in to kiss him, he tastes like beer. Tasting it second-hand from his lips is much more pleasant than drinking it from a glass.

"I have to go," I say, my voice casual.

"Oh, stay!" Jaya says. "No one should leave right before dessert!"

"I can't."

"Okay." Matt kisses me again.

"Can I borrow your phone to order a car?"

"You really need to get a new one," Matt says.

I remain perched on his lap while typing on his phone.

"I'll stay at mine tonight, okay?" Matt says. "I'll be late, and I don't want to wake you."

"Oh, you two are so cute. We need a photo." Jaya pushes her chair back and aims her phone at us. Putting the phone down again, she leans closer and puts a hot hand on my knee. Her dark eyes grab mine.

"Matt's told me all about your illness – it just sucks."

"Thanks." I move my knee to get away from her hand.

"But I have been wondering," leaning closer, she lowers her voice, "how's the sex? Sometimes even I am too tired for sex, so how do you do it, when you barely have the energy for anything?"

I laugh, as my face burns. I don't know if Matt heard her question. *Why does Jaya think about Matt having sex?* On her wrist, she wears a stack of festival wristbands, worn cotton bracelets in green, purple and yellow that she must have accumulated over several years. I didn't even save my wristband from the festival where Matt and I got together, but now I wish I had it as proof that it happened.

A ping from the phone announces the arrival of my ride, and I jump up from Matt's lap.

22

A week later, I curl up in a nest of blankets on the bench in the kitchen. Perching my laptop on my knees, I look at the photos from Matt's birthday that I have already viewed too many times. Jaya posted the one of me sitting on Matt's lap and captioned it:

'Lovebirds.'

Looking at the photo feels better than it did actually sitting there, but it's only a momentary distraction. My body remains poisoned, aching and heavy. The sadness cloaks me in a thick, tar-like substance; it must feed on exhaustion. My body is depleted enough to drag my mind down with it.

I can hear the others talking in the living room. Andrea shouts something, and I want to yell back: *shut up!*

With a few clicks on the screen, a calm voice fills the room.

"Count your breaths. Breathing in… one. Breathing out… two. Observe your thoughts without attachment, like clouds floating across a blue sky."

How's the sex? How's the sex? How's the sex?

When Jaya asked, I should have said something funny about making Matt do all the work. Jaya and I could have leaned closer together and laughed.

This is what I do. On particular days, I decide early in the morning. My friend Jas, she is a runner, and she has a whole routine to optimise her performance around a race. Extra rest and power bars beforehand, then chocolate milk straight after, because it has the optimal ratio of carbohydrates and protein for muscle recovery. The drawer in my bedside table is filled with power bars. My niece loves chocolate milk, so there's always some in the fridge, so I ask Matt to go get us some as soon as we are done. We clink our glasses together in a toast, and it makes us laugh. I'd lean even closer to Jaya and whisper: *but please don't tell Matt that it's never spontaneous anymore, planning and power bars are the opposite of desire and lust.*

Giving up on the meditation, I want to scroll back into the depths of my phone to find old texts I sent to Matt at the beginning of our relationship, when my body led the way like it's meant to, but those texts drowned in the pool in the summer.

On my laptop, I search again for Jaya's social media profile. Scrolling, I hunt for a photo that might not even exist.

For Matt's birthday last year, I naively booked for us to go on a kayak trip along the river, after an ad shouted at me that we could see the city from the water at night. When I booked it, his birthday was months away, and I couldn't imagine remaining sick for that long. When I couldn't go, he took a colleague instead, but I don't know who. I find a photo of Jaya and Matt around the time of his birthday last year, captioned 'celebratory birthday drinks for this oldie', but there are none from a kayak trip.

When Matt calls me now, I let the call go to voicemail. A text follows asking if he should come over tonight and stay over. I do not reply for a whole hour, then I say no. I don't explain, and he doesn't ask. I stare at the extensive collection of wines and spirits that sits on top of the kitchen cabinets.

The past week, I have tried to lift myself out of the ocean of sadness. On my laptop, I have watched a litter of puppies play in a garden, the golden balls of fluff tumbling on top of each other, nibbling at each other's legs and ears. I have leafed through the box hidden in the drawer of my bedside table and looked at the birthday candle and red underwear, but the objects are dead. The cardboard fork makes me miss Jas; the underwear makes me think of Jaya and Matt; and the pile of green sticky notes with my own reminders – *I believe, I believe, I believe* – just sit there in front of me and fail to come alive. I feel like I've partially died too, while simultaneously still being present to grieve my own death.

"We're going to the park!" Ellie yells.

"Okay!" I yell back.

Yesterday, Ailyn posted that she went to the park to go stargazing with Ina.

'I find it so comforting to feel how small and insignificant we are. Contemplating the thousands of years that humans have looked up at the same stars makes even a decade of illness feel like only the blink of an eye.'

I feel small and irrelevant too, but it isn't a relief – it's depressing. My mind hurls hard sentences at me. *Other people with this illness, they are a lot sicker than you – some can't talk, can't sit up in bed, can't take themselves to the bathroom, and they have to be fed with a spoon while lying down, and many have been like that for years, even decades, and just over five hundred days into your minor level of disability, you crack? You pride yourself on being strong, but you are not.*

Hearing the door slam shut behind Ellie, I push myself up and move a chair over to the kitchen counter and stretch up to reach a bottle of vodka. Pouring a measure of the transparent liquid into a kitchen glass, I mix it with juice and take a sip. The liquid leaves a trace of warmth. I take a second sip, before I tilt the glass back and guzzle it down. I want to drink until I am so senseless that I cannot feel this body and mind.

After another glass, I am spinning, dizzy. Lying down on the bench, I close my eyes. I have no idea now where tipsy graduates into light drunkenness and where that flips over into blacking out and if at any of those stages, I could feel good.

In the office, when Friday afternoons tipped over into evening and Jas, Jordan and I were still in the office, one of us would say we needed a drink, and Jordan would find a bottle of wine and three glasses in the kitchen. She would pour out an equal amount to each of us, white in the spring, rose in the summer and red in the autumn and winter, like a seasonal wardrobe. We would continue to work while sipping absentmindedly. It was better than any bar, just the three of us, united.

Now, half-sitting up to take another sip, I want to hurl the glass across the room and make it shatter against the wall.

Shuffling over to the sink, I pour the remains of the glass down the drain. I refill the glass with water and walk unsteadily back to my nest on the kitchen bench. I scroll to Jas's name in my phone, but instead of calling, I pick up the laptop again and go online to search for her. Jordan must have had her baby by now. I can't even check; I crash against the virtual wall she has erected around her online self to keep strangers out.

In a sun-filled square somewhere hot, Jas is standing next to a man in a suit. She's wearing a short white dress, holding a bouquet of white roses in one hand and his hand in the other. A blissed-out smile lights up the man's face. Jas posted the photo several weeks ago, at the end of September; I don't know how I missed it. The caption is minimal:

'Surprise!'

Underneath, loving comments flood the screen.

My hands shaking, I pull out her number and call. Listening to the ring tone, I tap my foot against the bench, fury pulsing. When it goes to voicemail, I find her work number and call that, but it only beeps and beeps. She never leaves her phone behind. She will be holding it in her hand, or it will be resting face-up at her desk, and glancing over, she will be looking at my name.

"Hello, this is Jas—"

"You got married without even telling me! I had to find out about your wedding from a social media post?"

A loud beep replies, and I realise I'm shouting at her voicemail. I hang up, seething.

'I can't believe you're screening my calls' I text.

Her reply is instant:

'Can't talk now, in meetings, will call you later.'

In the early evening, my phone vibrates and shouts Jas's name at me with lit-up letters. My head is throbbing. Sadness swims in my chest. I ignore the call.

On Christmas Eve during our second year at the consultancy, Jas and I sat next to each other in the office, the only ones there. Computer monitors glowing, we were each immersed in spreadsheets. Typing away, we were creating puzzle pieces we would then slot together. It looked like work, but it felt like play. I disappeared into it, with her, and we flowed.

Late in the afternoon, we stood up from the desks, wrapped up in coats and scarves, and walked outside into the dark cold, linking our arms together like penguins. We felt like the only ones left in the world; the square outside the offices was abandoned.

In the only café still open, we bought burnt coffees, plastic-wrapped gingerbread and crumbling mince pieces, which we carried back to the office, where we ate in silence, absorbed in our screens. We were connected like soldiers in battle, except our battle was with numbers and no one would die.

Late in the evening, we walked back to my flat, and she stayed over, the only time she did. When I told her that it had been my favourite Christmas Eve, Jas laughed and said it was hers too, but I couldn't tell if she was being ironic.

On Christmas Day, we sat at the kitchen table eating a silent breakfast of coffee, yoghurt and oranges. I opened my laptop while Jas read the news on her phone, but we sat there in two different silences then, and we both left shortly after; I went to Ellie's, and she went to have Christmas lunch in a fancy restaurant with her high-flying parents. I wanted to fly in formation alongside her forever. I wanted that like others want everlasting love.

'You got married without telling me' I text.

She tries calling again. I deflect it. If I open my mouth, the sorrow will flow out and leak onto everything around me.

'We didn't tell anyone' Jas texts now. 'That's the whole point of eloping.'

'You can tell people after.'

I breathe into her silence.

'You're right. I'm sorry. I should have told you.'

I stare at the screen. Jas never apologises.

Women sorry all over everyone, Jordan told us on our first day at work. *Don't apologise. If you're late, thank the person for waiting. If you've made a mistake, say thank you for spotting that.* Like everything, Jas took it to extremes and never apologised, even when she should.

'You don't believe in marriage' I finally text.

'Marriage can be many things' Jas texts. 'It doesn't have to mean what I used to think it did.'

'Congratulations then. I'm happy for you.'

'Let's meet up soon, okay?'

'Yes, let's.'

Years ago, when Jas was in a long-distance relationship with a man who lived in Geneva, he bought her a pillow that would pulse in tune with his heartbeat, the exact beat picked up by a bracelet he wore as he slept. He wanted her to 'fall asleep on top of an artificial copy of his heart'. She broke up with him, but if Sergei bought her the same pillow now, I'm sure she would keep it. We used to agree being changed by love signalled weakness, but now we both have; the only difference is that Jas has been elevated further, while love has only given me ugly qualities: I burn with jealousy every time Matt shares a work-related story, as I imagine Jaya sitting at the desk next to him, spewing out jokes like a conveyor belt of hilarities. *Is it even love then, if it doesn't transform you for the better?*

I text Matt. 'Take me out next weekend, please?'

23

In the front garden, I stand next to Matt, looking at the carrier on the back of his bike. The red paint has peeled off in big chunks. The sun shines on the patches of exposed metal. I shiver, as a forceful gust of wind hits me. Fluffy clouds streak across the blue sky. I have never sat on the back of a bike before, not even as a child.

I furrow my brows. "Are you sure that thing can hold me?"

Matt mounts the bike. "Come on, get on already! It will be fine. Trust me."

I climb on, the cold metal uncomfortable. I hold my legs up from the ground, and Matt starts pedalling. We wobble until he picks up speed. We are approaching the crossing with the main road, but Matt speeds up instead of slowing down. We zoom into the road just as the blinking green bike symbol turns red. We roll down the tree-lined asphalted path into the park.

Cool air whips my face. On the trees, the leaves glow orange and red and yellow, as if they are lit up from their core like lanterns. We are moving fast. My legs are seizing up, but I am a cloud, flying across the sky.

We bike along the main artery through the park. Colourful leaves litter the ground. A man in a suit is walking a long-limbed grey dog. A couple is intertwined on a bench. A small boy is holding his mother's hand and picking his nose with the other. My capturing is a frenzied thing; no filter separates the background from what matters. I'm like a starved person, eating anything and everything.

Abruptly, Matt swerves onto the grass. I bounce against the metal carrier. He breaks us to a halt, and I clamber off, before sinking onto the patchy grass. Placing the bike on its side like a resting animal, Matt sits down next to me. I slip off my shoes and dig my bare feet into the grass. The muscles in my legs throb in an unsynchronised rhythm, like those dance mats where different squares light up in a random sequence. The grass smells sweet. We lie down on the cool ground, and I rest my head on Matt's arm. The open space of the park is a vast savannah.

"I was almost expecting an alarm to blare out once you moved away from the house," Matt says. "You know, like people under house arrest who have those ankle monitors."

"Just don't tell my therapist."

"Are you not going to put your stopwatch on?" Matt says. "For your spreadsheet."

"I'm rebelling."

Matt reaches for my hand; he is warm, like a glove.

"So, I can't believe you never told me about this rare heart disease you had," he says. "I was talking to Aziza; she was very impressed with your resilience."

"Oh, that." Embarrassment expands in my chest. "It was stupid, I shouldn't have said it. But you should have seen the look on her face when I told her the truth… I couldn't stand it."

"Maybe you should talk to your therapist about needing to prove yourself to strangers?"

"He's not that kind of therapist. Anyway. Let's take a picture," I say.

"If only you hadn't drowned your phone," Matt mocks me. "Where did you even find that replacement phone? I didn't think they sold phones like that anymore."

"It's Hector's. You jealous?"

"Of what? Being cut off from the world even more than you already are?"

"Hey. Not funny."

Reaching for Matt's pocket, I slip my hand inside. Phone in hand, I extend my arm to capture our faces on the screen. We are close together against a background of emerald grass.

"You can post them, if you want," I say.

"Nah," Matt says, pocketing his phone.

Lying back down, I feel deflated. If Matt's life was small and narrow too, this would be easier. *Imagine if my illness was contagious; we could be connected in communal isolation.*

He pulls out a bottle of beer from his backpack and a green juice for me, then he extracts a game of bowls.

"I know it's a game for old people, but I thought this could work, if you just sit here and throw without moving?"

Pushing myself up on my elbow, I flip over to kiss him, as guilt explodes in my chest; I want to contract his world, while he's trying to expand mine.

Matt runs to collect the balls after each round, like a dog playing fetch. With each round, his throws fly further off the mark, as if he's not trying to make the balls land next to the tiny metal target, he's just throwing them as hard as he can.

"What are you doing?"

Matt turns to me, the ball resting in his hand. "Doesn't it ever make you angry?"

"What?"

"Everything. Your situation."

I laugh. "Well, yes. I threw my phone into the pool, didn't I?"

"You threw it? You said you dropped it."

I shake my head. Matt hands me the ball. "Throw it. As hard as you can."

I hurl the ball with full force into a high arch.

"Impressive," Matt says.

We take turns shooting projectiles into the air. Matt grunts like a tennis professional with each throw. We throw and throw and throw until I am shaking. Empty, I collapse onto my back. My body sinks into the ground like it wants to bury itself. Matt lies down next to me. I shiver with cold. Goosebumps prickle on my scalp. I push myself against his body.

After returning home, we lie next to each other in bed like fallen statues. Matt lifts my leg to rest on top of his. He strokes it gently, and I wince; the strained muscles shoot out pain. Matt removes his hand, but the pain lingers. Next door, George is playing an ethereal song on the piano.

"Hear that?" I say. "Private concert."

Matt strokes my hair. "I'm going to record it."

My mouth twitches, as an intense piano crescendo fills the room. We float on the music like we floated in the pool in the summer. I reach out to grab his hand. The erratic red numbers in the spreadsheet seem momentarily irrelevant. My legs can be as dead as prosthetics, but we are not.

"Patrick and my mom are separating," Matt suddenly says.

I roll over to face him. "When did you find out? Why didn't you say anything earlier?"

Matt shrugs. He twirls his phone in his hands. "I only thought of it now because Patrick plays the saxophone." He nods to the wall separating us from the piano. "Anyway, it doesn't matter. I barely know the guy anyway." His eyes water, and he clears his throat.

"What happened?"

"According to him, they just 'want different things in life', but he's the one leaving, so who knows if that's true? He didn't elaborate; he just sent a text. I tried to call my mom, but she won't pick up. When my dad left, she stayed in bed for months and didn't even shower or eat except for when I told her to."

"I didn't know it was that bad."

"Maybe nothing will come of it." Matt lights up the screen of his phone and blacks it out again. "People say things they don't mean all the time, don't they?"

"All the time," I say.

We elapse into a thick silence. I picture a tiny version of Matt pottering about a messy kitchen making macaroni cheese before carrying a tray into a bedroom kept dark by rolled-down blinds, where a lump on the bed indicates his mother. A falsely happy version of Matt's voice tells the hidden body he made her dinner, and then the unresponsive ball of limbs curled up under the blanket turns into me instead. Fear and confusion dance in the air, but they're not all mine this time. *How can I fix you? If you don't get better again, what will I do?*

I force myself to remain facing him. *Is this why you won't leave me? Because you hate the people who leave, and you don't want to be like them?*

183

His phone vibrates. Diving into the light of his phone, he types out a long text. I lean over to see who he's talking to, but the angle is too awkward.

"Who are you texting?" The words tumble out.

His thumbs hovering over the screen, Matt looks up and raises his eyebrows at me. "My mom. Why?"

The knot in my stomach unravels. "Oh, just curious."

Matt looks at me for a second too long before resuming his texting. After he puts his phone down, we lie in silence, until Matt asks if I want to come to Oliver's for Halloween.

"Who's going?"

"Oh, I don't know."

Will Jaya be invited? I bet she loves fancy dress.

"I can't," I say. "I will never get better if I keep doing things I shouldn't."

Picturing the aggressive red scars on the spreadsheet, guilt dances on top of my painful limbs. I want to grow the numbers, but they can only grow off a foundation of black stability, and I haven't even created that yet. I'm bouncing up and down like a yo-yo. *Every time you accumulate some energy, you must gift it to your body, so it can use that energy for healing. But also, don't cling to perfecting the numbers – that will only stress you out, and if your mind is stressed, your body can't heal.* The therapist makes it sound so simple to care without caring too much.

"The therapist clearly thinks you're doing a great job." Matt points at the glowing laptop screen, where a comment says exactly that in bold letters. Other comments litter the sheet:

'WELL DONE!'

'EXCEPTIONAL!'

'YOU'VE GOT THIS.'

"Yes," I say, my face hot. I snap the laptop shut to remove my own praise from view. "He's very encouraging."

24

Andrea runs into my room. Red blood drips from the corner of her small mouth, and grey half-moons glow under her eyes. She's wearing black leggings and a long-sleeved top.

"Look how scary I am!" She smiles. "Now, your turn!"

Holding a paint kit in one hand, she paints my face white with a sponge, her tongue peeking out of the corner of her mouth in concentration. The wet paint cools my skin. Andrea loves Halloween more than she loves her own birthday. Hector and Ellie have decorated the whole house: fake spiderwebs drape the walls, carved pumpkins sit on tables and windowsills and fake blood splatters the windows.

Moist whiteness covers half my face when the doorbell rings. Andrea throws the sponge and paint down on my nightstand and runs downstairs.

A minute later, she returns with her friend in tow. The other little girl, whose name I can't remember, has also painted her face white, and blood drips from her lips too, but she has refined facial features like an old-fashioned porcelain doll, and she isn't smiling, making her an eerie child from a horror film.

Andrea points to me. "This is my aunt; she's sick."

Her friend's eyes land on my face and pop open.

"What kind of illness makes her look like that?" she whispers to Andrea, as if I can't hear or understand, like an animal in a zoo.

"Oh, that's just make-up; the illness is only on the inside of her body," Andrea says. "Do you want to finish painting her face?"

The girl shakes her head.

"I'll do it," Andrea says. She moves over to the bed and picks up the sponge again to paint the other half of my face. Her friend hovers by the door.

"I'm not contagious," I say to the horror film child, as Andrea dabs my nose. The girl nods but stays by the door. *Has no one told you that the scariest things are invisible?*

Ellie pokes her head through the doorway. A high-necked black cape frames her white face. She smiles, showing off teeth stained with fake blood.

"Ready to go, girls?"

I follow them downstairs into the living room, where a vast collection of black candles flicker. I lie down on the couch. A huge basket of sweets sits on the table.

"Be generous!" Hector says, pointing at the basket. "There's lots more in the kitchen if you run out." He runs his fingers through his slicked-back hair and scratches a bloody gash on his cheek. His cape is identical to Ellie's.

When the door slams behind them, I open my laptop to watch a cartoon. I have never understood how animated films appeal to adults, but experiencing Ailyn's obsession first-hand makes it feel like I'm spending the evening with her instead of alone. This morning she posted a photo of a laptop like mine resting on top of pristine white sheets, and on that screen within a screen, she was watching the white blobs of the Moomins, just like I am now.

The doorbell rings. I grab a handful of wine gums and pop them into my mouth without getting up. Eating several chocolates, I stuff the wrappers in the pockets of my sweatpants. The doorbell rings again, but I remain horizontal. Ringing the bell for a third time, the kid holds down the buzzer, the shrill sound drowning out the cartoon. I shuffle to the door with the basket.

"Trick or treat!"

Lara grins at me. Dressed all in black, she clutches a bouquet of black roses in front of her with both hands, like a bride. She lifts her arms out to the side, and a set of black spider pincers rise from her petite body. Holding the flowers out to one side, she hugs me, then kisses me on the cheek with a loud smacking sound.

"You've got make-up on!" she exclaims. "Amazing!"

Handing me the roses, she walks past me into the house. Even the first time she was here, she acted as if it was her own home. Plopping down on the couch where I was just sitting, she curls her stockinged legs under her. I sit down in the other corner of the couch and place the basket of sweets between us.

"Great costume," I say, picking up a wrapped caramel.

"Black widow. The spider. Get it?"

"Oh, cool," I say, my smile freezing.

"Oh, your face!" Lara rolls her eyes. "Come on. You know it happened; I know it happened… it doesn't make it less real if we don't talk about it. And especially tonight! All Hallows Eve, it's meant to be a night for honouring the dead."

"I thought you were going to Oliver's? With Matt and everyone."

"I was, but on the way there I just got this feeling I should come here instead." Lara grabs a pink lollipop from the basket and unwraps the crinkly plastic. Popping it in her mouth, she only sits still for a minute before bouncing back up. I want to tell her to go to the party and tell me if Jaya is there.

"I'll put the flowers in a vase," Lara says. "Where do you keep them?"

"I have no idea."

"Okay, I'll have a little search." She floats into the kitchen with the flowers in her hand. Left behind, I feel useless. *I should be the one to get up. We shouldn't even be here; we should be out celebrating, like everyone else.* The numbers in my spreadsheet fill my head. Like a premature baby, it's hard to comprehend something that tiny can contain a life. At the top of the sheet, I've typed in capital letters: 'PREMATURE BABIES CAN GO ON TO ACHIEVE GREAT THINGS', even though some premature babies also die.

I speak to my prodigious therapist on the phone every other week, but he can't tell me what will happen first if I manage to shrink the numbers in every cell of the spreadsheet until my body can cope with the activity level without collapsing – will the temporary increase in limitations make Matt and everyone else abandon me, or will my body heal enough to revive my relationships? Will I even be able to shrink the numbers at all, when my body so often tricks me into feeling almost okay while I'm doing something and only shatters after I have stopped?

Tears stream down my face, soaking my cheeks. I try to hold them in, but they only pause for a fraction before they flow again. *Stop it, stop it, stop it.* I frantically wipe my face.

Lara walks over to me, oblivious.

"Here you go." She hands me a glass of juice I didn't ask for. As I take it from her, the tears flow again.

"I'm sorry," I say, my face hot, my insides squirming.

"Hey, what happened?"

Grabbing the glass from me again, she places it on the table and wraps me with her slender arms; the pincers that hang from them envelop me too. I wonder if it would be easier to be held if I was physically tiny like her. My tears wet her shoulder. I pull back and my insides wobble, but my eyes stop their uncontrolled leaking.

"I'm sorry." I wipe my face. "Don't know what happened."

"Saying you're sorry for crying is like apologising for having to eat or sleep."

Reaching for the glass, I sip the thick juice. My hand is shaking.

"Why don't I run you a bath?" Lara says.

While hot water pounds into the tub, I stand by the sink wiping off my distorted vampire mask. Scrubbing my red eyes, I envisage the illness being a costume that I can zip off and leave behind in a crumpled pile on the floor.

I sink into the cloud of bubbles that fills the bath. They smell like tropical fruits; the label on the bottle claims they provide rejuvenation. Pretending the bubbles are infusing me with energy, I let the hot water scald my skin. Ensuring I am covered, I shout out for Lara. Stepping into the room, she sits down on the tiled floor opposite the tub and leans against the wall, wrapping her arms around her knees. I search the blanket of bubbles for holes.

"Want to talk about it?" Lara says.

"Not really." The lump grows in my throat.

"Okay." Lara pauses. "I know feeling sad really sucks, but it doesn't mean anything is wrong with you."

"Everything is wrong with me," I say, indicating my bubble-covered body.

"I cried every single day for years, if that makes you feel better."

"I don't know why I'm crying," I say, as my eyes begin leaking again. "Today wasn't even a bad day." My defiant voice hangs in the steamy air. "I can walk for six minutes now, without collapsing after."

"That's so good," Lara says.

"I'm going to do eight minutes next week, maybe," I say, even though I can't control when the numbers will grow. I can't stretch towards them myself; I can only sweet-talk my body to move forwards, and it may indulge me or it may refuse.

On my phone, I've copied out the checklist my grandmother's doctor gave her of things she needs to manage if she wants to continue living independently. 'Cook, maintain personal hygiene, manage medications.' When she told me about the list, my grandmother scoffed and said that when she can't potter down to the shop to buy fresh bread every morning, it's game over and she will move in with my mother. I've googled the walk to the grocery store on the tiny high street down the road from Ellie's; when I can walk for twelve minutes, I will be able to make it there and back. Yesterday, I made my spreadsheet the background on my phone, replacing an old photo of me and Jas.

Lara leans forward and looks at me with her black-rimmed eyes.

"Last week, I picked up a sandwich for lunch and then remembered how David used to pack me lunches when I first started working... and I just broke down; the man at the till stared at me like I was crazy." Lara laughs. "I couldn't even eat the sandwich after that, but I couldn't throw it away either; I kept it in the fridge for days until it got mouldy."

I sink further into the water and look up at the white ceiling, where drops of condensation cling to the paint.

"When you feel nothing, that's when something is really wrong," Lara says.

I nod, even though nothingness sounds alluring.

"Hang on." Lara taps on her phone, then she holds it out to me. "Watch this."

Wiping my wet hands on a towel, I hold the phone high up above the water. *If I drop it now, will I get electrocuted?*

On the screen, a little boy steps off a train clutching his father's hand. The camera zooms in on the train window, until I see a stuffed bear laying abandoned on a seat. As the camera gets close, the animated bear jerks to life, jumps up on the windowsill and bangs desperately on the window, as the little boy walks away, oblivious. Fat tears slide down the stuffed bear's face, as his paws push against the glass.

I look up. "What is this?"

"Keep watching!" Lara gestures to the phone. "Isn't it just heartbreaking?"

"Why do you sound so excited?"

"Just watch it."

The camera is now focused on the little boy, who's arrived home. On his knees in his bedroom, he searches through his backpack, then starts bawling. His father pats him on the head. At night, the boy lies in bed, his wide-open eyes despairing. His father comes in with a bottle of what looks like cough medicine, sits down at the edge of the bed and holds out a spoonful of purple liquid to the distraught son, who gulps it down. The father stands in the doorway watching the boy close his eyes and drift off.

"What is this, an ad for sleeping medicine for kids?"

"Isn't it so sad?" Lara says. "That the little boy lost the bear?"

Handing the phone back, I stare at her. "Are you *crying*?"

Lara wipes her wet eyes. "How did you not find it sad?"

"Um, it's more disturbing than sad, isn't it? That they're encouraging parents to drug their kids? Where did you even find this?"

"It's one of the videos they show on crying retreats in Japan."

"Crying retreats? Are you joking?"

"It's a thing! Japanese people are even more emotionally restrained than we are, and so people want an outlet, a space where it's acceptable to cry. They watch sad videos and listen to sad songs, in a big group."

"You just tried to make me cry? On purpose?"

"I can't believe it didn't work. Your heart is made of stone."

"I do feel better now," I say. *I've not become someone who cries at anything, not yet.*

"The video worked on Matt and Oliver," Lara says.

"You made Matt cry?"

"He didn't start bawling or anything."

"Have you met Jaya yet?" I say. Saying her name, my heart pounds so hard it should ripple the water.

"Who?"

Relieved, I sink lower.

"Oh, you mean Matt's colleague?" Lara says. "Yes, she's come for drinks a couple of times. She's great, isn't she? Why?"

"Oh, no reason."

The bubbles are disintegrating, exposing patches of skin. *Of course you love her.*

Tell me everything. What's she like? What's so great about her, except the fact that she's healthy and full of boundless energy, like a Duracell rabbit?

"I should get out. My fingers are all wrinkled." I wriggle them in the air. "Can you give me a minute?"

Lara closes the door behind her. When I step out of the tub, I feel weak, like I always do now after being submerged in water, as if any energy I had before was soluble and is disappearing down the pipes. The bath salts have never delivered on their promise of rejuvenating me, but every time a tiny part of me still believes it may be different this time.

Wrapped in a towel, I cross the landing into my room. Lara sits down on the bed while I attempt to change into my pyjamas hidden under the towel.

"Oh, just strip already," Lara says. "Bodies are just meat suits for our souls. In Berlin, they even have naked raves — speaking of weird human rituals and retreats, didn't Matt go to one once? Before he met you."

I drop the towel. Lara applauds. Pulling my pyjamas on at speed, I sit down next to her.

Bodies may be just meat suits for our souls. But if your body is a prison, you can't express who you are, and eventually, you will change too until you are unrecognisable.

"Oh, I almost forgot, I want to show you something else." Lara taps on her phone screen and holds it out to me. Taking the phone from her, I look down at a video.

I am in the middle of a crowd of people at a train station, clustering around something I can't see. Experiencing Lara's shortness first-hand, I see only the backs of heads and bodies. Over the background noise, spirited piano music flows seamlessly. The frame shakes as the Lara holding the camera pushes through the throng to the front, until we both see George sitting at a piano, wearing the same corduroy trousers and white shirt that he wore last time we listened to him. His hands dance over the keys.

"Isn't it great?" Lara looks fondly at the phone screen. "I asked him out."

My eyebrows shoot up. "You did?"

She looks up at me. "Why are you so surprised?"

"I don't know, I thought…"

"David would have wanted me to meet someone. I would have wanted that for him, if it had been the other way around."

"Of course he would," I say. "I only meant… how old is George?"

I thought you would be celibate for the rest of your life and just pour excessive amounts of love onto your friends forever.

"Who cares? Age is such an arbitrary thing. Everyone ages differently."

"And bodies are only meat suits for our souls."

"Exactly." Lara grins.

25

"Do you think I'm ready for it?" I say into my new phone. I'm lying on the couch wearing jeans and a thick jumper that itches against my skin. The phone heats my ear. I have finally replaced the phone that drowned in the pool.

"You're the only one who lives in your body," my therapist says. "I can't hear what signals it's sending you."

"Well, I can't either," I say, exasperated. My mind and body bombard me with contrasting signals.

Let's do it!

No, we're not ready.

Come on, you're just scared – it will be fine.

We'll crash.

But I want to do it.

One is lying and the other isn't, but I still can't tell which is which. I'm meant to be listening to what I need instead of what I want. I have accumulated only black numbers in my spreadsheet for weeks now. 'Walking: nine minutes. Sitting upright: thirty-seven minutes. Talking: twenty-two minutes. Scrolling on my phone: fifteen minutes.'

"I'm afraid time's up for today, so let's pick this back up in two weeks?' the therapist says. 'It's great to have goals, but there's no time limit on them, remember. Slow and steady wins the race."

I want to tell him that I was born a hare, not a tortoise, but he has already hung up. Immediately, I click onto Ailyn's profile and watch her latest videos, as if she will be able to tell me what to do.

She's filming herself wrapped up in a thick coat and bubble hat at a Christmas market. Ina edges Ailyn's wheelchair through the crowd and past a wooden stall selling woollen sweaters in intricate patterns.

"Can we talk about wheelchairs for a second?" Ailyn says. "I just want to declare that I absolutely love mine. We named him Wilhelm." Laughing, she cranes her head to look up at Ina. "Do you remember why?" Ina shakes her head. "Anyway!" Ailyn returns to look at me. "I know it can suck to start using one, because accepting we need help – even if it's from a machine – it's so hard. It took me literally years to embrace the disability label for myself. But I'm so glad I did. If you think about it, needing a wheelchair is no different from using a washing machine or a car or whatever – we all use technology to help our bodies out.

"I mean, it feels so obvious to me now that it's a great thing to have Wilhelm, but it took me ages to shift my mind to think like that. With Ina too, at first, I massively resisted help. But now, when she helps me, I don't feel like a burden; I only feel so loved." The video cuts, and in the next snippet, Ailyn and Ina bite into opposite corners of a vast gingerbread heart they are holding up between them.

I watch the videos again, then I hold my phone up and experiment with the angle until my face fills the screen instead of Ailyn's. I press record.

"Hi everyone! So, I'm lying here debating whether to go to the shop down the road for the first time. I just spoke to my therapist, and he said I need to listen to whatever my body is telling me. I have no clue. So, I'm just going to do it anyway."

I push myself up. Holding my phone steady in front of me, I stride over to the door, grab Ellie's yellow raincoat from a hook and pull her wellies on. I step outside into the cool air. The rain drums on my hood.

"My sister loves Christmas – can you tell?" I say to the screen, as the camera captures the explosion of fairy lights that drape down the brick walls of the house like melting icicles.

Shuffling down the street, I'm still recording, but I'm not saying anything; I'm only watching my silent face bob along on the screen. Fairy lights adorn bushes and trees in people's front gardens. Someone has put up an inflatable snowman that grins through the rain. Fat droplets of water cling to the phone screen. I should have brought an umbrella, but my arms would burn from the weight of it. I keep my eyes glued to the screen, until I reach the church at the end of the road. I spot a wet bench in the corner of the paved courtyard.

"I'm just going to sit down and rest for a second," I say to the phone.

I sink down. The water from the bench makes my jeans damp. The bare branches of a tree hover over me, and rain drips down on my head. My mind itches to get back up; now that I'm still, my thoughts have too much space to dance. *You did know what your body was telling you, you just didn't want to listen.* I close my eyes.

"I'm going to do this visualisation my therapist taught me," I say. "My body is a golden shape, strong and glowing." The therapist's instructions sound odd in my own voice. I watch as I glide down the road and into the shop on the high street. Opening my eyes, I get back up.

"Okay, let's go," I say, locking eyes with myself on the screen.

I follow my golden self out of the courtyard. Reaching the high street, I stop in the middle of the pavement. Hovering, I stare at the tiny shop that glows on the other side of the road. I flip the camera around, so it captures the sliding doors. They swallow a woman my age and the toddler she's pulling by the hand. I cross the road, as if the woman is pulling me along with her too.

Stepping through the doors, my eyes drown. I'm assaulted by orange papayas and green mangos and purple grapes and brown kiwis and red apples and a sea of oranges and bananas and melons. Immobilised, I soak up the colourful abundance, which feels surreal, like I'm tripping on a psychedelic drug.

"The average supermarket now has fifty thousand items," I say into the phone.

"Excuse me?" says a woman behind me.

"Oh, sorry." I step to the side, blushing. Water drips from my coat onto the floor. A yellow sign warns customers the floor gets slippery when wet. I flip the camera so my face fills the screen again.

"We made it," I say.

I amble through the corridor of colourful fruits into the chilled section. I stop in front of a shelf of champagnes. The air from the open fridge cools my body. My arm aches from holding the phone up. I try to smile at the camera. A construction worker walks past and stares at me, and I rush the phone into my jacket pocket. Picking up a champagne bottle at random, I walk towards the till, as the phone records the inside of the pocket.

The teenage boy at the till takes the champagne from me. Angry red spots cover his thin face. As the scanner beeps, accomplishment thumps in my chest. On the counter, a blue plastic jar with a picture of a sad kitten begs for spare change for an animal shelter. Ailyn loves animals; when she recovers, she wants to move to the countryside and live on a farm. Impulsively, I extract a twenty-pound note from my wallet, fold it up and try to wedge it into the tiny slot on top of the kitten's head. The boy watches me struggle.

"Um, that slot is only meant for pennies?"

"I know." I keep pushing. "It's the season of giving," I add. I push and wiggle the note until it disappears into the box.

"See?" I say, beaming. "Persistence is everything."

"So, that's thirteen pounds seventy-five," the boy says, looking at me like I'm crazy.

Clutching the bottle in my hand, I step outside into the pounding rain. I pull the hood of the raincoat down, and a cool waterfall hits my head. Water slides off my nose and clings to my eyelashes. I extract my phone from my pocket and hold it out again, waving the champagne.

"Ta da!"

I float up the pavement, wondering whether I'm now drowning my new phone too. Ellie's overly decorated house glows through the rain. Three oversized plastic reindeer line the garden path. As I walk past them, my body exhales, and I suddenly notice my soaked hair; I'm freezing. My legs are throbbing.

"We did it!" I say to the screen, buzzing with elation. I'm soaring high, electricity bursting through me.

"Hello, Grace!"

I turn around, as George steps off his bike in front of his house. I jab at the red button to stop recording. *I've just ascended to the moon and back in the last fifteen minutes, just so you know.*

Balancing his bike against his body, George indicates the lights all over Ellie's house and the champagne in my hand. "Are they having a big Christmas party again this year then?"

"Don't think so, no."

"They haven't had one in ages, have they?"

"Well…" *Did you not watch Ellie waddle out of her house heavily pregnant, and then notice that no baby ever came home with her?*

"Not that I'm keeping tabs on them or anything." His face reddens. "They used to drop me a note ahead of each party warning of noise and saying I should feel free to pop over and join in. I mean, I never did, I'm not great with parties, but… it was nice of them. Anyway! See you later!" He waves and rushes up to the house, wheeling his bike alongside him. I try to align this awkward man with the person Lara described after their first date last week, when they went ice skating and sipped mulled wine. *He is such a multifaceted person. Data scientist by day, piano virtuoso by night – isn't that amazing? And he is so kind. His parents died when he was young, so he understands grief. I told him everything and he listened in the most beautiful way.*

Unlocking the door, I step into the house. Peeling off the wet clothes, I collapse onto the couch in my underwear and cover myself with a blanket. On my laptop, I type a new self-congratulatory note into the spreadsheet:

'FANTASTIC WORK! Walking: twelve minutes.'

Still electric with excitement, I replay the video on my phone, but it looks nothing like how it felt; my serious face

200

doesn't show even a glimmer of elation. I only look like I am complying with a demand. Ailyn makes it look so easy to record her life, but I've only made a weird silent film.

At night, when Ellie steps into my room with a bowl of pesto pasta, I sit up, grab the warm bottle of champagne from the nightstand and hold it out to her. Under the duvet, the electric blanket creates a cave of warmth for my exhausted body.

"For you!"

"I told you to stop ordering us wine and stuff," Ellie says.

"I know, but I just popped down to the shop earlier, and I wanted to surprise you with something nice." I wait for her to react.

"Thank you, that's so sweet. Sorry. I'm just tired." Ellie lies down on the bed next to me.

"It's a handy little shop," I say, the last word echoing between the walls. *The shop, the shop, the shop.*

"I'm slightly worried about Hector's alcohol consumption. When do you know if something is fine and when it's not?"

THE SHOP, THE SHOP, THE SHOP.

I wait. She looks up at the ceiling. "I mean, I don't even know what the recommended weekly intake is."

I give up trying to make her notice my achievement. "It's fourteen units. So, like a bottle and a half of wine."

"That's it? Even I drink that much."

"You should start having your parties again," I say.

"I don't think that's the solution if we need to cut down on drinking."

"But you love parties. Don't you think it's time?"

"Only if you do."

201

I look at her, confused. "That's what I just said."

"Are you sure?" She pops up, her eyes glowing now. "Hector did mention the idea of hosting a New Year's party, but... we don't want to... I mean, you shouldn't disrupt patients when they need their rest, right?" Ellie places her hand on the duvet on top of my leg, her warm eyes looking at me. My stomach drops.

"Don't worry about me!" My voice is too loud. "Have your party! Have two!"

My mind fills with all the celebrations that haven't happened over the last two years, all the people who should have been congregating in the living room, clutching drinks and laughing, their bodies moving to the beat of music. *I have killed so many experiences.*

"You could stay an extra few days at Mum and Dad's maybe?" Ellie says.

"Oh, I'm not going home for Christmas, didn't I say?"

She frowns. "Where else would you go?"

"Matt and I are going to spend it together. He never sees his family on Christmas anyway."

Her eyes pop open. "Really? I didn't realise... well, you should both come down then. He can keep you company if you're not up for celebrating with everyone."

"We can't; we have to stay here – he's flying out to Indonesia really early on Boxing Day. Ticking off another country."

The electric blanket stings me. I move to reach the switch dangling at the side of the bed, as Ellie closes the door. Emerging back up, I fire off a text to Matt.

'Ellie now thinks we're spending Christmas together, so don't give it away that we're not, okay?'

26

"Now, where is Matt?" My grandmother's face fills the phone screen. She adjusts her yellow paper crown, which is as wrinkled as her skin. "Let us say merry Christmas to him too! I can't believe I have never even met him. I might die soon; you can't keep putting off introducing us."

"He's just speaking to his mother," I say, nestling into the pillows on the couch and wrapping my dressing gown closer around me.

"It's so lovely that you two are spending the holidays together!" my aunt chimes in, half her face now showing on the screen.

"Yes, it is," I say. "Our first Christmas."

My grandmother bats my aunt away. "I'm speaking to Grace now!" She holds the camera so close to her face that I only see her eyes and nose.

"My friend Betty is getting a facelift," she declares. "Isn't that something? It's just horrible, looking like a shrivelled old thing when you remain the same person on the inside."

Her voice suddenly sounds frail to me. Watching my grandmother babble on about her friend's plastic surgery, it occurs to me that the disintegration of my body isn't wrong in itself, it's only happened decades too soon. *Is it easier for my grandmother to have her body decay because she always knew it would be this way, and it happens to everyone she knows? Or is it even worse for her because she can't hope to regain the body she still considers hers?* When I was little, she looked after me most afternoons after school and she was invincible then.

I hear Ellie's voice in the background. "Grandma, pass me the phone back."

Ellie's purple paper crown is askew, and her cheeks are flushed. "So, what have you decided for New Year's? Will you come back here or stay at Matt's or what?"

"Do I have to go anywhere? Can't I just stay here?"

"But…"

On my laptop, sitting on the coffee table in front of me, Ailyn starts a new live video. The sound is muted, and I watch her lips move against the backdrop of a Christmas tree covered in silver baubles. Her dark hair flows down her shoulders, and her red silk top shimmers. She speaks with red lips. I wonder if she's wearing a filter or not. I want her voice to envelop me; if we are both alone today, we could be alone together.

"I have to go," I say. "Matt's telling me dinner's ready."

"I thought he was on the phone with his family?" Ellie says.

"Multitasking. He says merry Christmas!"

"But you haven't said hi to Mum and Dad yet, hang on…"

"Merry Christmas!" I shout. Hanging up, I unmute Ailyn.

"My body is behaving this year so far, knock on wood. I might even be able to sit through all of Christmas dinner." Ailyn smiles and tosses her hair over her shoulder, exposing her slender neck. "But I know that's not something to take for granted. I'm so insanely grateful for it. I know holidays can be hard, there are too many expectations and social plans, and if your friends and family don't get your limitations then it's super hard to navigate."

Watching Ailyn, I munch on a chocolate, my tongue swimming in the sweetness of strawberry filling.

"A decade in, my grandparents still don't understand why I can't come to theirs tomorrow when we're all also getting together today," Ailyn says. "But that's okay. I love them and they love me, and that's enough."

Off-screen, someone yells for Ailyn.

"Okay, I have to go." She smiles, as two small children run through the frame behind her, laughing. "Cartoons are on – it's a big tradition here. Merry Christmas everyone, see you in a few days. I'm going offline to save as much energy as I can for actual human interactions. Not that you aren't human. You are the most beautiful, wonderful humans I've ever known, and I love you." She blows a kiss at the screen.

I snap the laptop shut. I am hot with shame now that Ailyn has disappeared to be with her own family; I should call Ellie back. The silent living room mocks me. *What are you doing here alone?* A monstrous Christmas tree fills the corner of the room, but no presents wait underneath.

I replay Ailyn's video from the beginning, and she declares she already misses Ina, even though it's only been two days since she travelled south to see relatives. Are some people made for that kind of closeness while others aren't?

Or have those of us who assume we aren't made for it just not met the right person yet? Ailyn makes love look so easy.

I text Matt, even though he's already on a plane thousands of miles away. He's flying when no one else wants to, moving towards volcanoes and jungles and strangers instead of his family.

"See you in a week! Take lots of photos."

Matt's mother asked if he wanted to come home again to visit. *Can you believe it?* Matt said. *She said it just like that, as if this summer was a success instead of a disaster. She doesn't even need me; Patrick hasn't left her after all.* Now, I find his mother's social media account. She has posted a photo of herself with Patrick and the twins in the middle of an ice skating rink captioned 'family is everything', and I want to message her and tell her to change the caption before Matt sees it.

My phone buzzes. Seeing Ellie's name on the screen again, I hesitate, before picking up. Our mother's face fills the screen. Her furious eyes contrast with the jolly reindeer design on her red sweater. Half of my father's face is in the frame too.

"Now, really! I know you are sick, and we are meant to give you extra allowances, but this is getting ridiculous! You weren't even going to wish us a merry Christmas?"

"I did! Didn't you hear me?"

Her eyes are dark. "You're not here, which is fine…"

"I'm sorry, okay? Merry Christmas."

"We love that you have finally found someone to spend your life with, *especially* now…"

"We're not 'spending our lives together', we're just… together."

"What does that mean? If you're spending Christmas with each other…"

My father squeezes his face into the screen, his cheek against my mother's. Seeing them nuzzled together, I suddenly crave being there too. I want to burrow up against my mother's anger. My father clasps her shoulder, and like he's pushed a button, she softens and smiles. My aunt says something I can't hear, and both my parents turn away from the screen, as if they've forgotten I'm still here. I watch the ceiling and my mother's chin; I can't hang up on them again.

"Oh, Grace, darling, I'm sorry!" My mother smiles down at me, her chin doubling. "I'll let you go enjoy your dinner with Matt. Send him our love!"

"Can you pass me back to Ellie?" I say.

I see my parents' socked feet, then Ellie's face.

"Hey," I say. "So, I was thinking, your New Year's thing, could I just join you?"

Ellie grins. Turning away from the camera, she shouts: "Darling! It's a Christmas miracle! Grace says she will be partying with us on New Year's!"

Hector whoops.

"See, God listens," my grandmother says. "I have been praying for her."

"You have been praying for her to want to party?" Ellie says.

"Is that Auntie Grace?" Andrea shouts. A second later, her elated face bobs around on the screen. "Why aren't you here? We're having so much fun!"

"You don't need me then," I smile.

"Say thank you for your present," Ellie prods.

"Thank you for my present!" Andrea echoes. "I'm going to listen tonight."

"I'm glad you like it," I say, papering over the urge to reach through the screen and yank the present out of her hands. On an old-fashioned tape recorder, I recorded myself reading all her favourite books. The project took months, and I wrapped the recorder up for her glowing with pride and excitement, but now it's just occurred to me I've made myself even more obsolete.

27

I sit propped up in bed, holding a glass of prosecco in one hand and my phone in the other. I have squeezed myself into a black sequinned dress. My legs look artificially tan under a pair of tights. The sounds of the party drift up to me, but I am lost in my phone screen, where Ailyn is wearing a silver party hat against a backdrop of fairy lights. Her skin glitters.

"So, Ina is at a party with her boyfriend tonight, and I'm so insanely jealous. Not of the fact that she has a boyfriend when I've never had one. That's all fine; it just feels weird, because we always spend New Year's together. I don't even know why I'm wearing this." She indicates the party hat. "She's really happy with this guy, and I'm so happy for her, obviously, but I'm going to have to count down to midnight by myself now, and it feels sad."

People are commenting on the video live:

'You're not alone!'

'I'm here!'

"You guys are the best. Really. So yeah, let's do the countdown together. I know I'm not the only one who's alone tonight; most of you probably are, because who has the energy to go to a party?"

'I can't stay up until midnight though' someone comments, with a string of crying emojis.

"When I say countdown, I should clarify that I don't mean actual midnight; I usually do it at like nine-thirty, because that's when I need to go to bed."

Someone knocks on my door. I look up, as Hector's head materialises in the crack, wearing an orange party hat.

"*Gracita*, come downstairs! You said you would join us, didn't you?"

"Yes," I reply. "Just a second."

"Come on, just put your phone down. They're nice people; no one will bite you."

"One second, I promise."

Rolling his eyes, Hector disappears again.

I type a message to Ailyn, as if I'm extending an existing conversation between us. I feel like I am; I have too many draft messages to her already saved on my phone.

'I don't know how you are brave enough to tell people you are jealous and lonely and sad – how do you trust people will still like you?'

Saving the message as yet another draft, I click onto Jaya's profile. In her latest photo, she's crammed into a photo booth with people I don't recognise, their faces half-obscured by props; Jaya smiles behind a cardboard cut-out of pouting red lips and sparkly silver glasses. I know it was taken at their office Christmas party because Matt told me about the photo booth the company had rented. I get out of bed, put on a pair of heels and walk downstairs, my heart pounding.

Loud voices mix with the music in the packed living room. I spot Ellie speaking to a petite woman in a long black dress that grazes her stockinged feet. Grey streaks her dark hair. On high heels, Ellie towers over her. They are both holding large glasses of red wine. The woman uses her arms extensively when she talks, as if her arms are a second mouth. From Ellie and Hector's wedding, I recognise her as Ellie's maid of honour. Wading through the crowd, I poke Ellie's shoulder.

"Hey! You made it." She smiles. "Fran, this is my baby sister, Grace." Fran flashes me a brief smile, but she looks annoyed to be interrupted. She's wearing a massive turquoise necklace that looks uncomfortably heavy.

"Aren't I too old for you to call me your baby sister?" I say.

"I'm saying it with affection." Ellie leans in and kisses me on the cheek; she must be tipsy already.

"So, as I was saying," Fran says, "visitor numbers are above expectations, but sales are lower than they hoped for. So, they are telling me I should be on social media to 'engage with people'. Apparently, I should be documenting my progress as I paint and post live video clips." Raising her wine glass, she takes a deep sip.

"Fran is an artist," Ellie says to me.

"Can you believe that people want to sit at home and watch other people paint?" Fran says. "Why? Why not do some actual painting instead of watching other people do it? It's ridiculous."

My face grows hot, as if Fran can know from looking at me that I am one of those people who spends too much time looking at the lives of others on a small screen.

"Anyone can make it online," Fran says. "If you're beautiful and willing to post endless shots of your perfect body and face, then, boom – you're a celebrity."

"That's true even offline though," I interrupt. "Objectively beautiful people with symmetric features get paid more."

"Is that right?" Fran says. "Either way, all this passive consumption through a screen, it's mad." Waving her arms again, the wine sloshes in her glass. "People need to create more and consume less; no wonder all millennials are depressed." She throws her arm out for emphasis, and a wave of wine escapes and floods the grey carpet.

"*Merda!*" Fran says, then laughs. She nudges Ellie with her elbow. "You shouldn't allow me to hold wine while I talk; you know I always spill."

She dries off the bottom of the glass on her black top. Ellie disappears into the kitchen for a cloth.

"It's very impressive," I say, "that you have made it as an artist."

Fran waves her hand dismissively. "It's not about making it or not. Creating the thing, that's what matters. The rest is just noise."

"What's just noise?" Ellie says as she kneels down on the carpet to attack the wine stain with a damp cloth.

"External success," I say. I turn to Fran. "If you don't want your success, can I have it?"

Fran laughs. "I like her," she says to Ellie, nodding in my direction. She turns back to me. "Let me tell you about Frida Kahlo. You know her, yes?"

I nod. "Of course, she's a feminist icon."

"Oh, you are a feminist, are you?"

"Isn't everyone?"

"Do you know her story? How she started painting? She was in a violent accident. On a tram, when she was young. It crashed, and a handrail, one of those metal ones, speared her like a pig for roasting. She survived, obviously, but she needed many operations and time to recover, and she had to stay in bed for months, and she was bored, and that's when she started painting. When you know this about her, so much of her self-portraiture becomes even more powerful, no?"

Fran reaches into her pocket for her phone, taps on it then thrusts it in my face.

"Here! Look! You tell me, doesn't she capture chronic pain so perfectly? Is this how it feels for you too?"

Heart thumping, I look at the photo. I can't impress Fran now. No one is impressed by a sick person, unless they achieve global success despite their limitations, like Frida. People say they are impressed by sick people's resilience in just coping with everyday life, but it's not an achievement when I didn't choose it.

On the screen Fran holds out to me, Frida's painted avatar is naked, her breasts visible between a set of thick white belts that wrap around her, as if they are holding her together. An exposed metal column has replaced her spine, and fine needles pierce her skin. Below her famous unibrow, white tears rain from her eyes onto her cheeks. A faint outline of a moustache sits above a sad mouth.

"See!" Fran says. "She is in pain, but she is not a victim; she is a fighter." Her voice is softer now, her eyes kind. "If it wasn't for her accident, she wouldn't have become what she did."

As if she is hosting an art tutorial, Fran continues to show me photos of Frida Kahlo's self-portraits. Looking at the paintings, I think of Jas, who used to have a photo of herself as the background on her phone. Jordan made a comment that it was narcissistic to look at your own face that often: *people pick up their phones every eight minutes on average. It's insane to look at yourself that often.*

"It's a bit narcissistic, isn't it?" I say. "To paint your own body and face over and over."

Fran stows her phone back in her pocket. "She wasn't painting herself; she was describing the human condition."

I blush. "I never understood art," I say. "I failed it in school."

Fran sighs. "You don't understand art; you feel it."

"See, I didn't even know that." I fake a laugh. Draining my glass, I twirl it in my hand like a baton. "If Frida Kahlo lived now, maybe she would just share photos of herself on social media. Instead of painting, she'd be an expert on filters and hashtags."

"Ha! Don't say that, that just breaks my heart. But you are probably right."

I wave my empty glass at Fran. "I need a top-up."

Weaving between clusters of people, I walk into the kitchen. Stepping out into the garden, the cool air hits me. Ellie is sitting on an inflatable turtle, a cigarette in her hand.

"Oh, hey, baby sister."

"I didn't take you for someone who escapes from their own party."

Ellie waves the cigarette in the air; it glows like a firefly. "Shhh, don't tell Mum." She giggles. I sit down next to her, and the plastic sags under us. A premature burst of fireworks sounds in the distance. *Ailyn will be doing her countdown to midnight soon.* I cross my arms against the cold, wishing I had brought my phone with me downstairs.

"Fran idolises Frida Kahlo, apparently," I say.

"Oh, big time. She even cultivated a unibrow for a while. Did you know, Frida Kahlo only started painting because she was stuck in bed for months after an accident?"

"Yes, Fran told me." I sigh. "I can't picture having the energy to do anything useful ever again."

"Oh, darling, you are already useful."

"No, I'm not."

"Fine, you're not. But you don't have to be productive right now."

"If I'm not useful, what's the point?"

"Huh." Ellie taps ash off her cigarette. I wish I had one to occupy my hands. I watch the orange embers on the cigarette tip instead of Ellie's face.

"I know what you need!" Ellie's head snaps towards me. She beams. "You need a funeral."

"What?"

"We held a funeral for Sebastian, and it's the best thing we did. Grieving is so important."

"Oh." I look ahead again, unable to face Ellie. "I never knew you named him."

Ellie throws the cigarette on the fake grass and grinds it down with her heel. She takes a deep breath and exhales with force. "We're holding a funeral for your old life, so you can accept that it's dead and move on."

"You can't be serious."

"Let's do it right now." Pushing herself up, Ellie scans the garden. She strides over to the large orange flowerpot that used to sit on the front step, bends down and drags it to the centre of the garden.

"Now we just need something to bury. Not your body, obviously. A photo, maybe?" She cocks her head at me.

"I don't print photos; I just keep them on my phone."

"Well, it can be anything that represents your old life."

"I have my office access card."

"Perfect. Run and get it. I'll start digging."

"I can't run."

"Yes, yes, I know." Ellie is already on her knees digging in the flowerpot dirt. "Amble along at your own pace."

I return gripping the plastic card, my legs throbbing. Still kneeling on the ground, Ellie grins up at me, her hands covered in dirt. A small pile of soil spills out next to her.

"So, we just bury this now?" I say.

"No, come on. You've been to funerals before, haven't you? We need some candles… then a eulogy. I can sing. It needs to feel like a ritual."

"I'm not doing a eulogy for myself."

"But that would be so cathartic."

I shake my head.

She sighs. "Fine, I'll do it."

Tapping on my phone, I find a video of a sea of flickering candles and hold it up. "Candles, done."

"We need real ones. We have spares in the kitchen cupboards somewhere, I think."

"It's my funeral." I place the phone on top of an upturned bucket next to the flowerpot. The screen flickers with the fake candles.

Ellie laughs. "Fair."

We stand with our backs to the kitchen, where a chorus of voices buzzes like cicadas. Linking her arm with mine, Ellie projects her voice at an invisible audience.

"We are here tonight to celebrate Grace's life. I have known her since she was born, so I have a million stories, but one of my favourites starts when she won the sprint race on sports day in first grade, and they gave her a chocolate medal.

"She was so proud of that medal, she even slept with it around her neck. Then she hung the medal on the wall. I thought she hadn't understood that chocolate was hiding under the shiny foil, but when I told her, she said in an exasperated voice that she knew that, but she had concluded she would get more satisfaction from keeping it on her wall.

She explained that she could only eat it once, but she could look at it every day for years if she had the self-control to not gulp it down.

"Then, a couple of years later, Princess Diana died. I was heartbroken; I had idolised her in a feverish, obsessive way. I sat on the floor in front of the TV watching her funeral procession move down streets packed with mourners.

"When Grace came into the room and saw me bawling my eyes out, she came over and patted my hand and told me it would be okay. When I didn't stop crying, she ran out of the room, and when she returned, she was grasping the medal. She peeled the gold foil off before offering it up to me, saying the chocolate would make me feel better. At this point, the chocolate had gone stale, it was powdery and specked with white, but that didn't matter, because—"

The door from the kitchen opens. "There you are!" Hector booms. "What are you doing out here?"

"Shhh, you're interrupting Grace's funeral!"

"I'm what?"

"Never mind, darling, we'll come back inside in a minute, okay?" Ellie blows him a kiss. Catching it, he blows her one too before closing the door again.

"Okay. Where was I?" Ellie looks down at the virtual candles on my phone screen. She clears her throat and starts singing over the piano. While singing, she looks at me, then indicates the flowerpot. Feeling ridiculous, I bend down and drop my office access pass into the hollowed-out hole, then grab a handful of dirt and throw it over the plastic card and lanyard. I don't know what I am burying – how far back do I have to unravel my life before I get to the foundation I should rebuild from? Am I burying just the consultancy years or everything that came before that too? Am I burying the people that belong to those years? Jas, Matt, Ailyn? Ellie keeps singing as I bury the card fully. When it's invisible, I pat down the soil and smoothen the surface. Standing back up, I feel naked.

28

The next evening, the remnants of last night's make-up still cling to my skin. A throbbing head and queasy stomach layer my deadened limbs, like I'm a Russian nest doll of pain, but inside the smallest doll, beyond the heavy shell of my body, I feel lighter than I have in a long time. My phone vibrates, and Matt's face fills the screen.

"Landed," he says. "Oh, it was the worst flight, so many screaming children. Who flies long-haul with a baby? They're like dogs – if one screams, it sets the rest of them off. Can't they give them tranquillizers?"

"Happy New Year to you too." We haven't spoken since he left for Indonesia, and hearing his voice, I want to extract him from the phone, like a magician pulling a rabbit out of a hat, even though I haven't missed him until now.

He pauses. "Hang on, my mom has sent me like a million texts."

While I wait, on autopilot I check whether Ailyn has

posted. As a new post from her fills the screen, I hear Fran's voice: *people sit at home and watch other people paint? It's ridiculous.* I click away from Ailyn's serene smile before reading the caption.

"Well, I was wrong," Matt says.

"What?"

"Patrick is actually leaving. He kissed my mom at midnight last night and told her it was his New Year's resolution to leave her."

I sit up. "What?"

Matt exhales. "It's just life, isn't it? Things end."

"Is she okay? What will happen with the twins?"

"They'll do joint custody, I guess." His voice hardens. "But why New Year's? It's my mom's favourite thing. She makes all these resolutions… she never keeps them, but she loves the idea of a blank slate, and now…"

"Come over," I say, holding back the words that swirl in my mind: *Your mother did get her blank slate; it's just even blanker than what she wanted.*

"Now? It's late. I'm still at the airport."

"Doesn't matter. There's a key under the flowerpot outside, just let yourself in and wake me up when you get here."

Hanging up, something like excitement flutters in my chest. In one of Ailyn's posts from years ago, Ina was lying in a hospital bed, grinning broadly with one arm in a sling, above a caption that explained how she fell from the trapeze and broke her arm and cracked several ribs, which meant temporarily she was also constrained. Ailyn declared that it felt nice to not be the only one with limitations. *I got to hold her up, for once.*

I should shuffle to the bathroom to wipe my face clean and brush my teeth, but I stay horizontal, recharging my insides instead of improving my outside. I fill my phone screen with a blue sphere that slowly expands and contracts, as if a being inside the phone is breathing. I synchronise my own inhales and exhales with the oceanic sphere, until my mind stills and my body softens.

When I hear the door unlock downstairs, I sit up, anticipation awakening my sluggish body. His footsteps come up the stairs two at a time. The door pushes open, and Matt steps into the room from the dark landing outside, smiling, as if everything is fine. I squint against the blinding light from the flashlight on his phone.

"Hello," he whispers, turning off the flashlight.

He extracts himself from his massive backpack and peels off his jacket, before crossing the room and bending down to kiss me.

"Oh man, I have so many photos to show you. We climbed the tallest volcano in Indonesia – it was incredible."

"I climbed the stairs three times yesterday," I say. "Our holidays were almost the same."

Matt laughs.

"So, Patrick, huh?" I pat the bed, like a perverted therapist.

"Yeah. It's pretty shit." Shrugging, he stretches out next to me. "How was last night then? Did you do the new year justice?"

"I went to bed at ten."

"Very wild."

I nod. "Do you want to talk about it? Your mum and everything."

"I don't know." He plays with his phone, twirling it between his hands. "I keep telling myself..." He takes a deep breath. "If I hadn't gone over in the summer, if I hadn't made her kick Patrick and the twins out, then maybe this wouldn't have happened." He exhales. "But it's ridiculous, right?" His eyes are huge, clinging to mine.

"We can't control everything," I say. "Really, we have so much less control in life than we like to think."

"Alright, guru Grace. Are you going to become a life coach now?"

"Okay, if you don't want to talk about it, can we sleep?"

I'm drifting off when Matt's voice fills the room again, his breath hot on my face. "All my peak life experiences have been with strangers. Does that make me defective?"

I drag myself back to the surface. His phone lights up his face.

"What strangers?"

"Here." Holding the phone so I can see, he scrolls through photos of a string of exotic locations.

Matt is surfing down sand dunes with three other young men. In the middle of another group of people, he's standing on top of a mountain as the sun rises above a green carpet of forest below. Standing next to a street food stall in the midst of a throng of people, he holds up a bowl of food next to two women.

"The top moments of my life, I'm always with people I don't know. We meet; we share these heightened experiences for a day or two, a week tops; and then I never see them again."

"You've had peak experiences with me," I say, but I can't think of any examples beyond the festival, and we weren't even fully together then. "Anyway, you always say it heightens the experience knowing you can't replicate it." Leaning over, I kiss him. "You're not any more defective than the rest of us."

I hear Matt's breaths elongate into sleep, but I remain awake hunting for peak experiences we have shared; there must be some. *Would he classify any of his experiences with Jaya as peak moments?*

Picking up my phone from the nightstand, I dig through Ellie's social media to find Fran's full name. Scrolling through a mass of recent photos of Ellie with Hector and Andrea, I find Fran in a photo Ellie posted a month ago of the two of them standing in a messy art studio in front of a massive canvas of turquoise waves. Stacks of canvases lean against the walls. Fran's jeans are splattered with paint, but her oversized white shirt is oddly pristine. 'So proud of you' Ellie has typed underneath. 'Can't wait to see your new exhibition in a few months. Add it to your spring calendars people!'

I follow the link underneath to a minimalistic website belonging to a boutique gallery. Fran's name is already on the website. I study the whole collection of canvases. An abstract painting of red and gold swirled together is the centrepiece of a collection titled 'I want to know what love is'. I stare at the painting. All I feel is my eyes hurting and my head aching, but I don't know whether it's art or love that I don't understand.

29

I curl up on the bench by the kitchen table. Tiny rivers stream down the windowpane. Green leaves already sprout from the trees beyond the garden wall; I don't know where the first months of the year have gone. Ailyn's husky voice streams out of my phone's speakers into the silent kitchen. She is sitting on her couch, a blanket enveloping her.

"So, next month will be an exciting one for me. Because... we're going to London!"

Hearing her elated voice, exhilaration pumps through me, and it isn't a forced mirroring this time.

"Best surprise ever!" Ina jumps into the frame. Her voice is sweet, like cotton candy. She smiles with red lips under blazing eyes; it's the first time I am seeing her wear make-up, and I wonder if she's going on another date today, and if so, whether Ailyn envies her boyfriend still.

Laughing, Ailyn turns to Ina. "It's about time – you're always the one surprising me."

"We're going to see the world's best trapeze artists!" Ina says. "And not just the public show, though even that's super cool in itself! I'll get to go to their trainings too and meet everyone and learn new moves."

"Influencer perks," Ailyn says to Ina, then turns to me. "But I'm going to be honest with you, I'm absolutely terrified to travel. Last time I tried to go abroad…" she fidgets with the blanket, looks down, then back up, "…my body couldn't handle it at all; I ended up in hospital. I think I am stronger now, but it's just scary to try."

"It'll be fine. I'll be there." Ina squeezes Ailyn in a sideways hug, then kisses her cheek. "I'll take care of you – it's what I do!"

Ailyn laughs, and Ina lets go. I can't decide if they are childlike or childish. Suddenly London feels close again, instead of a place far removed.

A doorbell rings. It takes me a moment to realise it is mine, not Ailyn's. I should rush to the door to let Matt in and shine my full attention on him the way Ailyn gives Ina hers. Since New Year's, our only notable experience outside the house was a cinema trip in February, where Matt ate buttery popcorn while I drowned in sound and colour. Sinking low in the plush seat, I closed my eyes halfway through, but even then, my body took weeks to recover; we have not left the house together since. Last weekend, we played Monopoly in the kitchen, pretending we were hipsters at a board game café. I drank mint tea and Matt repeatedly checked his phone. Only when the bell rings a second time do I remember Hector and Ellie can't let Matt in; they are having dinner at a friend's house.

"Sorry!" I say when I open the door. Matt is drenched, his hair plastered to his head. "The stairs, they're still a bit tricky sometimes; I have to go slow."

"I come bearing gifts!" Matt holds up a plastic bag. "Chinese."

He follows me into the kitchen, where my phone lies on the kitchen table, the screen glowing, betraying my lie that I was just upstairs, but Matt doesn't notice. We sit down at the kitchen table with the selection of plastic containers between us. We peel off the lids, revealing crispy duck and steaming pancakes, a row of spring rolls and wok-fried broccoli.

"Where are Ellie and Hector?" Matt says.

"Out," I say.

"Oh, okay." Matt looks disappointed. He has said nothing about the break-up of his mother's family for weeks. Whenever I have tried to mention it, he just shrugs and repeats that these things happen. I wonder if he confides more to Jaya when they work late together; several nights a week now, the whole team stays until long past dark.

"So, I follow this girl online," I say.

"Uh huh." Matt is focused on grabbing a large piece of duck meat with his chopsticks.

"She's got the same illness as me. And she's coming here, to London."

He looks up, swallows. "So?"

"I don't know." I shrug. "I could bump into her." I lift my own chopsticks to my mouth and fill it with rice. Last week, I walked to a café on the high street for the first time. I swam in the scents of coffee and fresh bread, then carried the takeaway cup of mint tea home as if it was sacred. *If I can do that, I can manage to go to wherever Ailyn will be.*

"Why do you want to meet a social media influencer?"

"She's not really an influencer. She only posts photos and captions that tell her story." I reach for a piece of broccoli. "She's real."

Matt looks up from the food again, rests his eyes on me for a second, then takes a large sip of beer. "An online profile is never the same as a person. It's always going to be edited."

"Why would she lie about being sick?"

"I didn't say she's lying; I'm just saying, you talk about this girl as if you know her." He puts his chopsticks down. "You just can't tell from a social media profile what's true and what's not. And people do lie about being sick. Don't you remember that blogger? Who pretended she had cancer so she could sell a juice detox programme she had healed herself with? She had never been sick at all; she had just shaved her head and eyebrows to make it believable."

"Here," he says, grabbing his phone from the table and typing something before passing it to me. "Look at this girl."

On the screen, an attractive teenaged blonde is posing on a white beach, her sticklike legs poking out of a black bathing suit. Hand on her hip, she is laughing at life. Turquoise water fans out behind her. I scan the photo and the caption, which is only a string of hashtags: globetrotter, digital nomad, bliss.

"Is this that blogger?" I ask.

"No."

"Okay, I give up. What's the catch?"

"Does she look real to you?"

I shrug. "It looks like any other social media profile."

"Ha!" Matt's face fills with triumph. "She's a character on a TV show. The actress updates it every day as if it's about a real life, but it's all just an extension of the show. And you couldn't tell."

"Fine," I say. "But that doesn't mean other people's profiles aren't real."

"But it does mean online people are not the same as real people."

"Real people edit themselves all the time, too."

"Yeah, I know. It's just... it sounds like you think this woman is your friend or something."

"I would love to meet people in real life," I snap. "But for me, it's either people through a screen or no people at all."

"You have real people who come to visit. I'm right here."

"Yes, but I can feel lonelier when I'm here with you than when I see Ailyn through a screen." I put my chopsticks down with shaking hands. Matt puts his chopsticks down too. He stares at me.

"What does that mean?"

I take a sip of water, even though I am not thirsty. "I don't know. This girl, her life feels like mine. Or maybe just how I would like this version of life to feel. Even if it's edited and through a screen, it feels... I mean, your life, everyone else's lives... you live on a different planet for healthy people that I can't access."

Picking up my chopsticks again, I grab food without looking at what I'm picking up. I chew while staring at the plate, as if I am absorbed in the act of eating. Matt resumes eating too, but the conversation isn't over. I can feel his unsaid words. Intense thoughts have a different consistency to air.

"Don't make me choose between you and her," I joke.

Matt nods. Slumping in his chair, he suddenly looks drained, like an old person.

"I didn't mean that I prefer Ailyn to you," I say. "But you spend time with other people... Oliver, Lara... and you have your colleagues too, Jaya and the others." Saying her name, my heart beats faster. Her name hangs in the air in bold, neon letters. "I just need some sick friends that are like me."

228

"Right. But she's not your friend, she's a random person online."

Matt picks up the last bite of duck from his plate before he gets up, strides over to the fridge and grabs another bottle of beer. I keep mechanically lifting the chopsticks to my mouth, chewing without tasting. Sitting down again, Matt reaches for one of the fortune cookies lying at the table between us. He rips off the plastic and cracks the cookie open. The silence itches and pinches.

"What does it say?" I ask.

"When you squeeze an orange, orange juice comes out, because that's what's inside."

"What does that mean?"

Matt shrugs. Reaching for the remaining cookie, I release it from the plastic and open it to pull out the thin piece of paper.

"Prepare for the unexpected," I read out loud.

Matt sips his beer.

"You can add them to your little shrine." He indicates the pieces of paper.

"Shrine?"

"Your shoebox. Your reminders."

"This isn't exactly an evening I want to remember." I smile, wanting to make it into a joke.

"What's with your voice?" Matt says.

I clear my throat of Ailyn's husky quality.

Finishing the beer, Matt says he has to go. Standing by the open door, I kiss him, but he offers only a dry-lipped peck in return. While he unlocks his bike, I remain in the doorway. Despite shivering from the cold air, I stay there until the blinking red tail light of his bike disappears at the top of the road.

30

The next morning, I reach out for my phone the moment I wake, hoping Matt has texted to clear the air. Words cover the screen.

'Are you okay?' My father.

'Just thought I'd check in. Are you safe?' Lara.

'Assume you're okay but wanted to make sure.' Jas.

Hands shaking, I scramble for my laptop and snap it open, as my mind immediately deduces what this handful of frantic texts must mean. It's an echo from a few months ago that promises only violent destruction. Opening the news pages, I scan headlines and photos.

In the photos, traumatised people are sitting on the ground wrapped in space blankets. At a bridge, terrorists have driven a van at speed into crowds of people. Afterwards, they stabbed other victims, in and around a bar that was heaving on a clear spring evening. I have been in that exact grimy bar before – it's close to the office, and it was one of the places I used to go to with Jas and the others when we wanted to save money, because they often did happy hour all night – but the place is so far away in time that the proximity in space feels negligible.

Picking up my phone, my anxiety rises with every ring. The bridge is only a distant location to me, not to everyone else I know. Matt shouldn't have been in that part of the city last night if he biked directly back to his flat after he left here, but maybe he didn't want to go home; maybe he texted someone else – *Jaya, Jaya, Jaya* – and they suggested he join them for drinks somewhere central.

"Hello?" Matt sounds rushed.

"Oh, you're okay!" My body softens.

"Come on, we live in a city of millions, the odds of someone you know being involved in the terror attack are minuscule." He speaks fast.

"But it has to happen to someone."

"Since when are you so anxious and irrational?"

"Being confined does strange things to a person."

"Ha, you don't need to tell me."

We elapse into silence.

"Are we okay?" I say.

"Yeah. Look, I have to go, but we're fine."

Hanging up, I find myself inappropriately glad for the zoomed-out perspective offered by catastrophe. I had forgotten that illness isn't the only thing that can derail a life, and at least I am now protected against the other categories of calamity. I do not walk outside at night; no one will shatter me with a speeding metal bonnet.

I reply to the texts from my father and Lara, before pausing on the text from Jas. My annoyance with her suddenly seems petty and our drifting apart just as much my fault as hers. I type out a long text, asking her how it

231

feels to be married, how work is going and if she is running the marathon again this year.

I walk downstairs. Hector is sitting by the kitchen table sobbing. His crying is as loud as his laughter usually is. My fear roars again.

"Did you know someone?" I say, frozen in the middle of the floor.

He looks up, his eyes red and puffy. "I'm fine." His bottom lip trembles. "I just... where I grew up, it was... volatile, is that the word? Attacks. Kidnappings. Bombs..." He takes a deep breath. His shining eyes look haunted and unfamiliar.

"Where's Ellie?" I say.

"Out grabbing coffee."

"Oh, okay." I hover, then sit down across from him.

"Apparently unstable bookshelves or scalding hot water coming out of the shower kill more people than terror attacks," I say, relaying one of the articles I just read.

Hector nods. He sits up straighter and clears his throat. "Yes, it's irrational, I know."

Tears start to leak from his eyes again; his body isn't listening to our arguments. His hand is so close to mine – I should reach out and pat it. I lift my hand, then change my mind and scratch my own arm instead. I hear the front door open.

"Hi, Ellie!" I yell.

Walk faster, come on.

"We're in here!"

"I heard you," Ellie says, annoyance in her voice. As she steps into the room, she spots Hector.

"Darling, what happened?" She rushes over and huddles in next to him. Without waiting for a reply, she strokes his head and kisses his forehead. I watch her. *When did you learn*

232

how to be a container for people's sadness? Why didn't I learn that too? Looking up, Ellie catches my eye, and I jump to my feet, embarrassed to have sat there watching them.

I walk back upstairs. I reach for my phone, but Jas has not replied to my text. I can see that she has read it, and it's as if we have walked past each other on the street and she has blanked me instead of saying hello. I realise only then that maybe she didn't write the earlier text specifically for me. She could have sent the same message to all the contacts saved in her phone, and I just happened to still be there, hidden in a list of hundreds. I suddenly wish friendship break-ups had become a trend. A clear abrupt cut would be easier to navigate than this slow disintegration, where I can't know if we are dead or only in hibernation.

I go onto Ailyn's profile. Has she seen the news of the attack? If the news has travelled that far, will it have scared her? Will it prevent her and Ina from coming to London after all? They don't seem like the kind of people to be deterred by irrational fear, but they could be.

If they did come, I could find out what trapeze show they'd be going to; it wouldn't be hard, they'll be posting all about it. I could buy tickets, meet them in person. Bumping into them accidentally on purpose, I would smile, shake their hands and say... *what?* I wouldn't want Ailyn to think I'm a stalker; I just want to see her expanded into a human being.

I have opened her latest post again, when I see a frantic comment where someone else has typed out my exact thoughts:

'Which show, when, where? I'll be there! Can't wait to meet you! Finally!'

Her desperation looks pathetic, bordering on deranged. I read a celebrity interview once where a singer mentioned

233

receiving locks of hair and baby teeth from her fans. She said those personal relics were disturbing but less so than the photos of strangers copying her haircut and outfits and make-up to look like her. I black out the phone screen.

31

Weeks later, I stand in line at the café down the road from Ellie's that I now go to once a week. I float on the smell of coffee and practise tuning out the assaulting whirr of the bean grinder when I notice the dark-haired young woman in front of me. The breeze from the ceiling fan kisses my face and plays with my hair, as I analyse the back of her head and body. Her tanned legs look too muscular, and I can't see a wheelchair anywhere in the room. Yesterday, I watched Ina push a grinning Ailyn through a modern airport, the caption underneath declaring: 'London, baby!'

"Decaf iced latte," the woman says without a trace of Ailyn's accent. I look away from her and scan the golden pastries instead, feeling a flash of irrational disappointment she wasn't who I wanted her to be.

"Really, it's super important that it's decaf," the woman insists. "I have a heart condition; I can't tolerate caffeine."

Heart dancing, I stare at the back of her head again, evaluating her body and stance and wanting her to turn around, because that was something Ailyn said once too, not that she had a heart condition, only that this is a lie she tells baristas when she orders decaf to make sure they get it right.

I stand next to the woman as we both wait for our drinks. Glancing at her face, I want to ask if she knows Ailyn, if she follows her or if she really does have something wrong with her heart. The barista hands the woman a plastic cup with a domed lid and a paper straw.

"Definitely decaf." He smiles reassuringly.

The woman strides over to a large armchair by the window clutching the plastic cup and straw. Sinking into the chair, she crosses one leg over the other and leans back, before plugging headphones into her ears. She sucks on the straw while watching her phone.

"Decaf americano." The barista hands me a paper cup that burns my fingers. I do not get the same caring smile.

Walking to the door, I glance back at the woman by the window. I grab the door, but instead of stepping through it, I hold it open for a tall woman with a stroller. Letting go of the handle, I turn around and walk back to where the woman is sitting. She looks up at me before I have even said anything, her eyebrows raised.

"Hi?"

"Could you tell me the time?" I say.

She looks down at her phone. "Eleven twelve."

"Thanks." I fidget with the lid on my coffee and half-turn away, before I swivel to face her again. "I couldn't help but overhear – you have a heart condition?"

"Oh yeah." She nods without elaborating.

If it was only a lie, would she have admitted to it now?

"Weird question, but do you happen to follow Ailyn?"

"Follow who?"

"On social media. Ailyn? She says she tells baristas she has a heart condition to make sure they give her decaf."

The woman stares at me. "I don't know who Ailyn is, and I really do have a heart condition."

"Right. Of course. Sorry." My face heats up.

Yanking her headphones out, the woman sits bolt upright. "When you next see her, you can tell your friend it's fucked up lying about that, okay?"

"Yes, definitely. I'm so sorry," I say.

Whipping around, I stride towards the door. I yank it open and pace down the pavement, the scalding liquid sloshing out of the cup and onto my hand.

Sitting on the couch sipping what remains of my cooling coffee, I see Ailyn has posted a shot of herself lying in a sea of pillows in a hotel bed. I should have defended her to the woman in the café, explained that Ailyn doesn't lie about heart conditions for fun.

'I haven't managed to leave the hotel since we arrived. But that doesn't matter. Just experiencing the airports, the flight and the taxi rides was sufficiently sensational for the trip to be totally worth it, and besides, we are here for Ina, not for me.'

Alongside the photo, Ailyn has posted a series of shots of Ina from the trapeze training sessions she has gone to while Ailyn has been lying inert in their immaculate hotel room. In a full-frontal shot, Ina is standing on a gym mat wearing a hot pink sports bra and leopard print tights. She is showing off abs that are so toned they look like she's drawn them on her skin with a marker. Grinning, she holds up red, blistering hands.

A short video captures Ina's flight through the air. As she is throwing herself from one trapeze to another, she is free from gravity, falling slower than a human should. She is made of clay, her malleable body an instrument primarily for play instead of a tool for production. I save the video as more evidence of what bodies can be moulded into.

I forward the video to Matt, then watch it again and again.

'Let's go on a first date next weekend' I text him. 'We've just met. You don't know me; I don't know you.'

'Oh, yeah? You sure you're up for it?'

'Yes.'

'Where are we going? A trapeze show?'

I hesitate. *It was his suggestion, not mine. If we happened to show up where Ailyn is, it wouldn't be my doing. I could trick myself into believing it would be close to a coincidence.* I remember the celebrity receiving locks of hair in the mail.

'No, there's this art gallery I want to go to.'

'Are you assembling a whole new personality for this date?' Matt replies. 'Since when do you like art?'

'I'm full of surprises.'

32

I step out of the car in front of the tiny gallery. Slamming the car door behind me, I spot Matt further down the pavement locking up his bike against a railing. Adjusting my black felt hat, I push the large sunglasses up my nose.

"You look like an incognito celebrity," Matt says, walking up to me. "Is your outfit part of this whole pretend first date thing?"

I lean in and kiss him on the cheek, leaving a trace of red lipstick. "You're not very good at pretending. It's so nice to finally meet you in person."

I lead the way into the gallery. A bell chimes above our heads. On the white walls are Fran's canvases that I have already seen online, but they are much larger in real life than I expected. I take my sunglasses off. A woman sits by a desk in the corner in front of a slim white computer.

"Welcome," she says in a zen voice, as if we have entered a spa. In her white silk blouse, she blends in with the wall.

Standing up, she holds out two glossy brochures, and I grab them.

"Excuse me," I say. "Do you have a chair I could borrow? I can't stand for long."

She blinks, and her eyes flicker onto my hat and heeled boots. "Of course."

In my costume, she will think I want the chair only because I am spoiled and want to sit on a throne. *It doesn't matter what she thinks; you will never see her again.* The gallerist disappears into a black door at the back of the room.

"If you don't mind me asking, why do you need a chair?" Matt says.

"Oh, didn't I mention it when we spoke online? I am disabled – my body doesn't work like it should."

"Really? I'm sorry to hear that."

"Oh, it's a dreary old story; I won't bore you with it. Look at these gorgeous pieces," I say, throwing my arms out to embrace the white walls.

Circling the room, Matt stops in front of an abstract painting made up of soft shades of turquoise fading into each other. He nods at it. "She's really captured the feeling of deep-sea diving."

I nod distractedly, while searching the walls for the canvas with the red and gold swirls. All the paintings in the room consist of shades of blue and green, her most recent collection, 'I am sixty per cent water'.

"So, you like diving then?" I say, pulling myself back to Matt. "Are you one of those adrenaline junkies?"

"I wouldn't call diving an adrenaline activity; it's very peaceful."

"Even our bones are one-third water," I say.

"Is that right?"

"Nothing is solid, even if it looks that way."

Reaching out, Matt snatches one of the brochures from my hand, just as the gallerist returns carrying a foldable white chair, her heels clicking against the floor. Taking it from her, I carry it under my arm into the back room of the gallery. Matt trails me, leafing through the brochure.

The vast red and gold canvas hangs in the centre of the wall. *I want to know what love is.* Without taking my eyes off it, I unfold the chair and sink down in front of it. I swim in the deep red paint; I want to dive into it as if it's love itself. No electronic barriers separate me from the world now. I want to feel the paint like I felt the music at George's, but I can't. Matt walks all the way up to the canvas and squints at the tiny white name card below the painting.

"What?" I say.

"Nothing."

"I want to touch it," I whisper.

"Then touch it."

I widen my eyes at him and jerk my head towards the gallerist.

"Oh, she can't see you from that angle," Matt says. "Besides, this new persona of yours strikes me as someone who wouldn't let rules prevent her from doing what she wants."

Getting up, I reach my arm out and place my finger on the surface, which is rougher than I expected. I stroke a golden swirl, following its twists, then jerk my finger away. Stepping back, I reach into my jacket pocket for my phone.

"No photos allowed."

I jump at the zen woman's calm voice, and my head whips around to where she has materialised in the corner. Smiling, she bows her head.

"Thank you."

"Sorry." Rushing my phone back to my pocket, I drop it, and it smashes against the tiled floor. *Did she see me touch the canvas?* I snap down to pick up the phone. A crack runs diagonally down the screen. The woman remains smiling as if nothing happened. She must be part of the exhibition, a piece of performance art. Unsettled by her impermeable calm, I point at the canvas.

"How much is this one?" I ask.

"£4200."

"Reasonable," I say, twirling my sunglasses between my fingers.

Turning around, the woman walks off. When she disappears from view, I lift my broken phone and snap a silent shot, the crack on the screen slicing the image in half.

"It's not a problem for you, is it?" I say. "My disability, I mean. I know it's not first-date material, but I'd rather be honest."

"No, it's cool."

Did he hesitate, even for a second?

"Just so you know, it may be permanent," I say.

He snaps his head away from the painting. "Really?"

"And it may not. I just don't know."

"I'm sure science will find out how to help you."

"I just don't want me recovering to be a requirement for you to want to be with me."

He nods slowly, then keeps nodding in the same slow rhythm, as if his head is stuck and will move up and down forever, like a perpetual motion machine. I gaze at the canvas without seeing it anymore.

"Matt, I…"

"What?"

I look at him, then back at the painting. My heart is hammering. *Say it.* I'm standing at the edge of a diving board that bends with my weight, but when I look down at the shimmering surface, I remember that water can feel like concrete if you jump from great heights.

"What?" he repeats.

"I'm hungry. Let's go for dinner."

"Can you handle that?"

"Probably not, but I don't care."

"It's only five-thirty. Places won't even be open yet."

"Come on, we'll find somewhere."

We are the only guests in the cheap Italian restaurant, except for a white-haired couple sitting in the corner. The man's walking stick is resting against their table, and the woman is wearing a clunky beige hearing aid. She bursts out laughing at something the man says, and he leans back and looks at her with proud contentment, as if not only the laughter but the whole woman is his own miraculous creation. I try to age Matt and myself next to each other, but we only fade into flimsy ghosts.

We peruse the sticky laminated menus in silence. I run my hand over a crease in the red and white chequered tablecloth. A waitress with colourful adult braces takes our order. She returns swiftly with a large glass of red wine for Matt and a lemonade for me.

"Cheers." Matt toasts his wine glass against my tumbler. "As much as I've enjoyed experiencing this posh art-loving persona of yours, can we stop playing the game now?"

"I did mean it. That I might never be fully normal again."

He takes a prolonged sip of wine, guzzling it down as if it's water. I mirror him. The cool sweetness fills me. Matt swirls his tagliatelle around his fork before piercing a prawn. I take a bite of gnocchi, spearing another piece as I chew.

"Come on, you can't give up," Matt says. "You've improved so much already."

"Yes, but… never mind."

His food still floating on the fork mid-air, Matt looks at me, opens his mouth to speak, says nothing and fills his mouth with food.

We eat in silence, like monks.

"Matt, I… Did I tell you Jas got married?"

He shakes his head, confused. "No, you didn't."

"Yes, she did!" I hear my manic voice as if it's someone else's. I ramble on.

"They eloped. She says they're going to do marriage their own way, whatever that means. Maybe they'll copy Frida Kahlo and her husband, who lived in two separate houses that were only connected by a walkway. I mean, it wasn't the best model, since they divorced, and both of them had other lovers throughout. But then they got married again to each other, later."

"Huh," Matt says.

The waitress comes over to take our empty plates. We order dessert, chocolate mousse for me, tiramisu for Matt. The restaurant has filled up; conversations bounce against the walls and ceiling. Bodies heat the air.

"Just have to pop to the bathroom," I say.

Over the shiny sink, I stare at myself in the mirror. Uncapping my lipstick, I paint my lips red. The water is glimmering far below me again. *Don't think, just jump.*

Exiting the bathroom, I step into the restaurant, and a rush of applause hits me. I am blinded by the eyes and smiles of a crowd of strangers. Startled, I search for Matt's face and find him winking at me, then wolf-whistling, fingers in his mouth. As I walk towards him, my face is a smiling mask.

My heart pounds. *Why did I babble on about marriage?* Sweat bursts from my palms. *Matt insisted he would never play the game of marital musical chairs, but now the music has stopped, and we were playing too, and I didn't know.*

Reaching our table, I sit down and zoom in on Matt's face, fading out the rest of the room. I search his shining eyes. Far away, the applause dies down. Conversations resume. Matt is grinning. His eyes are bright firepits. I lean across the table, my skin prickling.

"What's happening? What did you tell them?"

"I just stood up and clinked my knife against my glass and then told the truth. You know, you being sick, recovering... blah, blah, blah."

I laugh too loudly. My mind melts. Reaching for my lemonade, I drain it, as our waitress heads for our table. She's carrying a bowl of ice cream topped with a thick candle that spews bright sparks like a fountain. People are staring again, as she puts the bowl in front of me. When people start clapping, I blow at the candle, but the sparks keep returning. Watching the sparks, I stroke my bare finger, savouring its nakedness.

33

I'm lying in Ellie's bed looking at my phone. In a short video clip, Ailyn is sitting in her wheelchair in a leafy park amidst a cluster of fountains. Seeing her visibly placed in London for the first time makes her feel closer; her generic hotel room could have been anywhere in the world. I have been to those fountains before; I went the summer I first moved here. It feels like summer now too, even though it's only early May.

The video cuts to another clip, but now the camera zooms in on a man. I watch for only a fraction of a second, before my heart jolts, because the man originally belongs to my world, not Ailyn's.

George is sitting by a piano in front of the fountains, wearing his corduroy trousers despite the heat, the sleeves of his white shirt rolled up. The camera zooms out, and the frame holds Lara too now; she's standing close behind George, swaying to the music with a smile on her lips, her long flowing skirt dancing with her. They look like a couple that has been glued together for years. Next to them, a scattering of early morning tourists squint against the sunshine. Like Ailyn, they are capturing the music with their phones. George is absorbed in the piano. The video cuts for a second before it resumes. On top of the piano music, Ailyn's voice whispers in my ear: "So beautiful."

Happiness surges in me. My connection with Ailyn belongs to the physical world now. Our experiences are merging, just like I wanted them to. At different points in time, we have both sat close to George playing. My experience is still an electronic replication of hers, but her experience is also a replication of mine. Lara would call it a sign that Ailyn and Ina are in the same place as her and George at the same time as I am online watching that convergence happen.

Exiting the video, I order a car. I don't believe in signs, but I will surprise Lara – she will love it; I haven't seen her in months. Scurrying into my room, I hunt through my wardrobe for a summer dress.

As I step out of the house, the sun hits my face. It's a spotlight, moving with me as I walk. The air cools my bare legs. I hover on the pavement before I spot the car with the correct license plate driving towards me.

The streets are almost empty, but the car is moving in slow-motion. *By the time I get there, they will be gone.* I drum my fingers against my phone screen. I haven't saved up energy for today. The red numbers in my spreadsheet will expand so fast they explode out of their cells.

When the lights ahead turn orange, we slow down to a halt, and I want to replace the driver with another reckless one. Buzzing with adrenaline, I look out the window, then rewatch Ailyn's video on mute. *This is ridiculous. I should go home.* When the lights go green, I call Lara.

"You're an internet sensation."

She laughs. "I am?"

"I was just scrolling, and then there you were."

"Really?"

"George playing by the fountains, you swaying along. My friend posted a video, just now."

"Seriously? You can see us?" I picture her turning her head, looking for cameras.

"So, you're still there? He's still playing?"

"Yes, he'll play for hours; he says time doesn't exist when he's in the music." Lara laughs again. "Isn't that wonderfully weird that your friend happened to be here, and you happened to see it?"

"She's not really a friend," I say. *Do you see a woman in a wheelchair?* "Acquaintance is more accurate. We don't really know each other."

"Isn't he just a beautiful pianist?" Lara speaks in a honeyed voice I assumed would always belong solely to David. I wonder if George minds competing with a dead man, permanently etched into Lara's wrist and forever frozen at his peak.

"Are you in a car?" Lara says.

"Oh. Yes. Ellie's driving me to… church."

"You go to church now?"

"Yes, you know, at this point, why not throw everything at getting better? Okay, I have to go."

Walking through the tall gates into the park, my heart is pounding. I hear the music before I see them. As if time hasn't moved since I first watched the video, Lara is still swaying, and George is hunching over the piano, his hands dancing over the keys. As I stride towards them, my eyes hunt for a wheelchair and Ailyn's face, but she's not here. My heart drops. Closing in on Lara, I hug her from behind. She jumps.

"Grace! What are you doing here?"

People stare at us, as she embraces me like I have returned from war.

Hearing her exclaim, George stops playing. I wave at him, and he waves back and stands up, before plopping back down and diving into the keys again. Lara keeps her arm around my waist as we stand listening. I survey the crowd of people, but I see no wheelchairs.

When the song finishes, George gets up and walks over to us. He looks down, ignoring the applause that rains onto him. Lara grabs his hand. My eyes are on them, but Ailyn fills my mind. *The statue, that's where she'll be.* Like David frozen in time by dying, Ailyn is frozen in time by illness. 'I sometimes wonder if I'll never grow up' she wrote once. 'I'm a bizarre hybrid: parts of me are still a child, while other parts feel ancient'.

"Let's go for a walk," I say.

"Are you sure?"

No, of course I am not sure; I do not trust my body, and my body does not trust me. I do not know how to be out in the world anymore.

"Yes, I'm sure! Just a small one, down to the Peter Pan statue?"

George seems at ease again now that his hand is attached to Lara's. He moves his fingertips over her skin, as if she is a piano too. As we close in on the statue, I barely see the bronze shape of the little boy standing on a pedestal playing a flute. I scan the people around it.

"I adore this statue!" Lara bounces with elation. "Oh, look at the little rabbits climbing up towards him – they are so cute."

I scan the crowd of tourists. *She isn't here. Of course not;*

it's been a whole hour since I first saw her in the park; it's too long for her to be out in the world without repercussions. Heavy with disappointment, I focus on Lara.

"Do you want me to take a photo of you two?" I ask, indicating her and George.

"I want a photo with *you!*" Lara says. "Coming all the way here to surprise me... you're the best."

She squeezes me against her and we squint against the sun. She takes my hand, and we walk over to a bench overlooking the water, my legs throbbing with exertion. Sinking down onto the bench, I watch a white swan glide across the glittering water, as Lara is immersed in her phone. Out of the corner of my eye, I see her uploading our photo onto her social media, her other hand resting on George's leg. We are all floating in the Cloud now; Ailyn, Ina, Lara and me. Lara puts her phone away and leans her head onto my shoulder.

"I can't believe you're here," she repeats.

"Me either," I say, the sun warming my skin.

As another stranger drives me home, I tap on the phone screen and open a message to Ailyn, as I have done many times before, but this time I type fast, writing without considering how it will look to her. I fill the screen until I hit an invisible barrier and the screen rejects any more words. Before I can change my mind, I press send, placing my message in her inbox between too many messages sent by a multitude of strangers desperate to be seen.

34

I step into the therapist's waiting room. A woman is sitting below the sunset painting, holding her phone with both hands. I sit down across from her and try not to stare. *You are the first person I have ever met in real life who is like me.* Oblivious, the woman is staring at her screen without swiping or tapping. I realise then that tears are streaming down her face. She doesn't wipe them away or make any noise, as if the tears are separate from her. I want to ask if it's her first time here.

My phone vibrates. A tiny red heart has appeared next to the message I wrote to Ailyn. A second ago, she read my words and acknowledged them with a push of her finger on another small screen. Happiness jolts through me. I stare at the heart, my insides vibrating. *Any second now, words will follow.* For several minutes, I wait, buzzing, but the heart remains red and lonely. I can't will the words into existence.

I deflate. Ailyn will be reading someone else's message now, distributing more tiny hearts. Last night, she posted a photo of her and Ina sitting in a concert hall watching the trapeze show they came to London to see. I wonder if anyone who follows them online actually showed up there like they said they would. I reload my inbox. Ailyn's red heart remains glued to my own words.

I look up, and tears still leak out of the woman across from me. I lean forward and open my mouth. The woman looks up with dull and lost eyes. I bend down and pretend to tie my shoelace. Maybe she has been coming here for years, but instead of a progress curve snaking erratically upwards like mine, hers could be flat, like the ECG of a dead person. In my head, I practice repeating Ailyn's constant reassurances. *Recovery is possible!* But as I sit back up, my therapist calls my name from the doorway. I walk up to him and out of the room, and all the reassuring words I could have said to the crying woman remain only ideas. I wish I could give her an electronic red heart and then run away. The therapist is shorter than I remembered.

Stepping into the tiny box office, stale air hits me, as if the same molecules are bouncing against the walls as the last time I was here.

"I'm so glad you made it here in person." My therapist is beaming. "Because I have good news today. This is our final session. You're graduating!"

I frown. "Really? Just because I made it here in person?"

"Ha! No, no. I would have told you the same over the phone."

My chest tightens. "But I'm not better yet."

"You don't think you are better?" His pen poised over his notebook, he looks at me with raised eyebrows.

"I'm not recovered."

"No, no, of course. We have a while to go. But you

know what to do now. You can keep your slow progression going. It will add up."

I nod, as fear expands in my chest. I am only floating high compared to my sickest self. My ascension will be imperceptible to a healthy person, and besides, the numbers in the spreadsheet are too small to survive on their own. Walking: fourteen minutes. Sitting upright: fifty-five minutes. Talking: thirty-four minutes. Watching a screen: twenty-seven minutes. I have almost a thousand minutes in a waking day I need to fill with something. I am a house of cards; a single push of a finger, or even a breath of air, and I would collapse again. I can keep typing praise to myself in the expanding spreadsheet – 'YOUR REALITY NOW WAS ONCE WHAT YOU ONLY DREAMED OF!' – but I'm not sure it's enough.

"Is the funding running out?" I say.

His laugh is high-pitched. "You don't need me anymore."

"But…"

"Deep breaths, okay? You can email me if you need to."

"I don't feel ready," I say.

His eyes lock with mine. "Trust me, okay? I've been right until now, haven't I?"

I nod.

"Okay then. Let's go through your goals and your next steps. Have you thought more about what kind of work you might want to be doing, when you are ready for that step?"

I sink back down and fidget with my necklace. I look at the clock on the wall, which seems to have stopped.

You could be an excellent mattress tester, Matt joked, months ago, when I mentioned I couldn't envisage myself being employable ever again. I used to spend my days scanning vast amounts of information at top speed, manipulating numbers in a spreadsheet and assembling decks of perfectly symmetric presentation slides, but I can't envisage my brain ever being able to do that again.

Andrea rushed into my room a few days ago and declared that she wants to become an explorer when she grows up, and when I said that's not a viable choice anymore, since every bit of the planet has already been discovered, except for the deepest oceans, she only retorted: *that's fine then, I'll explore the oceans. Or space. Space would be cool. I like flying, a lot. And I'm not scared of heights.* I wanted to ask her how she could so easily dream without the boundaries of realism boxing her in. Maybe this is why people have children, to remind them to dream without limits.

"Can I have a rest break?" I say.

"Of course."

The therapist walks out of the room and shuts the door with a soft click. I lie down on the floor and pull out my phone. Online, I find a site that promises it will identify my purpose in life if I answer 108 questions. The length of the quiz itself feels insurmountable. I close the page and do another search for a random career generator, unsure if it even exists, but multiple sites instantly fill the screen, and I feel grateful for belonging to a generation of indecisive people so overwhelmed by choice they outsource life decisions to an automated website. I click on the first link.

'You are perfectly suited as a virtual assistant!'

The fake personalisation of the suggestion feels comforting. I scan several pages of description of what the role would entail. 'Apply you hunger for order, structure and control, without having to put on the perpetual smile required of an in-person assistant. By relieving others of their administrative burdens, you enable them to fly high.'

The therapist knocks on the door.

"Come in!" I say, stuffing my phone into my pocket and pushing myself up from the floor. The therapist sits down across from me.

"I want to become a virtual assistant," I say. Tasting the words, I wonder if it could be enough to enable someone else's flight instead of soaring high myself, while knowing it's all hypothetical, since a throbbing fog has descended just from reading the lengthy job description.

When the therapist finally holds his hand out for me to shake, I grab it forcefully again. I walk to the door, nerves fluttering. I still haven't asked him what I've been meaning to ask for months. I whip around.

"If I can make myself better now, does that mean I made myself sick, before?"

"Oh. Good question. Not necessarily. We don't always know why things happen. Some bodies fail and others don't, and it's not your fault if you happened to be given the former." He clasps his hands together and smiles. "Look, you know how to listen to your body now, and the rest, it's out of your control."

I nod and thank him, but my body remains tense. I step out of the room. If I had broken myself, maybe I could avoid doing it again, but if it's random, I have to rely on luck.

35

I walk down the residential road, as the sunset paints pink streaks onto the blue sky. Cars are parked bumper to bumper. I glance at my phone, which tells me I've walked for eight minutes and thirty seconds. I shuffle along, resisting the impulse to push further. If my body doesn't begin screaming at me later, I will have expanded my movement minutes to seventeen. I pause the stopwatch and sit down on a short brick wall that separates the pavement from a stranger's front garden.

'Want to come over tonight?' I text Matt.

'Sorry, have to stay late, we're way behind here.'

Jaya automatically floats into my head, but no pang of jealousy follows, only a niggling disappointment and an amusing thought: *Matt is converging with who I used to be. If I had stayed the same, we would be compatible now.* I try to convey the funny irony of this in a text to him, but it only looks like a passive aggressive comeback. I blank out the screen and stand back up.

I am halfway down the street when faint music drifts towards me from a parked car, a burgundy SUV that looks like Ellie's. The unmelodiousness of jazz gets louder as I move towards it. When I come up on the side of it, I peek into the car. Ellie is alone, staring straight ahead without seeing.

I tap on the passenger side window. Startled, she jumps and whips around. Seeing me, surprise floods her face, then a flicker of disappointment follows before she offers a weak smile. With a click, she unlocks the doors. I open the door halfway but remain standing on the pavement. I should have pretended I didn't spot her and kept walking; wanting to be alone must be the only reason she is sitting here drowning herself in jazz.

"You okay?" I ask.

"I don't know." Ellie drums her fingers in the palm of her other hand and makes a ticking sound with her tongue. "Can you just sit with me for a bit?"

She reaches her hand out to turn the music off, and I climb into the passenger seat. We sit there without talking, both staring straight ahead at nothing. Time expands.

In her silence, I insert horrible scenarios: Ellie has breast cancer. Hector has cheated on her. She has suicidal thoughts. *Don't they say it's often the outwardly joyous people who end up taking their own lives?* My therapist said I have to keep rewiring my brain to stop assuming the worst. *Naturally, humans spot negatives twice as often as positives, it's a survival mechanism, and now, after what happened to you, yours spot more negatives than most.*

"I'm pregnant," Ellie says.

Relief floods through me. "Congratulations!" I reach out for her hand and squeeze it.

"Yes, it's wonderful," she says, then starts crying.

I can't tell if her tears are happy or sad. Her crying is unfamiliar to me. I lean over the gearstick to hug her, and she clings to me, her grip desperate. When she lets go and sits back up, she dries her eyes with the sleeves of her sweater, leaving black trails of make-up.

"I just got back from the doctor," Ellie says. "I took a test last night at home, but... I didn't even tell Hector that the test was positive; I didn't trust it." She starts crying again.

"I'm so happy for you," I say uncertainly. Her tears keep flowing.

"Hey," I say, patting her arm. "I thought you really wanted another one?"

She nods. "I do. But I'm only five weeks, and we've been this far along so many times." She sniffles. "What happened with Sebastian... I can't go through that again."

I don't say anything. She babbles on about how it's impossible to die when you haven't actually been born, but to her, he was there, and he did die. She felt like she knew him, like a personality had already formed. She had never seen him, but it didn't matter, because she had felt him. He was lively, and she knew he would grow up to be a mischievous child. As she talks, her eyes continue to leak. She pauses to dry them.

"Ever since the test came out positive, I've just felt on the verge of panic."

Crying harder now, she can barely get the words out.

"At the doctor's just now, I asked if I could... you know, not go through with it."

Bawling, she gasps for air. My hand on hers feels inadequate.

"Hey, it's okay," I say.

"Right away, I said I didn't mean it. But for a moment, I actually did. I wanted the baby to disappear, just to be sure

I wouldn't have another one taken from me." Her crying escalates again. "I'm horrible."

I squeeze her hand. "You're not horrible. You were just scared. Even if you did decide to have an abortion – how does that make you horrible?"

Ellie turns to look at me. Her puffy eyes search mine. "I can't just give up on this baby because I am scared."

"If you think it would break you to lose another one, then you are allowed to stop. You could never be horrible." I shoot certainty at her. "I promise."

Ellie looks at me. "Okay. But I really, really want another one."

"Okay." I squeeze her hand.

She straightens up. "I need to tell Hector."

We drive back to the house without music. Once parked, we remain in the car listening to slow jazz until Ellie's eyes are no longer puffy and red. Thinking of the tiny seed forming within her, I picture it as the same baby that tried to make it four years ago, as if he has been floating in an alternate reality ever since then, and now he finally felt brave enough to give it another go.

Ellie follows me into the warm kitchen. Hector is stirring a huge pot on the stove and holding an almost empty wine glass in his other hand. Seductive spices fill the air. Another full glass of wine is sitting on the counter. Hector kisses Ellie on the mouth and holds the untouched glass of red wine out to her.

"Not today."

"No?"

Gaze locked with his, she shakes her head in slow motion. The edges of her mouth lift, as she keeps twisting her head side to side, eyes glued to Hector's. His widen.

"Really?"

"Really."

Emitting a yelp of laughter, Hector places his wine glass back on the counter without looking; it balances on the edge, before it falls to the floor. Shattering, the glass shoots red liquid everywhere. Hector doesn't even turn around to acknowledge the mess; he only wraps his arms around Ellie and lifts her off the ground. They stand in a pool of blood-red wine.

"Careful!" Ellie laughs.

Putting her down, he leans in and kisses her forehead. They keep each other wrapped in a tight hug. Andrea rolls her eyes.

"Come on! I'm starving. And you made a mess." She points at the broken glass.

I wonder if Ellie is crying silently into Hector's shoulder, or whether she is absorbing his uncomplicated elation. Andrea walks over to them and wraps herself onto their hug. I remain hovering in the doorway.

At night, the house is filled with the silence of other sleeping people. I float in my meditation bubble. A repeating thought pops into the calm emptiness of my mind: *what now?* I land back in my heavy body. *If the baby makes it all the way into the world this time, I have to move out; he will need his room back.* Fluttering my eyes back open, I reach for my phone. Holding it up to my ear, I listen to the periodic beeps as I try to connect to Matt.

"You're up late," he answers.

"I've got big news."

"Oh?"

"Well, it's not really *my* news. I shouldn't even be telling you." I lower my voice to a whisper. "Ellie's pregnant."

"Great." Matt's tone holds no excitement. "You called just to tell me that?"

"No… I called to tell you that if the pregnancy sticks this time, and she actually has the baby, I'll have to move out." I pause. "Want to try living together?" My palms are sweating.

"That is big news then," Matt says. "Can I think about it?"

Irritation surges through me. "You will cheat on someone just as an experiment, but moving in together you are not sure you want to try?"

Matt laughs. "Yeah, okay." He pauses. "Why don't you come stay here for the bank holiday weekend? As a trial run."

"Are you auditioning me?" I say, offended, even though I am auditioning him too.

36

The driver pulls to a halt across the road from the tower blocks where Matt lives. Trafficked roads surround the cluster of concrete buildings, trapping them. Through the car window, I spot Matt standing on the pavement in front of his building. As I step out of the car, he waves and runs across the street.

"You didn't have to come down," I say over the roar of traffic. "I remember where your flat is."

"I tried to call you. The lift is broken."

"Oh." I look at the vast tower block. The windows look impossibly tiny on the face of the immense concrete walls.

"Someone should come fix it later today," Matt says. "We could go wait somewhere until it works again."

"No." I shake my head. "It'll be fine."

"You sure?"

I nod. Heart pounding, I picture energy bursting from the centre of my chest into every limb. Bright pulsing light fills the muscles in my imagination.

Taking my weekend bag from me and slinging it over his shoulder, Matt locks us into the building. I shiver, as the cool air of the stairwell hits me.

We walk side by side up the wide concrete stairs. *Don't think about the number of steps, just walk.* I fall into a rhythm, marching like a soldier in slow motion.

I hit the first-floor landing and pick up the pace, repelled by a stinging smell. Matt only lives here because the rent remains laughably cheap, even though the area now qualifies as up-and-coming. Between the second and the third floor, we cross paths with an obese woman heading down. Matt files in behind me. The woman's laboured breathing echoes my own, we're a choir of struggling bodies.

"Burning legs," I say, as we hit the fourth floor.

Trailing Matt, I push myself up the next flight. *Some physical discomfort is normal, remember.* I stop on the landing. Hearing my footsteps disappear, Matt turns around; he's hovering on the first step of the next flight of stairs. "Want a piggyback?"

I shake my head, my breath ragged. "Just… need… a minute."

I want to sit down, but the floor is filthy and rubbish piles in the corners. I watched the marathon online again this year, hunting for Jas, in case she was running it again. I imagine her a couple of steps ahead of me now, pounding up the stairs, moving so fast it's like she's propelled upwards by an escalator. I latch on, letting her pull me along with a rope. I take each step artificially slowly. Reaching the sixth floor, my heart pumps elation into my limbs.

"And Grace is almost at the finish line now – she's headed for a record!" Matt's fake TV presenter voice echoes off the walls, as he runs up the last steps, then stands on the top with his hand outstretched as I take the final step onto the landing. I smack my hand into his so hard it burns.

Stepping into his flat, I sink down onto the worn wooden floor. I lie on my back and look up at the ceiling. My leg muscles are throbbing. My mind spins through my body parts, like a parent checking their child's soft skin for damage after a fall. *Legs, arms, chest, head, eyes. All there, all fine. You're okay.*

"Did I pass the first test?" I say to Matt.

He's looking down at me with concern.

"Don't worry," I say. "This isn't a desperate collapse. I could keep going if I had to."

"In that case…"

I hold my hand up to him and pull him down.

We sit half-naked on the couch. Our clothes lie in a pile on the floor. My feet rest on Matt's lap. I am wearing his T-shirt and no underwear. Matt's flatmate barely lives there; he travels for work so often that he must spend more nights away in hotels than he does in his own bed. The flat looks the same as it did the first time Matt took me here. The rooms are almost empty, as if Matt and his flatmate only just moved in. Matt's rusty bike is leaning against one of the bare white walls. The only furniture is a huge TV mounted on the wall and this plush green couch they got for free online.

"You definitely passed the second test." Matt kisses my shoulder.

I laugh. "Likewise. Flying colours." I reach for my phone and drape a blanket over my legs. "Do I get a medal?"

Wearing only his boxers, Matt reaches for the remote. On my phone, I check Ailyn's profile, but the photo of her and Ina at the trapeze show still remains the latest thing she has shared. Hit by an impulse, I open a comment and type in the same hurried way I wrote to her a few weeks ago.

Borrowing superlatives from Ailyn that I never use transforms the climb into someone else's experience, but I press comment before I can edit myself, solidifying the words onto the screens of all of Ailyn's followers.

'What an amazing day! I just walked up seven flights of stairs. I may pay for it later, but right now, it just feels incredible. My body is wonderful.'

I watch the screen, and instantly, strangers crowd around me. They congratulate me, sprinkling me with residues of the love they shower onto Ailyn. If I had an extraordinarily beautiful face or something to say, I would become an influencer too; it feels like being beamed on by sunlight.

"Oh, I forgot," Matt says, taking his eyes off the TV. "Want some chocolate milk? I bought some."

I laugh. "I'll get it."

"Well, look at you."

I walk from the bedroom to the kitchen on bare legs. A mosaic of wedding invitations covers the fridge. I scan the names written in elaborate cursive for ones I recognise, as if everyone overlapping between our lives will have copied Jas and are planning to get married without telling me. I stand in front of the open fridge and swim in the cool air until goosebumps cover my skin. I'm hit with a wave of longing for Jas, and for who we used to be together.

Returning to Matt with a cold glass in each hand, I reposition myself next to him.

"You have a lot of wedding invitations," I say.

"Yeah, absolutely mad."

"Am I invited to any of them?"

"Oh… yeah, I guess. But you wouldn't want to go to weddings of people you don't know, would you?"

"I know Aziza, kind of. From your birthday."

Matt laughs. "Aziza who thinks you are an event planner with a heart disease?"

"Yeah, okay. I won't come to that one."

Matt drums his fingers on the armrest of the couch, then looks at me.

"If we do move in together, what do you expect from me?" He shoots the words out.

I shrug. "More of this?"

"I need to know it wouldn't mean..." Matt hums the opening notes to the Wedding March and laughs nervously, then guzzles down chocolate milk. He is all knots.

I shake my head. "No. God, no. No, no, no."

Matt relaxes and smiles. "Okay then. Great."

I imagine myself sitting exactly here, hearing Matt's key in the lock at the end of a workday. Ailyn has said that when Ina comes home, she bounces off the couch, bounds to the door and greets Ina with the eager giddiness of a dog left alone all day. *At least that's what I do on the good days, when my body allows me*, she says. I can't picture doing that to Matt, and even if I did, he would say hello with a smile plastered on top of claustrophobia, and then he would begin coming home later and later until I would be asleep before his key turned in the door. We would only function if we both left early in the morning for offices and our separate lives were equally full, and I don't know if wanting to spend more time apart than together is healthy or dysfunctional.

37

Matt's phone rings out from where it's lying next to him on the couch. I can't see the name on the screen, but the microphone is set to loud, and I hear Jaya's bubbly voice stream out: "I'm just around the corner! Are you home? Can I pop by?"

"Grace is here," Matt says.

I strain to hear her reply: "Oh, okay. I don't have to come then."

"She should come!" My voice comes out shrill.

"Hang on," Matt says into the phone, before covering the microphone with his hand as he looks at me. "You sure? She doesn't have to. It's our last night."

"No really, it would be great to see her again." I will my smile to reach my eyes.

"Okay then. Did you hear that?" Matt says to Jaya.

We lie on the couch waiting until the doorbell rings. Matt jumps up. Jaya steps into the flat carrying beer bottles with colourful labels, two dangling from each hand. Putting the bottles down on the floor, she hugs Matt. Craning my neck to see, I count the extent of their embrace: three seconds.

"Hey," I say without getting up.

When Matt sits back down, he chooses the corner of the couch opposite me instead of sitting close. Jaya opts for the floor, where she sits cross-legged. She passes a beer to Matt and pops one open for herself, using a bottle opener from Matt's keychain that he offers her. They both take sips and comment on the flavours of the craft beer.

"Can I have one?" I point at the remaining bottles standing on the floor like bowling pins.

"Oh, of course!" Jaya says. "Sorry, should've offered, I just thought you didn't drink, with your condition and everything."

I struggle with the bottle opener. Jaya grabs it from me and twists the cap off with her hand.

"I have never seen you drink beer," Matt says to me, his eyebrows raised.

"Yes, you have."

"No, I haven't."

"At David's... you know." I take a large sip, and we sit in silence.

Jaya talks about a film she watched last night. When she talks, she uses her whole body; her arms are all over the place, and her facial expressions seem exaggerated.

"I'll order some food," Matt says, diving into his phone. Jaya and I drink from our bottles in silence before Jaya starts filling the air with new words: she tells Matt about a work project, and I can't comment now. Matt remains focused on the screen.

"Lebanese?" he says, interrupting Jaya's monologue.

"Oh delicious!" she says.

"Let's order from that place!" I turn to Matt. "I know you hate ordering from the same place twice, but it was so good. You know, the one where you talked to the waiter about your trip to Beirut and he proceeded to sit down and join most of our dinner."

"They closed," Matt says. "Ages ago."

"Oh okay."

"There's a place down a tiny side street not far from here," Jaya says.

"Great!" Picking up his phone, Matt starts tapping on the screen.

"Great!" I echo, picking at the label on my beer.

"So, Grace," Jaya says. Looking up, I let go of the label. "Matt tells me you might be moving in?"

"Oh. Yes. Maybe."

"Brave of you!" Jaya raises her eyebrows. "You sure you want to live with him?"

"Hey." Matt lowers his phone. His eyes are alight. "Why wouldn't she want to live with me?"

"You actually want a list?" Putting her beer on the floor, she starts counting on her fingers. "Self-centred to the point of rudeness…"

"Hey!" Matt is laughing now.

"See, exactly what I mean! Interrupting. Rude." Jaya grins.

Matt laughs again. I sit there, observing their effortless play.

"Only being silly," Jaya says. "I'm so happy for you guys." She turns to me. "You moving in, I think it's great."

"We haven't actually decided yet," I say.

When the food arrives, we spread the small mountain of boxes out on the couch and floor. Jaya remains cross-legged, dipping pita bread in the hummus. Matt attacks a pile of halloumi and tabbouleh. I bite into stuffed vine leaves, rice spilling onto my lap. I want to say something funny or insightful. My mind strains.

"Hey," Jaya says and throws a piece of pita at Matt's head. "Why so quiet? Do you still do that thing of tiring yourself out before you're seeing Grace?"

"What thing?" I say.

"It's nothing," Matt says.

Jaya laughs and turns to me. "Have you ever had a dog?"

"No. I'm not a pet person."

Jaya's eyebrows pop up. "Oh, I can't imagine not having one! Last year, I got a new puppy. We're allowed pets in the office, so I would bring him in, but he was hopeless; he wanted constant attention." Jaya takes a swig of beer. "So, I started playing fetch forever with him every morning, and then the rest of the day, he would be totally mellow and just sleep under my desk." She smiles at me. "That's what Matt does before he goes to see you. He runs and bikes so he's exhausted and can happily lie down with you and do nothing for the rest of the day. It's just the sweetest thing."

I look at Matt. His face is red.

"Very," I say. "Very sweet."

When Jaya pops to the bathroom, I lean over and kiss Matt deeply. We've been doing the same thing. He's been exhausting himself before coming to see me, and I have been resting more before seeing him. Opposites, but the same.

He kisses me back for a while before pulling away, but we have nothing else to say to each other after that. Until Jaya returns, the room feels too quiet. Watching Jaya launch into a story about a friend's disastrous date at a bar that turned out to be a strip club, the momentary feeling of closeness with Matt evaporates. Weariness floods me.

"I'm going to bed," I say brightly, getting up.

"Okay," Matt says.

"Thanks for letting me interrupt your evening." Jaya smiles at me. Jumping up from her cross-legged position, she wraps me in a forceful hug. I reciprocate half-heartedly and pat her on the back.

Walking towards the bedroom, I'm conscious of them watching, but they start talking again immediately. I close the door behind me and lie down in bed. The soft sheets smell of detergent. The springs of the mattress dig into my side. The lights are off, but there are no curtains or blinds, and the lights from the office buildings, streetlights and passing cars glow into the room, making it feel like falling asleep in front of a muted TV.

I got the timeline wrong. The realisation spins around in my exhausted mind. My relationship with Matt has felt fragile ever since I got sick; one more wrong step and we would come apart into thousands of pieces too small to be glued back together. The lack of greatness could be explained so easily. But we were always fragile, even before my body became fragile too. Ellie said that her miscarriages had brought her closer to Hector, even though she thought they could not become closer than they were when they got married. Their love is an alchemist that can take anything thrown at it and turn it into gold, while Matt and I were always a sculpture made of ice. We could be beautiful for a while, but we would always have melted, eventually. I have assumed we would have shone and glimmered, if I hadn't moved us out of the blistering sunshine of health, but instead, we would only have melted faster. Tension in my body and mind eases, as if I'm releasing a physical grip on an object.

I lie in silence for several minutes, before I grab my phone from the bedside table. My fingers press and swipe on the screen. I want Ailyn to have liked my comment about climbing the stairs, maybe even responded to it. Only strangers have showered me with hearts, but Ailyn has uploaded a new post.

Ina is lying in a hospital bed wearing a sky-blue hospital gown. Under white sheets, she is smiling and giving thumbs-up with both hands, one wrist circled by a plastic hospital bracelet. The photo is an echo: I remember her arm in a sling in a similar shot after her trapeze accident last year. *What part of her is broken this time?* Her arms look fine. She's not wearing a neck brace.

Scanning the caption below the photo of Ina in the hospital bed, I see only keywords: *Collapse. Seizure. Tumour. Brain. Tests. Cancer. Operate.* The phone shakes in my trembling hands.

38

My heart thunders, as I read the full caption.

'She collapsed days ago, but we didn't want to share anything before we knew more. Ina is okay. I'm at the hospital with her, currently lying down across three chairs we have pushed together to create a makeshift couch. Ina collapsed by the breakfast buffet on our last day in London, so we're still here. They want to operate urgently. She's being sliced open here in a couple of days.'

Making the screen go black, I hold down the button to shut the phone off completely, something I haven't done in years. I don't even want to leave the switched-off phone next to me, as if the phone itself contains cancer.

Tightness spreads in my chest. I cry so hard that it's difficult to breathe. Tears block my nose. The crying wants to be loud, but I force myself to stay silent. If Matt or Jaya hear me, they will run into the room and ask what's wrong, and the intensity of this fiery grief is inappropriate: I barely know Ina – she's not even a friend of a friend, because Ailyn is something other than a friend. I sob with an intensity that should be reserved for this happening to someone I love.

When my tears finally stop, they dry on my face, and my skin feels hardened, as if I'm wearing a face mask. My insides wobble. While Ailyn has seen my name and words and acknowledged me by pushing a heart-shaped symbol on her screen, Ina will not be aware of my existence. Hundreds or thousands of messages like mine will flood Ailyn every day; she wouldn't have shared mine with Ina. Anger throbs in the midst of my despair. Each intimate cluster of people should have a limited amount of bad luck, and over the last decade Ailyn has absorbed the illness share allocated also to everyone she loves.

I hear Jaya's and Matt's voices come closer; she must be leaving. They talk in indecipherable voices before I hear the door open and close. She would have hugged him goodbye. When she did, how many seconds did they linger? Three, four, five?

My chest remains tight, and my muscles tense, but the jealousy now is only an echo.

Minutes later, Matt enters the darkened bedroom. As he slips into bed next to me, I deepen my breathing, before changing my mind about faking sleep and turning to face him instead. Opening my eyes, I see him lying on his side, facing me, his eyes open. Lights from the city dance on the ceilings and walls. I force words into the room.

"You know that influencer I follow? Her best friend just got diagnosed with cancer."

"Ah, that sucks. Unlucky."

Sitting up abruptly, I look down at him. "Unlucky is your response to hearing someone is dying?"

He sits up too, facing me. "You didn't say she was dying. Most people who get cancer don't die."

"Yes, well, she's got brain cancer so she might be."

"Look, I don't know her. I can't care about every single person who is sick and dying. Millions and millions of people die every year."

"But most of them are old. Ina is younger than we are."

"Millions of kids die in poor countries every year, but you've never voiced any concern about them."

"What happened to Ina could happen to us."

"And if it did, I would be upset."

Lying back down, I look at the ceiling, not at Matt. He does the same. In graveyards, spouses are buried next to each other. If Ina dies, Ailyn will want to save the adjacent spot for herself. I can't imagine any other name on my tombstone than my own.

"Look," Matt says, his voice loud in the silent room. "What's happened to you... David... that's different." His voice breaks. "I'm not saying I don't care about that."

"I know." My heart is racing, and my stomach feels hollow. I push the words out: "Do you like her? Jaya?"

"What?" Jerking back upright, Matt looks down at me.

"Do you like Jaya?" I repeat, filling with an unexpected calm.

"What's Jaya got to do with anything?"

"Nothing. But there's no good time to talk about it."

"I like her as a person. Obviously. We're friends."

"You know that's not what I mean."

"But don't *you* know that if I was into her, I would have told you?"

"It's hard to leave a sick person."

"It's harder to stay with them." His words come fast, then he sighs. "Sorry. I didn't mean for that to sound so harsh."

I smile, because I have feared those words for years, and yet they did not sting.

"No, I get it. Honestly. If I were you, I would have left me a long time ago."

I force my eyes away from the ceiling and onto his face; he looks lost and exhausted. I want to hold him and stroke his head.

"So, you have thought about it?" I say. "Leaving?"

"Sometimes. Have you?"

"What, me leaving or you leaving?"

"You leaving."

"Well, I can't really leave to go anywhere."

"Come on, I'm serious."

"Yes. Sometimes. What we have, do you think this is it? Are we as good as it gets?"

"You're sick, so it's different."

"But if I wasn't sick."

"But you are."

"I'm trying to remember the beginning, before everything."

"Exactly. We were great then."

"Were we?"

"Do you not think so?"

"It's not meant to be great only in the beginning," I say. "It's meant to get even better over time… Ellie said that with her and Hector, the hardest moments have strengthened their relationship, but…"

"It's not a competition."

"I know, but don't you think if you're going to spend your life with someone, it can't just be about waiting for the parts where nothing is going wrong? We may be waiting forever."

Matt falls asleep with his arms around me. His breath smells of beer, and I grow too hot, wrapped by his warm body. I look at the lights from the street dancing on the wall. We never sleep intertwined, but now I let myself be held. My mind feels soft, the sea of thoughts finally flat.

Part 3

1

Glued to my phone, I am curled up on the couch in the early morning quiet, obsessively refreshing Ailyn's page every few minutes. The door slams behind Hector and Andrea, while Ellie is still pottering about in the kitchen.

I woke at dawn, alertness instantly flooding my body – in a hospital only miles away, Ina is being sliced open. They will find the tumour and extract it, and the surgeons will recreate a healthy version of her. Terrifyingly tiny margins separate successfully removing the lump of cancer and removing essential parts of Ina. It feels suddenly laughable that I considered excelling at work so essential when the worst thing arising from not delivering would have been my own bruised ego and other people's disappointment.

Only minutes after I woke, Ailyn posted an image of Ina sitting in her hospital bed. Head tilted to one side, Ina grinned at the camera, her right hand forming a peace sign, as the sunrise lit up the left side of her body. Flower-filled vases of different shapes and sizes covered her bedside tables.

'Strangely, we laughed a lot this morning' Ailyn said. 'We cracked up at things that wouldn't have been funny on any other day. It must be a survival mechanism of the mind, allowing you to laugh at anything to keep you afloat on the hardest days.'

Hearing Ellie's footsteps approach, I look up from the screen. She's cradling a huge mug of tea and her face is drawn. She's only wearing black cotton leggings and a loose grey T-shirt without a bra; I can see the faint outline of her nipples. Her belly isn't visibly rounding yet, but the tiny creature growing inside her lets us know it's there by altering Ellie's behaviour. Some days, she walks around with an angelic smile on her face for no apparent reason, but on other days, like today, the dark circles under her eyes are so pronounced they remind me of her vampire make-up on Halloween.

"Are you not going to work?" I say.

Ellie sinks down into the couch and curls up in the opposite corner; she looks like she never wants to get back up. She's always running late for work; I find it surprising she hasn't been fired yet, but I can't tell her that when she looks like this.

"I have a check-up today," she says.

"Isn't Hector going with you?"

"I didn't tell him." She slurps the steaming tea and plays with the tag of the tea bag that's hanging off the edge of the mug. She looks up at me. "It's not really a check-up. It's an extra test you can take privately, to see if everything is fine."

She picks at a stain on the couch with her nail. "No reason why it shouldn't be. We used to say those tests were ridiculous, only for the rich and hysterically worried. And they can't even predict miscarriages. It's a waste of money, but…"

"I can come," I say instinctively.

Looking up, Ellie's eyes are wide and childlike. "Really?"

"Sure. Which hospital?"

She tells me, and I feel a wave of disappointment: *it's not the hospital where Ina is.* If it was, I could have been in the same building as Ailyn and Ina; even if they wouldn't know, I would be close. They don't need me – if I showed up, they would be alarmed, not relieved – but I could offer unseen moral support.

In the waiting room, Ellie and I sit next to each other on bright orange plastic chairs. She is leafing through a magazine without reading anything. I close my eyes. I want to continue my surveillance of Ailyn and Ina, but my phone died while we were driving.

"Can I borrow your phone?" I say to Ellie.

Nodding, Ellie unlocks it and passes it to me. Frantically, I tap on the screen.

Ailyn has posted, and I scan the caption before seeing the image, my heart beating faster, but she only writes that the operation is still ongoing.

'Time has never in my life passed this slowly. I'm wearing Ina's purple sweater, as if using her things can anchor her to life while she is unconscious.'

In the photo above, Ina is balancing barefooted on a slackline in a park, leafy trees overhead casting dappled shadows onto her. Wearing ripped denim shorts, her legs are all muscle. *When Ina was healthy*, I think, then remind myself that there was a lag between the origin of the cancer and us knowing about it; the tumour was already there, we were just oblivious.

283

I glance at Ellie's soft belly. Why do some bodies grow cells that create life, while others only grow the wrong kind of cells that might end it? And why do some bodies, like mine, have cells that inexplicably go into hibernation for years? I still don't know whether all of this – mine, Ailyn's and Ina's illnesses and Ellie's miscarriages – was determined at birth or whether we could have prevented it if only science had progressed further and we were informed.

"How's Matt?" Ellie says. "We haven't seen him in a while."

"Matt?"

She indicates the phone in my hand. "You're texting him, aren't you?"

"No." I put the phone down in my lap, my hands suddenly clammy. Only the Internet is aware of my obsession with Ina's fate: the ads that pop up on my social media feed now promote cancer support groups. Unaware that the cancer isn't mine, the algorithm is also oblivious to cancer differing from electric blankets and silk pyjamas; even if you searched for it once, it's not something you want to be reminded of every time you go online.

"We aren't together anymore," I say.

Ellie's eyebrows fly up. "What? Since when?" Her brows furrow in confusion. "But you just stayed at his a few days ago. What happened?"

"We decided we aren't right for each other. It's been brewing for a while."

A doctor calls out Ellie's name. She jumps out of her seat, then pauses, turns and looks down at me. "Are you okay?"

I nod. "Go, go." I wave her towards the waiting doctor, a short woman with round glasses.

"Okay, but let's talk after, okay?" Looking worried, she hovers for a second.

"I'm the one who ended it," I say.

Her eyebrows fly up again, before she nods and crosses the room. When she disappears down the corridor, I float off to the last morning at Matt's, when we stood embracing in his hallway next to my packed bag for the longest time, breaking up without words. I miss Jas just as much as I miss Matt, but no one has asked about her.

Returning from the consulting room, Ellie radiates. I sit up straight.

"You got the results already?"

Her eyes bright, she shakes her head. "I didn't even take the test. I just spoke to the doctor, it was like a therapy session. No test can guarantee that everything will be fine, which is what I want."

I rush after her, as she powerwalks through the waiting room and into the cool air of the grey car park.

"I don't know what got into me!" she exclaims. "I'm going to drive to Hector's office, okay? He's what I need, not a medical test."

Arriving at the car, she yanks open the door. She starts driving as soon as I shut the door behind me. As she navigates the traffic, words shoot out of her like a geyser. We've been driving for almost ten minutes before she stops talking.

"Oh!" She hits her forehead with her palm. "I'm sorry. I completely forgot. Matt! What happened? Are you okay?"

"Yes, I'm fine."

"Really?"

"Yes, I promise. I told you, it was my choice. I mean, it was mutual, but I initiated it. I've been meaning to, for a while, but… it's a good thing. We're still friends," I add, not knowing whether it's true.

We drive in silence. Seeing Ellie like this, so desperately wanting to see Hector, any doubts that Matt and I made the right choice evaporate. We stop for a red light.

"Really, this had to happen at some point. We should have probably ended it years ago. We weren't right for each other."

The silence extends.

"I was never sure about you two," Ellie suddenly says.

I turn to face her. "What? But you and Hector love him."

Ellie throws me a quick glance. "Yes, but I'm not sure you did?"

I don't reply. The cars behind us beep their horns; the light has flipped to green. Ellie drives on.

"You were always kind of distanced with each other, whenever I saw you at least." She steals a glance at me.

"Eyes on the road," I say.

"You didn't seem fully free, or maybe not really fully at home. I just never knew if that meant it wasn't really love or whether it was only because you don't express your feelings out loud like I do."

I look out the window.

"Hector will be upset though," Ellie says. "He adores Matt."

"They can still meet, if they want."

"You know what will never happen."

Speeding up, Ellie fills the silence with more words about the baby; it's now the size of a blueberry, which sounds impossibly tiny, like something that could be easily misplaced and never found again.

"It can't be as simple as either you love someone or you don't," I interrupt. "Love must be a spectrum. The kind of love that you and Hector have... it's not normal. You can't just say that everything else isn't love. What else would you call it?"

"A half-love, maybe."

"Does it have to last forever to be love?"

"Of course not."

Close to Hector's office, Ellie parks in a spot marked for stopping only.

"Stay in the car? I'll be quick, promise."

Slamming the door shut, she hurries down the pavement; every few steps she breaks into a little jog.

Ellie has left her phone in the cupholder. Ina must be out of the operation soon; another hour has passed already since I checked. Picking up the phone, I stare blankly at the six empty spaces of the passcode request, before it seems obvious which cluster of numbers Ellie would have chosen. I type in her wedding date, and the barrier dissolves.

In a new post, Ailyn sits in the passenger seat of a car. *Another synchronicity. We could have crossed paths just now.*

'Operation done. All well. She's not awake yet, but I'm going to see her now. If this car stays stuck in traffic for much longer, I may jump out and just sprint to the hospital. I'm filled with the hysterical strength that enables mothers to lift cars off babies, even though no one needs me to save Ina.'

Exhaling, relief floods me like a drug. The silent emptiness of the car feels wrong. Reaching my hand out, I turn on the radio and jazz streams out. I drum my hands on my thighs. My foot jiggles. When I finally see Ellie walk down the pavement again, I wrench open the door, step out of the car and run towards her, tackling her with a hug; she wobbles.

"Hey!" She laughs. "What's going on?"

I squeeze harder. She strokes my hair.

"You'll be okay," she whispers, mistaking my elation for sadness.

287

2

I am lying in bed, my body warm after a bath, when Matt's laughing face fills the screen of my vibrating phone. I stare at the photo of him for several seconds before I pick up.

"You will not believe this," Matt says, excitement filling his voice. "Hang on, let me turn the video on, so you can see."

He talks as if nothing has changed, as if it isn't the first time we are speaking since we broke up. I had no things to return to him; he hadn't even left behind a toothbrush or an old T-shirt, there were no physical traces of him spending several nights a week in this room for years.

I move my phone away from my ear so I can see the screen again, where a blurry living room filled with equally blurry people appears. I immediately identify the white wall and generic black-and-white print of a city skyline.

"Recognise it?" Matt's voice is loud above the blend of voices and music. Moving the camera, he catches the kitchen counters and a large glass table covered in bottles and glasses.

"What are you doing in my old flat?"

"So strange, right?"

Abruptly, Matt's face fills the screen again. He runs his hand through his hair, which is shorter than the last time we saw each other. I want to reach out and touch him, stroke the stubble on his jaw.

"It's my friend's housewarming. Looks totally different in here now." The camera flips back to show me the rooms I used to live in. "I'll give you a tour."

In the bedroom, a colourful patterned throw covers the bed. A large tropical plant sits on the bedside table. A mosaic of unframed photos is tacked directly onto the wall above the bed. It could be the same bed I used to spend my days in when I first got sick; I rented the flat furnished. The last time I was in that room, lying on what could be that exact mattress, I felt like I was dying, and I was under the illusion that Matt and I were made of metal, not ice.

"Hey Matt!" says the voice of a stranger from somewhere outside the frame.

Matt's face fills the screen again. "I'm gonna go, okay?"

"Okay." I smile back, surprising myself with how easy it feels to speak to him.

"Hey, are you coming to Lara's birthday next month?"

"Yes. It's only next door, remember? She moved in with George last week."

"Oh, yeah. Cool. I might see you there then."

I've just hung up, when Ellie comes into my room, knocking half-heartedly on the door even though she is already walking through it. Her hands are empty. She sits down on the foot of the bed and starts talking, making it

289

look as if this is how we have always been with each other, popping in and out of each other's rooms for no reason.

"Matt just called," I say. "It was strange."

"Speaking to him again? I bet."

"No, not that. It was fine, actually."

I explain about the house party in my old flat.

"Seeing those rooms again was weird. I can't remember how I felt when I was last there, when I was at my worst. As if it never happened. I know it did," I add. "But I just can't recall the feeling of it anymore. Shouldn't I remember it?"

Ellie shuffles up the bed. Leaning against the headboard, she turns to face me.

"After giving birth to Andrea, I vowed to never do it again. The pain was just out of this world. The fact that lots of women around the world die in childbirth suddenly seemed understandable, almost relatable. But then less than a year later, I told Hector I wanted another baby. When he reminded me that I had said I would never give birth again, I laughed it off." She smiles. "I could remember saying it, but I couldn't recall the pain itself anymore, and so it felt like I must have been exaggerating, even though I knew I hadn't. We're probably made like that for a reason – who can cope with constantly reliving that level of pain?"

"I have to move out," I say.

"Why?"

I point at her stomach.

"Don't jinx it," Ellie says, stroking it. She has announced she is buying all new maternity clothes; after we came back from the hospital, she threw out the ones she used last time. She doesn't want to know the gender this time, as if doing everything differently will guarantee a different outcome.

"We're not kicking you out," Ellie says.

"What are you going to do, build me a shed in the garden?"

"I would!"

"I'm kicking me out."

"But where will you go?"

"I'll figure it out."

Ellie lies next to me for a while. I lie on the side of the bed that used to be Matt's. On my laptop screen, Ailyn has squeezed herself into Ina's hospital bed. Ina's hair is shaved short on the side of her head that is visible. A small bandage traces a half-moon shape across her exposed skull. Ina looks even more exhausted than Ailyn: her eyes are narrowed, and her smile is weak, as if her facial muscles are only strong enough to barely lift the edges of her mouth and eyes. They look like children having a sleepover.

'She's been sleeping most of the day' Ailyn says. 'I've sat here watching her, resisting recurring impulses to wake her up just to check she's really alive. She laughed once today. She's so drained that her laugh was more just a smile with an exhaling sound trailing it, like a whisper, but it was still a laugh, and it was the most beautiful sound I've ever heard. She's still here; she's still herself.'

I start typing another message to Ailyn.

'Are you jealous of Ina? Do you envy her? Not for the cancer, but for the immediate and extensive care that has come with it.'

I used to think my jealousy of Jaya was ugly, but envying a healthy life when you are sick is at least understandable, even if it's unattractive. *If even that is nasty, what is envy of another sick person, a sicker person?*

When I was lying in that bed in my old flat, I would have given up all my superfluous body parts – hair, a kidney, teeth – in return for the care they have given Ina.

291

A doctor instantly confirming on a screen that it's a tangible, physical thing that made your body collapse, and then, immediately, a whole team of medical professionals rush to remove the wrongness from you. While you wait, you are put in a bed, and you feel safe; you do not need to worry because there's a button you can press, and someone will come and hold you up. No one is insinuating that what you feel is not real.

After many tests, a doctor says that they do think it's all in your head, but it's a different kind of all in your head, a good kind that means the physical wrongness is all lumped together in one place. The rest of your body and mind is perfectly fine and still yours.

But then, Ailyn and I, we can at least cling to the possibility that our bodies can be fully restored. We don't know when, but it could happen. *When everything is uncertain, anything is possible*, Ailyn wrote once. Ina may be told it's only a quick, downwards spiral before it ends, and that sliver of hope that she might not have that we do is why I have been left to navigate this strange half-life on my own, while Ina is crowd-surfing.

'We don't know yet if Ina gets to stay or not' Ailyn writes. 'Three weeks, they said, before we will know how aggressive the cancer is, but for now: she is here, alive and herself. I am here. We are here.'

3

I step into George's empty living room and straight into Lara's open arms. She smells of flowers.

"Happy birthday," I say into her ear. We hold each other for a long time, as George hovers behind her.

"Hey, you've gotten better at hugging," Lara says as she releases me. "You didn't try to pull away."

George nods at me. I nod back. The grand piano stands in the middle of the living room now. Large green plants sit on the floor in huge pots and vases of cut flowers balance on side tables.

"Come through to the kitchen!" Lara drags me by the hand. "I'll make you a drink."

In the kitchen, Lara mixes a mocktail in a large plastic cup. She adds mint leaves and ice cubes.

"How is it going with you two?" I ask, indicating the living room, where George has sat down by the piano.

Lara looks up with a dreamy gaze. "It's been a little like

taming a wild, solitary animal. You have to do it slowly, otherwise, you startle it and scare it off."

"Slowly?" I raise my eyebrows. "You moved in after, what, eight months?"

"Ten and a half, if you count from our first date." Lara laughs. "I would have moved in after a week." She hands me the drink. "So, how do you feel about seeing Matt tonight?"

"Oh, fine." Taking the plastic cup from her, I take a sip.

Lifting her own cup, Lara touches it against mine, just as the doorbell rings.

Over the next half-hour, the room fills with people. Sipping my drink, I'm surprised by the number of faces I recognise. Before coming, I was anxious about speaking to strangers, but now seeing people I used to know feels worse; they think they know me, but they don't, not anymore. A friend of Lara's from school spots me across the room, and her eyes go wide.

"You're alive!" she shouts.

"I'm alive!" I reply.

She crosses the room and stands next to me. "So, what are you doing now?"

Before I can answer, another of their school friends comes over to join her.

"Do you remember Grace? Matt's girlfriend, from way back."

"Ex-girlfriend, actually," I say.

"Oh, really? Shit, I didn't know, I'm sorry."

"It's fine. We're still friends," I say.

The woman looks at me with a slight frown and narrowing of her eyes, then she snaps her fingers. "Hey, you're the one that got sick, aren't you?"

"Yes, that's me."

"But you're okay now?"

I'm about to start explaining – *I am not recovered, not yet; I may look fine, but it's an illusion, and actually, I've been saving up for tonight for several days, and I will have to pay for this extravagant evening of socialising later with hours or days of pain that no one sees* – but then suddenly I don't need her to understand.

"Yes, I'm much better."

I hear Matt's voice then. Automatically, I whip around. My body reacts instinctively to the sounds of him, as if it has forgotten that we are no longer each other's person, if we ever were. His loud voice exclaims an animated hello to someone I don't know. Seeing him, I don't want him to spot me – how are we meant to be around each other now? We can't go back to being the kind of friends we were before. Maybe we can go forwards to being a different version of friends, but suddenly I don't know how we can do that; I barely know how to retain friendships of any kind. Turning back to resume my conversation with Lara's two friends, I find them talking to a man I don't know, leaving me adrift.

I turn again and walk towards Matt. He spots me and smiles.

"Well, hey there," he says with ease, as if we bump into each other all the time. We hug, but his body against mine feels odd, and we let go quickly.

"How are you?" we say simultaneously, then laugh.

Lifting my drink to take a sip, I find it empty. "Drink?" I ask.

In the busy kitchen, Matt lifts a bottle of beer out of an ice-filled bucket that sits on the counter. I mix myself another mocktail in my plastic glass before we are again standing next to each other without anything to say.

"Want to go outside?" I nod towards the dark garden. We step outside, and the cold air hits us; it's only the beginning of autumn, but it feels like winter. We stand next to each other, holding our drinks and looking ahead, our breaths visible. Above us, a thin sliver of moon hangs in the sky.

"So, how have you been? You good?" Matt says.

"Fine, thanks. How's work?"

"Yeah, good." Matt turns to look at me. "You're really better?"

"Not recovered or anything, but it's the direction that matters, isn't it?"

"That's great. Really great." He takes a sip of his drink. "And Ellie, Hector, Andrea, the baby?"

"They miss you. You can go visit you know, if you want. I mean, they're right there." I point to the wall I used to be on the other side of. *Knock once for A, twice for B.*

"Yeah, maybe."

I look up. A handful of stars is scattered across the dark sky. "Hey, didn't you always say you wanted to go stargazing in a dark reserve?"

"Yeah, I really want to go to this desert in Peru; the stars you can see there are meant to be out of this world. Literally."

"Well, I can't offer you Peru, but do you want a taster session?" I point up.

Matt tilts his head back. "We can barely see anything."

"Our eyes will adjust. Come on."

Placing our drinks on the ground, we lie down next to them. The cold seeps through my clothes, but I like the solidity of the hard ground. Matt takes his phone out of his pocket.

"They must have an app," he says. "That shows us the constellations." The screen lights up his face. I look up at the dark sky.

"Hammock," I say, extending my arm and pointing.

"What?" Matt looks up from his phone.

"There." I trace the shape of a hammock with my finger in the air. "Those stars, they look like a hammock."

Laughing, Matt puts his phone down. "Alright." He points. "Spoon."

"Wine bottle."

We continue to match made-up constellations to earthly shapes: *tent, tree, bowl.* We are making up names that no one else will ever use to describe those clusters of stars. Almost instantly, we will forget them too, but for once, I don't mind the impermanence. Hunting the sky for shapes, my world feels vast.

The feeling will not last, just like the names we are inventing, but if I fall back into despair, that feeling will not be permanent either. I will not ascend on a straight line. My world will expand and shrink on repeat, until hours and days of feeling healthy may extend into weeks, months and years. That may not last either – anything I create can disintegrate – but for now, I am here.

Inside, someone turns up the music. A minute later, someone opens the door from the kitchen, and an unfamiliar female voice calls out: "Matt? You out here?"

"Yeah." He turns to me. "I might go inside; it's cold."

"Okay."

He gets to his feet and looks down at me, extending a hand to help me up. "You coming?"

"I'll just stay for a little while longer."

"Alright." Picking up his beer bottle, Matt walks back into the kitchen. "See you later then."

The door closes behind him, muffling the music. Remaining on the ground, I continue to make up constellation names on my own, as my eyes adjust, and new tiny pinpricks of light pop up.

Acknowledgements

Thank you to everyone who has supported the creation of this novel.

Thank you to Cornerstones and editor Susannah for your insightful feedback and enthusiastic support for the project. Thank you to the whole team at Troubador Publishing for turning the manuscript into a beautiful physical book.

Thank you to friends who read extracts and earlier drafts: Alice, Charlotte, Jackie, Jemma, Jo and Katy. I'm forever grateful for your feedback and encouragement. A special thank you to Evie for the myriad of insightful comments, grammar checks and the most inspiring conversations about writing. Thank you to Ailsa for cover design brainstorming.

Thank you to the incredible social media community of people living with and recovering from chronic illness. I am so grateful to have been virtually surrounded by all of you over the last years. An extra thank you to the wonderful creatives Julie, Rachel and Sarah (and Evie – again) for sharing your art with the world and inspiring me to do the same.

Thank you to all my friends who journeyed through the chronic illness years with me, for trekking across London to visit, for phone calls, voice notes and texts and for letting me rest on your beds, couches and laps. Aisha, Alenja, Amanda, Diddle, Eleni, Ioanna, Jackie, Jemma, Jo, Karoline, Katie H, Katie L, Kristin, Liza, Maria, Naty and Sarah – I love you all.

Sofie, thank you for the alarm clock and for sitting in the hotel lounge with me so I didn't have to be alone. (And for the best wedding present idea. Sorry I wasn't ready in time, but it was still the best.) You are so there it's insane, and I love you.

Thank you to my parents for surrounding me with books when I was little (literally) and for putting the old computer in my room so I could write tiny stories. For endless support over thirty-one years and for reading the book draft – thank you.

Thank you to Kjetil for being the best big brother anyone could wish for, and for believing in my writing dreams enough to give me an artist stipend. Thank you to Ingvild for conversations about life and for your excitement over the short story about Gjespetrollet. Thank you to Tomas for modelling how to carve out your own life path.

Thank you to my wonderful parents-in-law, Cheryl and Steve, for all your support.

Thank you to my host parents, Chuck and Diane, and my host sister Nicole for choosing me to join your family. The year with you made me dream in English and expanded my world.

Most of all, thank you to Nic, for reading many, many drafts of this book, for printing even more versions of it and for making everyday life magical, even during the crying years. I am the luckiest to be journeying through life with you, and I love you every day always.